THE JINNI KEY

THE JINNI KEY

Copyright © 2019 by Bethany Atazadeh

Contact Info:

www.bethanyatazadeh.com

Cover Design : Eight Little Pages

ISBN: 978-0-9995368-6-5 (paperback)
978-1-7332888-3-5 (ebook)

First Edition : December 2019
10 9 8 7 6 5 4 3 2 1

THE JINNI KEY

BOOK TWO IN THE
STOLEN KINGDOM SERIES

BETHANY ATAZADEH

GRACE HOUSE PRESS

ALSO BY

BETHANY ATAZADEH

THE STOLEN KINGDOM SERIES :

THE STOLEN KINGDOM

THE NUMBER SERIES :

EVALENE'S NUMBER

PEARL'S NUMBER

THE CONFIDENT CORGI

PENNY'S PUPPY PACK FOR WRITERS

MARKETING FOR AUTHORS SERIES :

HOW YOUR BOOK SELLS ITSELF

GROW YOUR AUTHOR PLATFORM

BOOK SALES THAT MULTIPLY

SIGN UP FOR MY AUTHOR NEWSLETTER

Be the first to learn about Bethany Atazadeh's new releases, get exclusive content, updates, and more!

WWW.BETHANYATAZADEH.COM

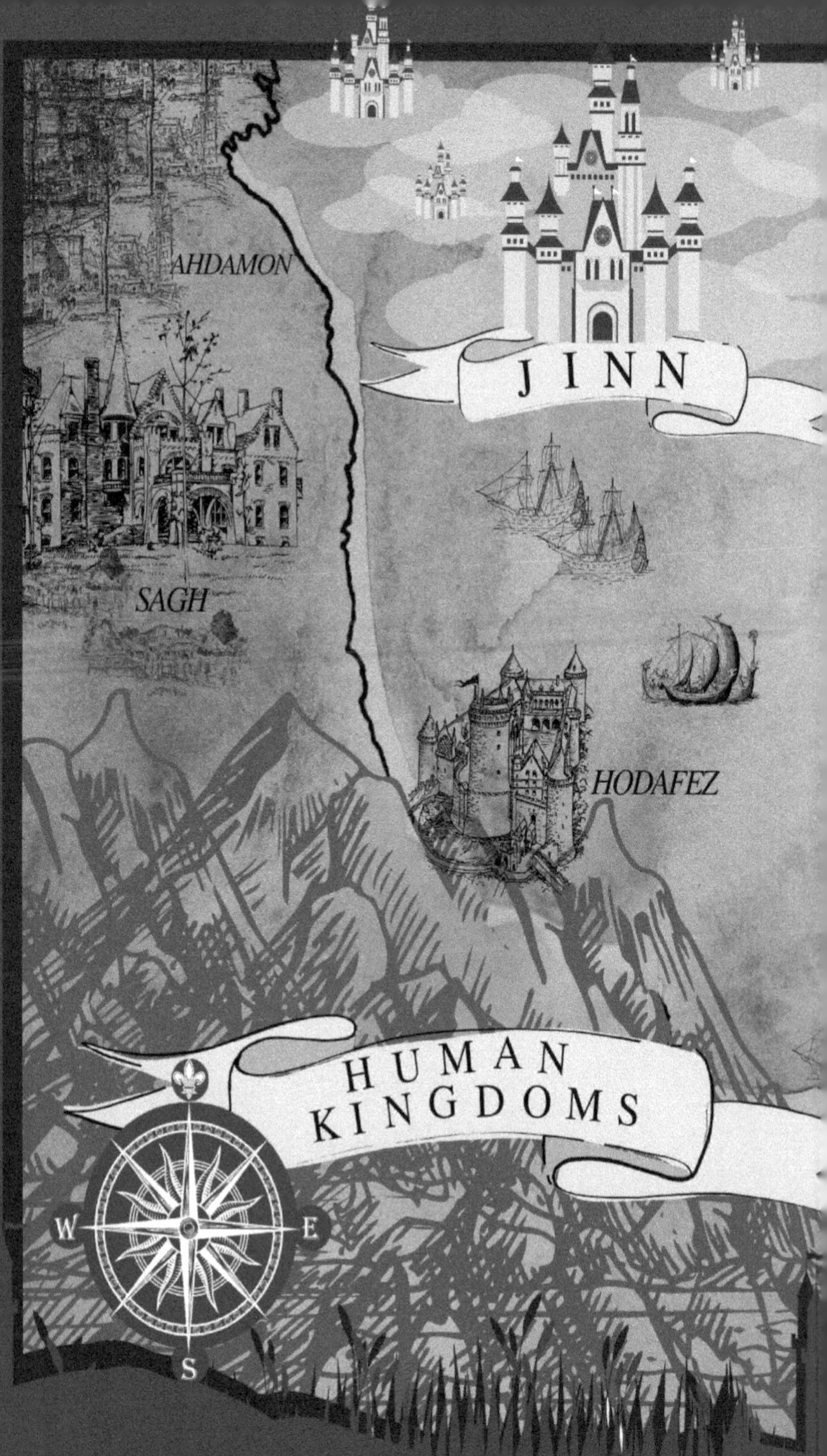
AHDAMON
JINN
SAGH
HODAFEZ
HUMAN
KINGDOMS
W
E
S

RUSALKA

DRAGON CLIFFS

KESHDI

AZIZ

PIRUZ

BARADAAN

Chapter 1

Rena

JUST A SHORT YEAR ago, on my birthday, I met him for the first time. My family sent me off covered in pale ceremonial shells, fixed to me from my neck all the way to the tip of my tail. My mother adjusted the colorful crown of vibrant ocean flowers before I waved her away. Nearby Merefolk stared, unashamed, as I swam past. My long, red hair flowed behind me. *Regally, I hope.* The heavy attire weighed me down. With effort, I swam on, waiting until I reached a deep canyon that curved out of sight before I shucked the ensemble to swim faster. This was the day I *finally* saw the surface.

As a young Meremaid, only sixteen, I'd looked forward to this rite of passage my entire life. *Watch out for sharks or stray squid,* my father's voice echoed now as I swam alone through dark caverns, slowly leaving the depths behind. I clutched the remaining shell necklace around my neck. Occasionally I stopped to rest, but other than a passing whale, the hours of swimming passed without incident.

Breaking the surface, a light breeze hit my skin and air filled my lungs. I feasted my eyes on my first sunset and gasped. *Yuliya was lying. The color is nothing like her pet fish. I've never seen anything like it.*

I only had an hour or two before I'd have to return to our underwater kingdom. So, I'd make the most of it. A small rock jutted out of the water a short distance from land; I dragged myself up onto it.

Outside of the water, I felt heavy. The rock dug into me far more than it would at home. *Nadia said the human world would lose its charm quickly.* I pushed the thought away, settling onto the rock, savoring the sunset. My sisters wouldn't ruin this for me.

The burning orb hurt my eyes; I took a break from staring at it to admire the rest of the sky. Brilliant blues with streaks of orange, gold, and pink.

I almost missed him. A dark shape fell through the clouds and splashed into the ocean in the distance.

For a moment, I almost turned back to the sunset, but my curiosity got the better of me. Diving into the water, my powerful tail carried me to the spot in moments. The ripples on the surface above me showed the impact, but nothing else. Below, drifting toward the ocean floor, I spotted him.

Was it a human or a Jinni?

Either way, I knew the rules: stay away.

I touched the shells around my neck. No one was around. *Maybe I'll swim a little closer. Just to see.*

The fallen creature was a male with pale skin, almost translucent, and deep black hair like I'd never seen back home.

A Jinni.

According to the elder-Mere, they were far worse than humans. But this one wasn't doing anything particularly evil, that I could tell.

Fascinated, I swam closer to admire him. His eyes were closed and he continued to sink. Bubbles escaped his mouth. I chewed on my lip, growing worried when I noticed his lack of gills. *Is he drowning?*

I didn't know what to do. A Jinni in the sea was on my mother's list of the vilest things that could ever happen. Interacting with him was, if possible, even worse. But I couldn't let him die.

I swam closer and reached out to poke him. Nothing. Feeling skittish, like he might open his eyes at any moment and surprise me, I swept up behind him and pulled him by the arms. He was heavy compared to the Mere. Larger and taller than me, and muscular. I kept my tail away from those strange legs as I began to swim back toward the surface. Who knew what he might do?

Our heads burst above the water and I inhaled a deep breath for him, showing him what to do. His head lolled to the side.

Glancing around, I found my sunset-gazing rock. I tugged him through the waves and dragged him onto it. Flopping him onto his back, I lay my tail alongside him, leaning in. The longer he didn't move, the less I worried about my mother and the more I worried about him.

I pulled myself even closer until I could lean down and listen to his chest for a heartbeat. My mother said they were heartless—did she mean literally? I nearly gave up, but then I heard it, faint, but beating. As I lay on his chest, staring at the shadow of a dark beard on his chin, and that sharp jawline, I was puzzled. *Why isn't he waking up?*

It dawned on me that his chest wasn't moving at all. His heart might last a bit longer, but he needed to breathe!

Sitting up, I pushed him onto his side and beat on his back. It was like hitting a whale. No results, no reaction. I let him drop onto his back again and eyed his lips.

It was just a fairytale. Told at bedtime to little-Mere. Kissing didn't really bring humans back to life. And he wasn't a human anyway, so even if it did work, that solution didn't apply... *Did it?*

I licked my lips. Reaching out, I touched one finger to his mouth, softly, tracing the shape. Putting my hand on his chest to stabilize myself, I leaned forward, bringing my full weight over him in a hurry. I tilted my face toward his, prepared to do the unthinkable, when he coughed. Water spewed from his mouth and hit my face. I jerked back as he vomited up what seemed like half the ocean.

When he finally fell back, his eyes were closed and his breathing came in ragged gasps. I pulled my tail away, prepared to leap into the water the moment he saw me, but he didn't even open his eyes. *I should stay to make sure he's okay. And to see what color they are.* The way he lay there unmoving made me think he might still need a kiss.

"What happened to you?" I whispered, mostly to myself.

"Banished," he spoke between ragged breaths, startling me again.

Mother always said my curiosity would land me in the belly of a shark. Instead of listening to her and leaving him to his exiled fate, I slid a few inches closer, carefully lowering my upper body onto the rock next to him. Propping my head in my hand, I said in an even softer whisper, "Why?"

When his eyes flashed open, I froze. Just inches away from my face, they were light blue, the color of the icebergs in the north.

They closed as suddenly as they'd opened. "You're so beautiful," he said, and my heart fluttered. No one called me beautiful. Not when they'd seen my sisters. "I must be dreaming."

Half of me wished he could see me in the ocean, where my hair would swirl around me instead of hanging limp and wet on my shoulders, and the water would make my tail shimmer. The other part reminded me that Mother would kill me if she found out what I was doing. A dream would be better for both of us.

"You *are* dreaming." I smiled down at him. He blinked in confusion, squeezing his eyes shut again, rubbing a hand across his face.

I wanted to lift my tail and let the beautiful red scales shine and sparkle in the sunlight to convince him further. But my mother's voice in my head stopped me. The Mere and the Jinn didn't get along very well; it wouldn't do to upset him in his condition. Thinking this, I tucked the Jinni Key I always wore underneath my thick shell necklace to hide it before he opened his eyes again. Better not to overwhelm him.

"What's your name?" I asked to distract him. Those blue eyes flew open, landing on my face. I brushed my hair back, feeling self-conscious. Nobody looked at me like that back home.

He sighed, staring openly in his supposed dream state. His eyes traced the shape of my face, my lips. I blushed, thinking about how I'd done the same thing a few minutes ago. But he didn't know that. *Did he?*

"Gideon," he told me. His eyes were growing more alert and his breathing came easier now.

I should go. Can the Jinn use their Gifts outside of their land? That made me nervous all over again. He hadn't done anything yet... but would I see it coming if he did? *Would I even know what to look for?*

"What's your name?" He rolled over to face me. The sudden movement made me flinch and slide away instinctively. "It's okay," he said, reaching a hand toward me. "I won't hurt you."

But I panicked.

Leaping off the rock, I dove into the water away from the hand that had almost touched me. *A Jinni hand.*

He leaned over the rock and peered down into the deep, searching for me. I let myself sink lower, into the protective darkness. Though his face was distorted, he looked sad. I sighed and watched the bubbles float up to him, jealous of them. But my mother's voice in my head held me back.

I stayed close, as the water grew darker. The sunset was ending. I'd missed it. The whole reason I'd come here in the first place. But for some reason, I didn't care anymore.

Gideon gave up looking for me and crashed into the water, swimming like a little-Mere toward the shore. It was only a short distance away, but at the rate he was going, it would take him a while.

I'd never answered his question. "Rena," I whispered, wishing he could hear. "My name is Rena."

* * *

THE JOURNEY HOME FELT ten times longer than it had when I'd left. Back to the center of the sea, then down to the depths, miles below the surface, where the Mere Kingdom of Rusalka stretched across the ocean floor. At the edges of our kingdom, the stone sentries stood tall, guarding our home from predators. The statues' fierce expressions and enormous heights made most sea creatures turn back, unless born and raised here. We could fight off sharks or squid if need be, but we couldn't very well risk a whale swimming over the tips of the palace spires. The coral grew so delicate at those heights, it would snap in two.

I paused to rest my hand on the stony waves of the nearest sentries' hair, which reminded me of Gideon's—except their heads were ten times larger. I desperately wished I could see him again. Make sure he was okay. But besides crawling onto the human shores after him, there was only one way I could think to check on him.

I didn't waste time thinking about how it could go badly. I had to try. Swimming through the lower levels of the city, I cut through a school of fish, ignoring the stingrays that trailed after me hoping for a hand out.

Under a tall arch, I found the group of Meremen right where I thought they'd be. "Has anyone seen Yuliya?" I asked them.

At my eldest sister's name, they lost interest in their fish races and whatever bets they were placing. "Not recently," Ruslan answered, swimming toward me, not bothering to hide his eagerness to win favor with the royal family—both with my sister and with me, the holder of the Jinni Key. "Why do you ask?"

"Just between us, I think she's lonely." I sighed, shaking my head and dropping my gaze instead of meeting their eyes, hoping they wouldn't see through me. "Don't tell her I said anything, of course, but… if you find her, maybe one of you could keep her company?"

"I'll find her," Egor volunteered immediately.

"If she's lonely, then the more of us, the better, don't you think?" Dmitri swam off without waiting for an answer, and the others followed.

I waited until they were out of sight before I smirked. They should keep Yuliya busy for quite a while. In all fairness, I didn't think she'd mind.

Swimming toward Yuliya's rooms, I listened carefully before entering.

My eldest sister was a master of spells. Most Mere could only use ocean shells that were already spelled for a particular use. Or, if they were a bit more talented, maybe they could learn to copy a spell that another Mere had done in the past. But Yuliya's creativity over the last few decades had led to her creating some extremely unique spells.

Somewhere in these rooms, my eldest sister kept an oyster shell the size of my head with an especially useful spell.

It was far too large to wear around her neck with her other prized shells, which meant it was available to use—*if* I could find it.

I dug through a treasure chest Yuliya had taken from a sunken ship. There were dozens of shells inside. Most of their purposes were a mystery to me.

The oyster shell was missing.

It didn't surprise me that she'd hidden it. This wasn't even the first time I'd tried to steal it. Though it took ages, I swam along the ceiling and then the floor of the large room, searching for a disruption to the coral and stone; an anemone out of place or a starfish too strategically set. Finally, I found a strange crevice along the wall, where the coral seemed almost intentionally meshed together. The thin gap in the rocks behind the coral held the oyster shell. Its jaws opened easily, as it was uninhabited. No pearl inside either, only two empty wings, but as I held it open before me, it began to shimmer.

"Show me the Jinni I met today," I whispered. "Show me *Gideon*."

It lit up. The Jinni was even more handsome when he was wide awake. Those sharp blue eyes and long dark hair made nearby humans turn to look as he strode anxiously through their city.

I stroked his cheek in the image. "What worries you?" I whispered, though he couldn't hear me. "Is it your banishment?"

One human was so startled at the sight of him, she dropped her baskets. Instead of mocking her or moving on, Gideon bent to help her pick them up. I couldn't look away. His words came back to me: "I won't hurt you." Remembering the way he'd tried to find me in the water, I found that I believed him. At least an hour passed as I watched, and I couldn't look away. He was so kind.

Voices in the hall made me shut the shell in a rush. I hid in a corner of the room until they faded. *That was too close.*

Yuliya could be gone all night or she could be on her way back to her rooms right now. It was risky to stay here. I tucked the shell under my arm, slipping out into the empty hallway, swimming away from my rooms toward the lowest levels of the palace.

I had many hiding places near the ocean floor that Yuliya would never think to look. And she *would* come looking. But I hadn't seen enough. There was something different about Gideon, something that spoke to me. He was like no one I'd ever met before.

I had to know him.

Chapter 2

Rena

"WHAT DID YOU THINK of the surface, Reens?" my sister Dina asked the next morning, grinning as she circled me, flipping her vibrant diamond-covered tail across my face just to annoy me. "We didn't see you anywhere last night."

"I'll bet you a jellyfish sting she had to go straight to bed because she stared right at the sun." Misha giggled, circling the other way. Her long, dark hair swirled around her tail, which was a darker shade of the orange sunset I'd seen the day before.

Yuliya swam between them, taking my hands and pulling me away. I let her. *What does she want now?* The top half of her white-blonde hair was pulled back from her face by a delicate gold crown that twisted through her hair and across her forehead. We sank onto a soft green bed of woven-kelp. Her shimmering black tail brushed against mine, and her eyes touched on the Jinni Key around my neck before drifting away. "Ignore them," she murmured with a sweet smile. "Tell me everything."

Yuliya's unusual kindness put me on edge. *Maybe she's discovered the oyster shell is missing. Does she suspect me?* My sisters were only nice when they wanted something. I'd considered telling them about Gideon, but now I wasn't sure I should. "It was fine. You know. Air… feels strange. The sun hurt my eyes—"

"Told you," Misha snickered and pinched both Sasha's and Nadia's bare shoulders just for swimming nearby. Sasha yelped and swam away, but Nadia hissed at her.

"Sisters." Yuliya waved a hand covered in gold bracelets for them to settle, and they did—with glares. She brushed away a long strand of hair that floated over her arm. "Go on, Rena."

Misha flipped her orange tail and swam toward an enormous shell chair like nothing had happened. She dragged her hand along the wall of plankton on her way, waking them up until the room held a soft glow. Mood lighting, since Mere could see in the dark. Trying to make me feel relaxed. I preferred my sisters when they were mean; at least then I knew their intentions. This only strengthened my resolve not to say anything about Gideon.

"That's really all that happened." I shrugged, pulling my tail up to hug it, scratching at the red scales to clean them, even though I kept them impeccable. "It was boring on the surface. Just like you said it would be."

Yuliya played with one of the shells around my neck. "Hmm. I don't believe you."

I snatched it out of her hand.

That only made her more confident. Her green eyes narrowed as she smiled. "You always try to tell us your stories, no matter how boring. So, what are you hiding?"

"We have ways to make you tell us," Nadia chimed in, touching the shells on her necklace. Though she hid her collection under a heavy assortment of gold, charms, and other jewels, she held a wealth of magic around her neck. Her hand grazed a curling shark-eye shell—spelled to imitate the fear and adrenaline experienced during a shark attack—then slipped over to a tiny oyster-drill shell.

I flinched at what that one could do, pushing off the bed of kelp. "You wouldn't dare!"

Their hands pulled me back down, keeping me in place. I considered thrashing. My tail could knock some of them out, but that'd be asking for it. For the moment, I let them hold me there, clenching my teeth.

"Tell us, then," Nadia said, as she tickled one of the many brown-and-white-striped fish she kept as pets because they matched her tail. "What secrets are you keeping?"

I glared at her and the rest of my sisters. "Fine. I stayed too late," I lied. "I wanted to see what stars looked like. Are you happy?"

Nadia rolled her eyes and swam lazily over to a more comfortable coral seat covered in soft starfish for cushion. "That's boring. We all did that."

Sasha floated down to sit in one of my tall, open windows where she could smile at passing Meremen, while Dina admired herself in my oval mirror, adding a bit of my stash of jelly to her hair to give it more shine.

But Yuliya stared at me. "I think you're lying."

I swallowed, trying not to react. "I'm not."

I'd paused too long.

"Yes, you are!"

This time, when she reached out to grab my wrist, I was faster. Swimming at full speed, I crossed the cavernous room and raced through the door, ignoring the Mere in the hall. *If I can just make it to one of my hiding places*—a hand brushed the tip of my tail and I pushed even harder.

Through the coral palace corridors, taking the fastest way outside, I squeezed through a tiny window, meant more for little-Mere than someone my age. I shot downward, aiming for a hiding place my sisters had yet to find near the base of our enormous home, less than a minute away.

A spell hit me at full blast.

I spun off course, with the breath knocked out of me, eyes stinging.

"Got you!" Yuliya trumpeted, gripping my arm in a way that would leave bruises. My other sisters cheered as they caught up.

"Little sister." Nadia shook her head. "I'll never understand why you think you could be faster than us. We've years on you."

"Decades." Misha laughed.

Sasha didn't say anything. Only eleven years my senior, we were closest in age, and no doubt she remembered all too well when she'd been the youngest. I wondered if they'd been this vicious when she was 16.

"I'll tell mother," I said, but my voice lacked real confidence. Mother wouldn't care. As long as we didn't die, she considered our 'games' to be good practice for leading our people.

"Go ahead," Yuliya smiled, all teeth. She quoted our mother: "If you're not shark bait every now and then, how will you learn to stand up to a shark?"

"When was the last time Rena was shark bait?" Dina asked, lifting one of her sharper shells.

"No! Stop," I whined. "I don't want to!"

I shouldn't have reacted. Sometimes indifference would make them leave me alone. But my protest only made them more eager.

"Don't worry, Rena. This will be fun!" Yuliya grinned, not waiting for Dina's shell, pulling out her sharpest shell instead. In one swift motion, she sliced it across my open palm adding a new scar to the rest.

I hissed in pain.

Blood seeped into the water. As red as any other mammal. And far more pungent. The unique tang of bitter mixed with sweet was in the water. There was nothing stopping it now. A Mere's blood spread faster than any other creature's.

With a giggle, my sisters waved and fled in all directions. "Good luck!" Yuliya called as she disappeared within the palace.

I didn't waste any time. Clamping my hands together, I ignored the pain and tried to hold the blood in as much as possible as I swam awkwardly toward the ocean floor. But I knew I left a small trail of blood behind me.

My heart pumped fiercely and I aimed for the thick kelp below to wrap around my hand and stop the bleeding.

I hadn't even reached it when the alarms sounded at the kingdom borders.

Slamming into the sand on the ocean floor, I snatched at a tall strand of kelp that waved nearby. I ripped it out of the sand to twist around my palm, once, twice, three times, knotting it tightly to stem the bleeding. It would make my trail fainter, but it wouldn't be enough.

With a flip of my tail, I swam into the deep canyons of the lower city, where dwellings were built into volcanic rock and coral. I headed for the lowest level of the palace where I'd intended to hide earlier.

In the distance, along the borders of Rusalka, the sentries stood their ground as usual, but their stony faces didn't deter the ravenous sharks this time. Not when there was blood in the water.

A few smaller sharks, a hammerhead, and a great white that was larger than three Mere put together, all swam in my direction. Mere blood reeked for miles in the ocean and the sharks' dark pupils widened in their frenzy until their eyes were completely black.

Nearby Mere reacted quickly, using spells to defend themselves or attack the intruders. I swam on, hoping to make it without incident.

One solitary tiger shark zeroed in on me. It spanned at least a dozen feet and blocked my path completely.

I flipped and swam in the opposite direction, toward the upper palace where the spires stretched for miles and miles toward the surface.

Glancing behind me, I panicked. The tiger shark was gaining. The shells around my neck were supposed to be for instances just like this, but in my terror, I couldn't think of a single spell.

Desperate, I aimed for the nearest safe room with bars of steel, pulled from the hulls of sunken ships. They'd been melded together with Mere magic into a careful design that allowed a Mere to slip through, but nothing larger.

I raced by dozens of palace windows. Later, it would physically hurt that so many had seen my shame, but in the moment, I didn't care. I hit the safe room at full speed, not caring when the coral and rough iron bars scraped my skin.

The tiger shark slammed into the side of the bars only seconds after. Flakes of coral drifted through the water, shaken from the walls, but the structure held.

Soon, I was surrounded by more sharks, all in a frenzy and determined to get to me. The attack lasted only a few more minutes before nearby Mere finished off the last one, most of the others having been chased off.

We'd eat well tonight… at my expense.

Chapter 3

Rena

"I'M TERRIBLY DISAPPOINTED IN you, Marena Yuryevna Mniszech," my mother repeated what she'd said to me publicly after I'd crept out of the cage in shame. But this time, we were in her chambers, without an audience. She didn't know my sisters were responsible; I'd told her I cut myself.

"To flee an attack…" She sighed, rubbing a spot on her brow below her crown, as she shook her head. "It's not just shameful. It's a sign of poor leadership. Poor judgment. A complete lack of effort."

"But, Mother, it was more than twice my size!"

Her gaze hardened. "That's what your spells are for. You're forever forgetting to use them. Do you even practice?"

I touched the shells around my neck, spelled for different attacks and necessities. She was right; I always panicked when I needed them.

"Don't be so hard on her now," my father said with a laugh as he swam into the room. "Remember our first shark attacks?"

They chuckled, sharing some dark joke. Mother and Father were both in their second century and covered in scars. Did they even remember being my age? Had their siblings treated them the way mine treated me? I'd never had a chance to find out since all my aunts and uncles were stationed across the seas and never visited.

Outside the coral palace window, a large group of Mere swam by and Father plucked his favorite trident—spelled with perfect aim—off the wall. "The plans are finalized for the shark hunt. Today's attack was proof it's overdue. I'll be back in a few weeks. Maybe a month." He swam toward the door, not bothering to kiss either of us goodbye in his eagerness.

"Let the others go after them," Mother called out, swimming after him. She'd begged him not to go for weeks, but my father loved the hunt and this latest incident was just an excuse to go. I trailed behind, forgotten. "We need you here."

"Nonsense." Father smiled over his shoulder. "You'll be fine." We reached the halls and he joined the others.

Mother's hand clamped down on my arm. Dragging me in the opposite direction, we swam toward the lower levels.

Even as we sank, I knew what she wanted.

At the bottom of the ocean floor, underneath the palace where only starfish and anemone lived, my mother gripped a conch shell around her neck, whispering a unique spell she'd created. A bubble of air appeared before us and slowly grew until it made a cavernous little pocket of space before us on the ocean floor. A tiny room of air, meant for me.

"Please, mother," I begged, trying feebly to pull my arm from her grip. "I don't want to."

"Just this once, my sweet urchin." She didn't let go. Smiling down at me, she added, "Do this for me. I know exactly what I want, and it will hardly cost a thing."

She waited, staring at the Key that hung around my neck. Sighing, I lifted it out from underneath my shells. The top of the large Key was shaped like a crescent moon, designed after the land it was from. And it was spelled with Jinni magic.

I'd grown up with the Jinni Key and knew its power better than anyone. I pursed my lips, staring at the bubble of air before us. Mother thought herself ingenious for creating this spell. *It will keep your blood out of the water,* she'd said with a grin when she first showed me a few years prior. I wished she would search for a way to stop the pain instead.

The Key would fulfill someone's greatest desire, but there was always a cost. A small cut for a small desire, like a delicious meal of squid or shark. A deep gash for a deeper desire, such as my mother's youthful appearance. Every desire was paid for with blood. I'd learned through harsh experience which kinds cost more, and when the price was too high.

Maybe the cost of using the Key would've been more tolerable, if I could've used it on myself. But there were limits. It would *never* allow me to bend another being's will to fit the desire.

And what I'd wanted most over the years had not changed.

When I was a little-Mere, I'd tried to use the Key to unlock my mother's love. But it couldn't go against her will. It couldn't make her hug me, or turn from her advisors to listen, or stop my sisters when they picked on me.

As I grew older, sometimes my greatest desire would shift to my father's love, or even, on rare occasions, my sisters.

The Key would show an inky black vision of them meeting my gaze and seeing *me* for once, instead of the Key and how they could use it. And though I knew it wouldn't work, I still slipped the Key into the lock below the vision, hoping just this once it might turn.

It never fit the lock.

Still, the Key gave me power in the ocean. Mere would bring me gifts, hoping I'd deign to unlock their own desires. When I was a little-Mere, I often did. Mother would say yes or no, and I'd comply. It was a strange version of the love I wanted, and if it was all I could have, I would take it.

Over the years, I said no more often. Yet the Mere still doted on me more than my sisters, which infuriated them. Especially Yuliya.

To the Mere, there was always a chance I might say yes. No one wanted to be on my bad side. There was only one I couldn't say no to: my mother.

She waited patiently now for me to give in.

Pulling the Key off my neck, I gripped it and whispered my mother's name. It shifted and bent as its long spine melded into a new shape. A vision appeared before us like the inky cloud of a squid but with a tiny image of my mother's greatest desire unfolding inside:

My father, seated on his throne at home instead of hunting. He lounged beside my mother, rubbing her golden tail affectionately.

His lips moved in the vision and I could almost hear him saying, *"Whatever you'd like, my sweet anemone."*

As we watched the scene, my mother grinned. "Yes," she whispered, mostly to herself, "That's exactly what I want."

She didn't seem to care that in the vision my father glowered at the deep-sea storm raging outside, which tore at the coral walls and would soon make the outer rooms uninhabitable. She didn't care if he stayed for her, she simply wanted him to stay, and a storm conjured by the Key would force him to return.

Again, I found myself wishing I could use the Key on myself.

"Unlock it for me, Rena," my mother commanded.

"No, please," I moaned, "It'll hurt too much!"

"You'll be perfectly safe," my mother argued, ushering me toward the pocket of air. "It's a very small desire. As long as you're out of the water, nothing will come for you here, and I'll visit you until you heal."

"Promise?"

"Of course, little starfish. You're my favorite after all." She winked at me and gave me a push. I fell into the bubble, dropping onto the soft sand, forced to drag myself up to a sitting position.

The price for such a large desire would be steep. The Key needed fuel, after all. It had to come from somewhere.

I swallowed, my gills fluttering anxiously, as I lifted the Key. Underneath the inky vision, a tiny keyhole appeared, the perfect fit for this latest mold. I pushed the Key in, feeling the pressure, and gave it a twist.

* * *

EVEN THOUGH I SCREAMED in agony, clutching the broken scales where blood oozed from my tail, my mother only reached through to pat my head before smiling absently. "I'll bring you some bandages and dinner shortly," she said as she swam away, not even waiting until my tears dried.

The Key always took blood to perform the spell. Sometimes, quite a bit. This time it left me feeling faint with a long but shallow cut along the side of my tail. I dragged myself through the sand to the other side of the air pocket where soggy kelp splayed out, caught in the air pocket and dying. Wrapping a long strand around the wound as a makeshift bandage, I curled up in the rest of the kelp, already feeling dried out myself. And lonely.

Would Mother even remember to bring dinner? No doubt Father had returned just like she wanted. I'd seen the Key work its magic enough to know it never failed.

My mother had told me that the Key was a gift from the Queen of Jinn. Right as I'd been born at the tail end of the Silent War, they'd bartered a fragile peace between the two nations during the Treaty of Contempt. As a gesture of goodwill, the Queen of Jinn had offered a rare treasure to the little-Mere still strapped to her mother's chest. To me.

Whatever someone *most* wanted, this Key could unlock it. For a price. And it could never be stolen; only given away. Mother used to mutter bitterly that they gave it to me, the littlest, so that the Key would be useless to our kind for as long as possible.

Mother didn't bring dinner.

Stomach growling, I tried to sleep and found myself thinking about Gideon. He'd never treat me this way.

I dreamt of him and woke smiling at how strange he'd looked without a tail. When Mother did finally bring some fish, she tossed it into my small bubble of air, where it flopped on the sand, still alive. "I'm so sorry, my little polyp, but I can't stay," she said, already swimming away. "You'll be healed in just a few days. The time will fly by."

It didn't.

I spent the hours thinking about Gideon, imagining him with me—his skin was so clear that I would tease him about how he nearly glowed underwater. We would have long conversations where he cared what I had to say instead of waiting for his turn to speak like my family. He called me beautiful many times again, although of course, none were as sweet as the first time.

Hours passed as I imagined staring into those pale blue eyes. I held up the Jinni Key, considering it. I hadn't tried to unlock my own desire in years. Why bother, when it hadn't changed?

Still. Tapping the Key in thought, I took a deep breath and wrapped my fingers around it, whispering my own name. It shifted to fit my greatest desire, and when the inky vision appeared before me, there he was. Gideon stared into my eyes the way he had on the rock, seeing the real me. He didn't even know the Key existed, but he loved me anyway. Heart beating loudly in my ears, I lifted the Key up to the lock and pushed it in.

But it wouldn't turn.

With a huff, I let go and dropped back onto the kelp, letting the vision disappear. My greatest desire hadn't really changed. The Key still couldn't give it to me.

Even so, Gideon was different. Maybe the Key couldn't help me, but as soon as my tail stopped bleeding, I wanted to see him again.

* * *

AFTER A FEW MORE days of solitude, the scab on my tail finally healed enough that swimming wouldn't make it crack open and bleed again. The moment it felt safe, I left the pocket of air and swam back to my rooms.

No one had missed me.

I considered the oyster shell that would let me see Gideon from afar. More than anything, I wanted a glimpse of him—but not just through a soundless screen. I wanted him to see *me* too, and this opportunity was too perfect. No one would even know if I left.

Slipping out of the palace and past the stone sentries, I swam toward the surface. What if Gideon was looking for me too? *Maybe this time, I'll be brave enough to speak with him!*

I reached the shore where he'd crawled out of the water. Slipping behind a small boulder, I stared at the village beyond. The land grass was dull here. Only one color, and barely moving unless a strong wind came by. Everything felt too bright, but my eyes adjusted over time.

Though many villagers took boats out to catch fish, Gideon was absent. Maybe he hadn't stayed after all.

My hopes sank with the sun, until finally, avoiding the fishermen, I gave up and swam home.

My only consolation was knowing I could visit the hidden oyster shell periodically to see him again.

* * *

I SWAM TO THE surface often, but never saw Gideon again. Those stolen moments watching him in the shell were all I had.

One day, Gideon simply sat staring out at the human world, shoulders slumped. He seemed so defeated. *Is there a chance he's looking for me too? That he wants to know who rescued him?*

I bit my lip to stop myself from grinning at the thought over dinner. Nothing my sisters said or did could ruin my mood. Even when Yuliya came home from a shark hunt and tortured me for information on her missing shell, I never told her or anyone else about him.

As the months wore on, though, I grew more desperate. I'd never been terribly interested in any of the Meremen before, but my sisters had loads of experience in that area.

I found Yuliya in her room, seated on a twisting coral chair like it was a throne, surrounded by my other sisters. They didn't notice me enter, too busy weaving sea flowers through their hair, trying on different shells and seaweed wraps. Each of them could pass for a siren with their stunning beauty, yet they still played with dyes, inks, and all kinds of jewels to accentuate their looks.

I drifted over to listen.

"Egor is the handsomest, but Ruslan is stronger," they were saying. I rolled my eyes at them.

"Rena," Yuliya sung sweetly. She hadn't missed my entrance after all. "I feel certain that your Key would help me decide which Mereman I like more. Perhaps you'd be willing to use it for your big sister, hmm?"

I sighed. She tried to make me use the Key almost as much as Mother, although I rarely said yes.

Once, Yuliya had even stolen it from me when I was still a little-Mere.

"Ha!" she'd sneered at me then, "It's mine now. I'll be the favorite and you'll be nothing—"

Before she'd even finished speaking, the Key had vanished from her hand and returned to its original place around my neck.

"Mother said the Jinni spelled the Key so it could never be stolen," I'd reminded her in a mocking tone, stroking the Key, which had only infuriated her more. I'd paid for that. Still, no one tried to steal it from me after that.

Now their eyes were on me. Waiting. Yuliya's held a hint of buried anger that made me want to avoid stirring up any more sand. I took a deep breath and my gills fluttered nervously as I nodded.

It wouldn't hurt to peek at her greatest desire. Only to fulfill it. Which I wouldn't do.

Pulling out the Key from the shell where I'd taken to hiding it, I wrapped my fingers around the long stem, feeling it warm like blood, twisting into a new silhouette as I spoke Yuliya's name over it.

The inky black cloud appeared with a vision of Yuliya inside. In it, she plucked the Key from my outstretched hand, holding it up in triumph as the new owner, while I slumped back. She wanted me to give it to her willingly—the only way she could ever get it.

"Your greatest desire hasn't changed," I told her on a sigh. Shaking my head, I braced for a wave of anger. "And I'm still not giving it to you."

Though she scowled, she didn't say anything right away.

After a long pause, she turned back to her mirror, lifting the long, red flower crown from her head to replace it with a sea urchin crown, which she kept alive while she wore it for the soft blue glow of its long tentacles. "What are you here for, anyway?" she asked calmly, as if the last few minutes hadn't happened.

"Nothing," I said, clearing my throat and letting myself sink onto a nearby coral bench. "I just overheard some talk of Jinni last week and was curious to know more. You're old enough to have been at one of the treaties. Did you ever see a Jinni face to face?"

Yuliya scoffed. "Of course."

She adjusted the crown, ignoring the way we all waited. Even my other sisters were intrigued at the mention of the Jinn.

"Are they as dangerous as Mother says?" I dared to ask.

Yuliya smirked at that. "Hardly. We are their equals at the very least. Believe me, they wouldn't have given you that Key as a goodwill offering to the Mere, if they didn't fear us enough to want peace."

I played with the pointed tips of my tail as I took in Yuliya's words, feigning indifference. "Would you really know? I doubt you ever had to fight one."

That earned me a glare. "This coming from a girl who's never met a Jinni in her life."

I looked away.

Out of the corner of my eye, Yuliya's hand stilled when I didn't immediately agree.

"Is it true they're as large as a whale?" I asked to throw her off the scent.

* * *

MONTHS PASSED, AND I didn't dare ask Yuliya or anyone else about the Jinni again. Instead, I found excuses to disappear to the small caves underneath the palace, where I'd hidden the oyster shell.

"Show me Gideon," I'd whisper, and spend hours watching him. He was searching for something. Or *someone*. It was hard to tell, without any way to hear him.

One thing I knew for sure though, without hearing a word: he never hurt anyone. He was nothing like the Jinn in the stories. I wished I could've seen their legendary home in the clouds, or even better, that Gideon could somehow come visit me here.

Every so often, I'd use the Key to see if my greatest desire had changed. It never did. Gideon continued to appear, unwavering. If anything, the vision grew stronger. More focused. And more importantly, this was the first time that my desire seemed as if it might truly be possible. If only I could meet him again.

On the one-year anniversary of meeting him, after an unremarkable feast in the dining hall with my family and a few hundred other Mere, I decided to celebrate my seventeenth birthday with a gift to myself. Using a small woven bag, I snuck the oyster shell up to my rooms so I could see Gideon again.

He was already asleep when I called up his image. I set him on the bed, curling my arm under my head as a pillow, and touched his cheek. "I wish I could see you," I whispered. "Do you even remember meeting me?"

My door burst open and my sisters swam in without warning. "Your birthday isn't over yet, little sister! Time for—" Yuliya cut off. "My shell! You little—"

"What's this?" Nadia interrupted, catching my wrist before I could slam the oyster shell shut and hide Gideon. "Or should I say, *who's* this?"

"No one," I said, tugging at my arm without success. "Just a Mereman."

"Just a Mereman," Yuliya repeated slowly, floating closer. She picked up her oyster shell carefully, studying Gideon's face as he slept.

I kept my hands away from the shells around my neck, wanting to appear poised and confident, though my fingers twitched.

"Look who has a crush," Misha purred, grinning as she settled onto my bed.

Sasha swam over to sit by the door, closing in the last opening of the semi-circle they'd made around me. "Why haven't you told us about the Mereman before Rena?"

Nadia let go of my hand, but Yuliya was too suspicious to believe me so easily. I had to let her stare at Gideon, studying him.

"This is no Mereman," she said finally, bringing her gaze to mine. "Rena is staring at a Jinni."

Chapter 4

Rena

"COME," YULIYA SAID, WAVING toward the bed. "Sit with us and tell us about this Jinni. How did you first see him? Was it while you were using your Key for someone?"

I hesitated.

Glancing at Dina where she reclined in the windowsill, and then at Sasha who blocked the door, I admitted defeat. I followed my other sisters over to the bed. They raced me to it, leaving only enough room for me to perch on the edge.

Still I kept calm, at least on the outside. "You guessed right. I saw him with the Key—"

"Whose greatest desire was it?" Nadia interrupted.

"Ah... it was—it was a while ago, so I don't remember..."

Misha's eyes narrowed. "You're lying."

Yuliya was already bored. "You know what?" she said, flicking a hand through the water as if tossing my words away. "I think I'd prefer to see for myself."

She snatched the Key from my neck, snapping the string, clutching it in her hand as she spoke my name over it.

Misha and Nadia held my arms. "It will come back to me," I yelled, thrashing in their grip, but they only held tighter.

Gideon appeared before all of us in the inky black vision, standing before an image of me. I looked like one of the humans, standing on land, gazing up into his eyes. He lifted one of my hands to his lips and kissed it, smiling down at me. My heart ached at the sight.

The Key vanished from Yuliya's hand, disrupting the vision as it returned to its original place around my neck. Just like I'd said it would, but not quite in time.

"Who. Is. He?" Yuliya's voice was low.

I heard the threat. Her hand lifted toward her shells.

Before she could attack, I acted first. Grabbing the shell nearest my belly, I spoke the spell in a rush.

A blast of air blew out from me, slamming into all five of my sisters, knocking them off the bed and across the room. Yuliya hit the wall. Hard. I winced, but caught myself. I didn't want to grovel. Instead, I tried to make myself seem bigger, like a pufferfish, floating higher with a little flip of my tail.

"You little witch!" she hissed as she got her breath back. "You're going to regret that!"

Her hand lifted to her neck where she kept her own assortment of shells—some of which were new to me and held unknown torture.

I yelled without thinking, "Wait! I'll tell you!" So much for not groveling.

"Don't listen to her," Nadia snapped, pink as an anemone with fury. Her small school of pet fish churned around her anxiously. "No story will protect you from paying for that."

I rolled my eyes, lifting my chin high. "So dramatic. I guarantee you'll change your mind."

Sasha's gaze turned from repairing her hair in the mirror to watch us with interest. Misha was less convinced, but considering, as she crossed her arms over her shell-covered chest—she had almost as many as Yuliya and was equally quick to use them. Even Dina stopped fixing the loose diamonds on her tail to pay attention.

But it was Yuliya who spoke next, surprising me. "Alright. Tell us about the Jinni—every single detail—and I'll consider a truce." She drifted back to lounge on the bed, the picture of ease, as if nothing had happened. Only the tip of her black tail twitched back and forth, exposing her true feelings.

Sasha swam closer, choosing a comfortable spot on the kelp where she could lean back and listen, while Nadia sighed so deeply that bubbles flowed from her gills.

"Just let her tell her story," Dina said as she sank down next to us, patting Nadia's dark tail, not quite affectionate, but not quite a slap either.

I regretted offering up my secret. I'd held out for a full year. Then, in one hour of weakness, they'd caught me. But after seventeen years with my five elder sisters, I knew there was no backing out now.

I shrugged, leaning back to rest my head against the bedpost. "His name is Gideon."

Their stunned silence was almost worth it. I grinned.

"You *spoke* to him? You're an even bigger idiot than I thought," Nadia said with a chortle. Her pet fish rubbed against her, soaking up her delight.

Misha had gone a bit pale. She and Yuliya had lived more than a century; long enough to have experienced more than the one small Jinni war.

"How are you still alive, may I ask, dear sister?" Yuliya lifted a jaded brow. "Considering you can't even face a catfish, let alone a Jinni? Was he dead?"

"No!" My cheeks reddened. "It was when I visited the surface on my last birthday. He was a little… unconscious. But not the whole time!"

Yuliya exchanged a knowing glance with Misha, and they burst out laughing. "Her greatest desire is for a Jinni who wasn't even awake to meet her!"

"He *did* wake up!" I yelled back. "And he said I was beautiful, and he was kind, and I love him!"

I froze as I heard my words. I'd never said it out loud before. My sisters stared at me, glancing between themselves, wide-eyed.

"Did she just say she's in love with a Jinni?" Dina gave a soft laugh of disbelief.

Yuliya only shook her head. "I feel sorry for her. Rena doesn't even know what love is."

"I do too!" I snapped, flinging myself off the bed away from them. "If I could get to him, I'd prove it."

"Ha. Love is just a tale for little-Mere, Rena. It isn't real. And certainly not with a Jinni. The Jinn are liars. They have their supposed code, but they also have a million ways around it, especially when it comes to dealings with the Mere. They can't be trusted." Yuliya was more serious than I'd seen her in years. "If you'd spent more than a short little sunset with him, you'd know who he really is. You're a fool to even consider him."

"I *have* seen who he really is," I reminded her, crossing my arms.

My sisters shook their heads at me, but I didn't care. I'd been watching him for a year now. I did know him, and he was better than all of them combined.

Yuliya fiddled with her shells, thoughtful, and finally broke the silence. "You believe he could actually love you?"

"Yes," I hissed. I wasn't as unlovable as they seemed to think. And Gideon would recognize me as the one who'd saved him. I'd wondered many times if the search he seemed to be on was for me. Maybe he loved me a little already.

But Yuliya wasn't done. "Would you go to the surface for him? Leave the ocean?"

My eyes flashed to hers. I crossed my arms as my other sisters drew closer. "What do you mean? Like use the Key?"

"Better," she said, holding up a shell she'd always worn but I'd never seen her use. "I used this only once, years ago, when we visited Jinn. It will get rid of your tail and give you two stumps instead."

"They're called legs," I snapped. I knew at least that much. "And the Key could do that for me." *If* that became what I wanted most and most likely with unbearable pain for such a high price. But I didn't mention that.

"Sure." She waved a hand in dismissal. "Legs. Whatever you prefer to call them. This spell is far simpler than your precious Key. It will guarantee you can wander around the human world to find your precious Jinni."

I couldn't help but touch my tail. The beautiful red scales shone from careful attention. *What would having legs feel like?* My eyes narrowed. "Why do you want to help me? What's the catch?"

"Why does there have to be a catch? Can't I help my little sister? All you'd have to do in exchange is give your Key to me. Willingly."

"That's not a fair trade, and you know it."

"Fine," she said, shrugging. "I'm feeling benevolent. If this Jinni truly loves you, you can keep your Key. But, if you're wrong, it's mine. And of course, we will need a deadline."

"What kind of deadline?"

"Once you have legs," she continued thoughtfully, as if she hadn't heard me, "you will have only one month to find your Jinni and get him to fall in love with you."

I tried not to smile and give myself away. That didn't worry me at all. Like most Mere, I had tracking spells that would help me find him easily. And after our first meeting, I felt confident a month would be ten times longer than I needed. In fact, it was quite possible Gideon would know me instantly. But on the other hand, I'd never been to the human world. Who knew how large it was and how long it might take to reach Gideon?

"Two months," I bargained.

"One." Yuliya's voice was harsh and unbending.

"What if, for some reason…" I tried to find the right words. "He's shy and needs more time?"

"Or if he says he can't stand your ugly face?" Nadia added with a chortle.

I glared at her. "He won't do that!"

"*If* you do not have some proof of his love for you after one month on land," Yuliya crossed her arms, "then you will forfeit the Key to me. No exceptions."

My other sister's eyes widened at Yuliya's words, disbelief written in the glances they exchanged with each other.

The Key was nearly all of my magic. I'd never grasped the full scope of the sea magic; I hadn't needed to.

"It won't work to bend someone's will, you know." I squinted at her. I'd never understood why she wanted it so badly. Everything she wanted most involved manipulating others. "And you'd never use it for anyone else. So it wouldn't help you at all."

Yuliya just laughed slightly. "The Key is valuable for many reasons, and you know it. You think you're the kingdom's favorite because you're the baby? Just wait and see how things change when you can't give anyone what they want anymore."

For once, I couldn't disagree. The silence was heavy. Yuliya waited, brow arched, as she fingered the shell with the impossible spell. To have legs... To finally be able to search for Gideon and speak to him again...

I let a smile stretch across my face and nodded. This could be everything I'd dreamt of for the last year. "I swear on Rusalka and every fish in it." I reached for the shell.

Yuliya didn't give it to me. Instead, she tilted her head, considering. "We'll have to make it binding."

I drew back. I'd had no intention of keeping my agreement, and she knew it.

She held out her hand. "Hair."

I knew why she asked. She wanted to meld the spell to fit me specifically. Once she did, I would be compelled to keep my promise.

Pursing my lips, I stared at her, wanting to refuse. But if I did, she'd know I hadn't meant it. And besides, a month would give me more than enough time, wouldn't it?

With a sigh, I reached up and yanked a strand of my red hair out, handing it over to her. I wasn't in a position to bargain. But I touched my tail, struggling with the idea of losing it.

Yuliya took ingredients from a bottle around her neck. Closing her eyes, she held them in a tightly clenched fist so none of us could see, holding the shell and my strand of hair in her other hand, making a spell on the spot.

I envied her ability to do this. It was one of the reasons no one challenged her. Many spells were entirely internal and secret, belonging only to the one who'd come up with them, and impossible to replicate unless the creator chose to share. Which of course, Yuliya never would.

Even though we all leaned in, Yuliya took precautions, not opening her hand until all the ingredients had melded into the sea and over into the shell. We grudgingly waited for her to explain. I felt a flutter like a tiny school of fish in my belly all panicking at the same time.

"I've changed the spell," Yuliya stated the obvious as she opened her eyes, enjoying our anxious tension. "It's still spelled to give you legs whenever you choose. But now, you must have proof that he loves you enough to ask you to stay *or* the spell will break. If that happens, you will forfeit the Key to me and lose your legs."

That would force me to return to the ocean. How vindictive. Not only would she get the Key, but she'd make sure I didn't have any second chances with Gideon either.

"If you accept this shell, the binding spell will require this proof, otherwise it will exist as evidence that you gave the Key to me willingly." She smirked as her words sunk in, then said it anyway, "At that time, ownership of the Key will transfer to me based on your giving it to me in this moment."

I swallowed. To say goodbye to the Key forever? I'd never considered it before. But then again, legs to walk on land and find Gideon had never been an option before either. And I wanted that chance. Badly. Pursing my lips, I nodded and held out my hand for the shell.

"One last thing," Yuliya added as she dangled the shell above my hand, "if you speak of this agreement and reveal the terms to *anyone* before you have your proof, you will also forfeit the Key to me."

My free hand flew up to clutch my throat as if it had a life of its own. To not be able to speak of it… She was putting me in a very difficult place, and she knew it. But she'd also seen my greatest desire, and knew what I would say.

I cleared my throat, not letting myself think about it any longer. "Fine." I didn't want to live here anymore anyway. I wanted to be with Gideon. To be with someone who would truly love me. I pictured him the way I did every night and various times throughout the day, smiling at me the way he had in the vision, and I grinned. Taking a small bag from my closet, I packed a few items. Extra shells. A little jewelry. An ocean flower for my hair.

"Rena, I should warn you," Yuliya added, when I held out my hand for the shell. "Don't let the humans see your magic. If they find out what you can do, they won't like it. And what they don't like, they *eliminate*. Understand?" My other sisters nodded gravely. I resisted the urge to roll my eyes.

"In accepting this shell, you accept our deal," she intoned, opening her hand to reveal the shell.

Swallowing, I picked it up. The water shimmered around our hands and the binding contract settled over me.

It was quiet. My sisters glanced between each other, wide-eyed. Nothing like this had ever been done before. Yuliya gave me the words for when I was ready to use the spell, to get my human legs. I could use it anytime I wanted for the next month.

I squealed and swam a giddy circle around the room, and then another. My gills spasmed in excitement. "Tell Mother and Father I've gone to our cousins in the south," I said as I swam toward my window, not wanting to waste another minute. "I'm leaving immediately!"

As I passed the stone sentries at the edge of the kingdom, it felt like my life was finally beginning. I patted one of them on a rocky shoulder in goodbye and grinned. "I hope I never see you again."

I swam through underwater canyons, hands on the shells around my neck, just in case I ran into a predator. There were no safe dwellings out here. It had been months since I'd last risked this journey to the surface. Where to even start? My instincts led me to the same place I'd first met Gideon—the human kingdom closest to that rock where I'd watched my first sunset.

I surfaced by the beach. The human buildings shimmered in the early morning dawn. Taking a deep breath, I blew it out, gripped the shell from Yuliya, and whispered the spell that would give me legs.

It was agony.

My tail felt as if it were being ripped in two. Though there was no blood, it hurt far worse than any wound the Key had ever given me. My vision blurred as spots appeared and I passed out.

I woke underneath the water in the shallows, gills still spasming in pain. They hadn't gone anywhere. But as I moved to swim, I found two long scrawny legs where my tail had been. Wide-eyed, I touched one of them, feeling the fleshy skin in awe. Carefully, I kicked them apart. They looked ridiculous.

As I pushed off the sand, I broke free of the water and stumbled to shore where I stared down at the two stubs. It looked like I was standing on two extra arms. I laughed and shook my head. I'd only taken a few tentative steps down the beach, when I heard a splash behind me.

My hands flew to my mouth. *Is it Gideon? Has he found me already?*

Hopes high as the blue sky overhead, I spun around, nearly tripping in my haste.

It wasn't Gideon.

Instead, I found a human girl standing in the water, fully clothed. She didn't even notice me as she strode onto land and bent to twist the cloth around her legs.

Frowning, I took a few steps closer. Most humans seemed to cover their legs for some reason. I didn't want to stand out in the human world, did I? "Where can I get some of those?"

Chapter 5

Rena

A WEEK HAD PASSED since I'd entered the human world. I pulled my hand away from my mouth to find I'd chewed my nails so short they were bleeding again. This bad habit never would have lasted underwater, but here on land it was only getting worse and was a constant reminder of my anxiety.

I stared up at the vaulted ceilings of the Hodafez castle, where I was now a guest of Queen Arie—the girl I'd met that first day in the water.

When I'd trailed her home to her castle that day, she'd been trying to save her father, as well as avoid an arranged marriage with King Amir of Sagh. I'd butchered her plans—

by accident, of course. At least it had all worked out in the end. Well, avoiding the marriage at least, not as much her father's condition.

King Amir's Gift of Persuasion had left a permanent mark on Arie's father's mind. He'd slipped into a coma with only a handful of waking moments over the last week.

Standing, I crossed to the large window in the king's bedchamber. The room felt more like a tomb. I'd tried some of my limited spells on his ailments, wanting to make myself useful, but it only seemed to slow the inevitable.

I dropped into a chair and let my head fall into my hands. My red hair fell forward, creating a curtain to hide my face, even though there was no one here to see. No one conscious anyway.

Every time I helped the king, Yuliya's words would echo in my mind. *Don't let the humans see your magic.* Arie still believed what I'd told her in the beginning: that it was my presence alone that helped her father. If she'd been able to read my mind with her Jinni's Gift and learn that I was out of spells and her father was still fading, she might not let me stay.

I shivered at the thought. Good thing she couldn't read my mind. The sea's spells had protected the Mere from the Jinn for centuries, and they were equally helpful protection from the rare Gifted human.

Because I was desperate to stay.

I'd exhausted every possible spell to track Gideon over the last week and not one of them had worked. He was in the human world still, but it was impossible to nail down an exact location. It baffled me, until I finally realized he was flashing across space and time, the way only a Jinni could. The few times I'd caught a glimpse of him and prepared to set out in one direction, he would suddenly shift far away to another and ruin everything.

That was why I'd spent every waking hour over the last three days with the king, even though my spells only required a few minutes, because the last time Gideon had flashed into the castle, he'd come here. To this room.

Arie had been with her father at the time, while I'd been outside in the courtyard—where Gideon had *last* appeared—chatting with a boy named Bosh. Gideon had brought news regarding his search for a way to heal the king—or rather a lack of news. Arie had casually mentioned this over dinner, hours after Gideon had already left.

I sighed, moving my chair into the square of sunlight streaming into the room. At least while I waited for Gideon to return, I could soak up these glorious rays.

Each day here was a constant battle between trying to find Gideon, yet not reveal the true reasons for my search. Yuliya had been wise to include that restriction in our agreement. Every single day I regretted agreeing to it.

I dozed in the warm sunlight all afternoon until the door clicked open. Arie stepped inside. Her thick brows were drawn together and she went straight to her father's bedside to check on him, her long, black hair brushing the blankets as she sat on the edge of the bed. "Anything?" she whispered, as if he truly was just sleeping.

I shook my head. It surprised me to find that this made me sad. None of my sisters could've evoked that feeling in me. I didn't know Arie well enough to trust her just yet, but I almost felt as if she was becoming a friend.

I chewed on the inside of my lip, trying to keep quiet while she tucked the blankets more carefully around her father. When she sighed a second time, I took it as an opening. "What's wrong?"

"I just spoke with Gideon. He still hasn't found anyone in the human world who knows a cure, and he…"

I stopped listening. My body grew cold like I'd swum through ice water. Gideon had come back again? *How do I keep missing him?*

"When did you talk to him?" I inserted at the first opportunity when she paused to listen to her father's breathing.

"Just a few minutes ago."

The ice water in my veins flashed hot and then cold again as I took that in. "Where?"

Arie turned at the tension in my voice, meeting my eyes for the first time since she'd arrived. "In the throne room. Why?"

"I—I just—no reason really." I forgot to be polite in my haste. "I have to go."

I ran down the long castle corridors, slowing to a fast waddle whenever a servant appeared, until I reached the grand throne room with its enormous ceilings, white marble floors and pillars, and walls full of golden accents wherever you looked.

It was empty.

After a thorough search of the rest of the castle, I finally made my way to my private room where I screamed into my pillow in frustration.

✱ ✱ ✱

YET ANOTHER WEEK PASSED. I paced the throne room of the Hodafez castle, kicking at my heavy skirts and struggling to hide my anxiety.

It was raining outside and I'd spent the afternoon watching water fall from the sky and beat on the enormous glass windows. Arie held a stack of papers in her hand, sorting through them in some random fashion.

She insisted on holding court six days a week, despite the fact that no one in her kingdom wanted to bring their grievances before her—before a girl with a Jinni's Gift that let her read their minds. Once again, I found myself thankful the Mere were immune to the Gifted.

I wiggled my human toes in the slippers, enjoying the strange feeling. Arie glanced up at my fidgeting, but she assumed it was nervous energy from the rainy day, because that's what I'd told her.

A knock sounded on the tall wooden door, catching our attention. Arie opened it to find a servant with her hand poised to knock again.

"Yes?"

The servant trembled under Arie's stare. Arie's lips tightened, and then stretched into a smile as she placed a reassuring hand on the servant's arm.

Curiosity pulled me closer to see what made this human so nervous. Halfway there, I remembered that Arie's Gift made even her own household uncomfortable. My feet slowed.

"Letter for you, your majesty," the servant barely spoke above a whisper, handing the folded correspondence to the queen before bowing low and scurrying away.

Arie didn't waste time, breaking the red seal and unfolding it.

I snuck up behind her and peered over her shoulder. The few rows of wiggly lines scrawled across the page meant nothing to me. "What's it say?"

Arie sneered at the page, crumpling it into a ball as she shook her head. "King Amir wants to discuss an accord between our kingdoms to *renew goodwill*." She laughed once.

"Why is that funny?"

"Just that he thinks I'd consider letting him back into Hodafez under any circumstances." Arie shook her head again and threw the letter into the fireplace, returning to her work.

I picked up the book I'd abandoned the day before and dropped into a chair with a huff.

The Land of Jinn

Or at least, that's what Arie told me it was called. She'd asked me to read it, to see if there was any mention of how the Jinni cured a poisoned mind.

Every few minutes, I flipped a page, making sure to rustle it a few times. The little black letters meant nothing to me. But the pictures were pretty.

I was helping Arie's father as much as I could with my spells already. If Arie needed to think I was reading a book to do so while she tried to rule her kingdom in her father's place, I'd play along. My real reason for staying here in Hodafez though—my only reason—was to find Gideon.

That moment on my first day was still the most I'd seen of him. In the middle of Arie's wedding-turned-coronation, he'd crashed through the doors with a group of humans. A fight broke out. While everyone lost their minds and chaos reigned, I'd withdrawn to a corner where I'd held the Key in my hands and whispered his name over it.

Gideon.

I hadn't admitted it before that moment, even to myself, but I'd hoped his vision would be the same as mine: that he'd been looking for me too.

Instead, in the inky cloud I saw him standing before a large gate made entirely of pearl. Instead of grass or dirt, he stood on white curling whisps of thick smoke which I realized were clouds. On each side of the gate, walls stretched into the distance and out of sight. I could only assume it was Jinn, since I'd seen nothing remotely like it in the human world.

In the vision, Gideon pushed the gate open and stepped through—then something hurled him back out and he nearly fell off the cloud. I reached out a hand toward him instinctively, even though it wasn't real. Then, the Key showed me his greatest desire: the gate before him began to open. He was welcomed in.

I'd blinked as the vision faded, confused. In the moments that I hesitated, pondering the best way to approach him with this knowledge, I missed my chance. Gideon vanished.

"He'll come back," I told myself that day through gritted teeth. "Next time you'll talk to him."

But the days on land had ticked by until one week became two. Today the second week ended. I had only two weeks left to find Gideon and convince him we belonged together. It felt like years since I'd stepped out of the water on two legs and begun navigating the human world. Each day I tried to locate him without success, and at this point, I was running out of ideas.

It'd been a while since I'd turned a page. I flipped the yellowed parchment, letting the pages slide together so Arie would hear it.

The next page had a picture of a Jinni. Without being able to read the words, I had no idea what it meant, but it reminded me of Gideon. Of my looming deadline.

"This seems like a terrible waste of time," I complained when I couldn't stand listening to the rain any longer. "We should ask Gideon to force your subjects to attend court." That seemed like a completely reasonable suggestion; it could solve both our problems at once.

"And why do you want to see Gideon again?" Arie murmured without taking her eyes off the papers.

I clammed up.

No way I would let Yuliya have my Key because of a simple slip of the tongue. "No reason." I shrugged, like I did every time she asked. "I just think the Jinni are fascinating. That's why I decided to visit the human world, remember?" I repeated the lie I'd told her when we met. "Because no one knows where the entrance is to Jinn, and I certainly won't meet one back home." I paused, just in case she wanted to respond, and when she didn't, I continued, "Anyway, I'd really like to meet Gideon. He seems like a great place to start." My voice sounded strained to me, but Arie either didn't notice or didn't care.

"Mmmhmm," she agreed absently. "He's bound to come by soon. Be patient and you'll get to meet him."

"That's what you said last time," I whined, too frustrated to censor myself. "You really don't know how to reach him?" In the large room, my voice echoed.

Arie's eyes lifted to meet mine. Toss me on land and take my tail, it was *so* hard to keep a secret! I stretched my lips in a smile and shrugged. "I wouldn't want to overstay my welcome, but I so badly want to meet a Jinni before I go home."

A wrinkle formed between Arie's brows and she sighed, letting the papers fall to her lap. "Last time we wanted to find Gideon, we searched for a Jinni artifact. They naturally call to the Jinn. The problem is, I don't know if they need to be close by to sense it. I don't even know if they call to every Jinni or only some. Not to mention, I don't even have the artifact anymore—there are so many variables, I honestly wouldn't know where to start."

I mulled that over. Something old from Jinn? Did my Key count? It was undoubtedly Jinni, not to mention ancient, and terribly powerful at that.

I grinned as my hopes rose. I bet it would be strong enough to call to Gideon like the artifacts Arie described.

But it was currently hidden from prying eyes, including the Jinn; my mother had made sure of that before I'd even learned to swim by putting a cloaking spell over the Key. I held in a groan. *How do I uncloak it?* I'd never thought to ask.

I couldn't sit still anymore. Standing, I clutched my thick human skirts as I paced.

An idea came to me, and I paused. "You said 'we.' Does that mean others were looking for artifacts as well?" *Maybe I can get them to help me.*

"Yes..." The corners of Arie's mouth turned down. "Kadin and I—and his crew, of course."

I grinned. That was perfect. One of Kadin's crew members, Bosh, came to the castle almost every day to give updates; I could ask him for help.

Arie's frown deepened as she stared out the window.

"You don't like Kadin very much, do you?" I asked, feeling proud of reading her well for once. In my opinion, Kadin and his crew were all far nicer than any Mereman. But Arie had let me stay here and helped me navigate the human world, so if she didn't like him, I'd stand by her.

"What?" Her brows rose and I had her full attention now as she unconsciously crumpled the papers in her hand. "Why would you say that?"

"I can tell from the way you won't talk about him, won't let him come visit, and you always look unhappy when people mention him." I ticked the reasons off on my fingers.

"Ah..." she stared down at her papers, not shuffling them anymore. "I don't hate Kadin at all," she finally whispered. "The opposite. But I have to do what's best for both of us."

The opposite. I scrunched up my nose. Humans were riddled with inconsistencies.

Without thinking, my hand lifted to the Key around my neck. I waited until Arie was engrossed in the papers again before I wandered past the thrones toward a window behind her. Once out of sight, I wrapped my fingers around the spine of the Key and whispered her name.

Arie.

When we'd first met, the Key had shown me her father in good health. But people often had more than one desire, and sometimes the stronger ones would battle for priority. Maybe Arie's had changed.

The inky vision appeared before me with Arie on the same throne, but my lips parted when I saw the man sitting beside her: Kadin.

"You... love him?" I muttered to myself as the vision faded away. Interesting.

Making my way over to the thrones, I dropped into the one beside Arie, ignoring the way she stiffened. No one else was here; who cared if I sat on a throne? I leaned on the arm, propping my head in my hand. "Why do you love Kadin?"

She sputtered. "What? I never said I loved him."

"But you want to be with him," I said, frowning. "Isn't that love?"

Arie regained control of her emotions, lifting her chin as she returned her focus to her work. "I think you're reading into what I said quite a bit."

I couldn't tell her about the vision, but I knew what I saw. Another thought hit me. "Do you think he loves you?"

"I have no idea," Arie snapped. She was sensitive for someone who didn't care.

I thought of Gideon again. "Have you ever been in love?"

Exasperated, Arie dropped the papers in her lap to rub a hand across her forehead. "Love is complicated. I barely know Kadin so how could I love him?" She stood, taking the papers with her. "Clearly I won't be getting anything done here today. I'm going to retire to my chambers."

I SNUCK INTO ARIE'S rooms in the middle of the night, passing the outer chamber where her servant snored. Crawling into the bed the way I had back home with my sisters when I'd been a little-Mere, I poked Arie's shoulder.

She squeaked as she jumped away from me. "Who's there?"

"It's just me."

"Who is... Rena? What're you doing here?" Arie reached over to light a candle. I'd forgotten she couldn't see in the dark. My eyes could make out the room just fine. Born in the depths of the sea, the cozy darkness almost made me feel like I was back home instead of in this castle. Which was very dry.

For a moment, I was sidetracked, picturing a lovely late-night bath. Just a couple minutes. A tiny soak. But the servants probably wouldn't appreciate that. They found my constant immersion strange.

A hiss of a match striking was followed by a warm yellow light burning bright between Arie's fingers as she lit the candle on her bedside table. It lit up the little circle of space around us, illuminating Arie's big canopy bed and her worried face. "What's going on?" she repeated, now that she could see me.

"I couldn't sleep." The truth was I'd been trying to figure out how to unveil the Key so it could call Gideon, but I hadn't made any progress and was hoping Arie might give me a clue.

Arie fell back against her pillow with a sigh. "So you decided I shouldn't sleep either?" she mumbled, covering her face with her arm.

"Tell me more about Kadin," I said, ignoring her complaints. "Is he still in town?"

Arie stilled. "I don't know."

"But you're the queen." I pulled back the blankets so I could put my feet underneath and warm my toes. When I tucked myself in, it almost looked like I had a tail again. "Shouldn't you know where your subjects are? He wouldn't leave, would he? Or does he not care as much as—"

"Okay!" Arie interrupted, dropping her arm, fully awake now. She sat up and leaned against the headboard next to me. "He's here in town. In the Khov Inn."

I smirked. "So you *do* keep an eye on him."

She shrugged.

"Does that mean you might love him after all?"

"Rena, we've been over this." Arie played with one of the colorful threads decorating her blanket. "You have to know someone to love them, and they have to know you. And how could we possibly have had time to do that when we met barely more than a month ago?"

I sighed. She sounded like my sisters. That was ridiculous. I already knew I loved Gideon, and there was a very good chance he loved me too.

"I might... *like* Kadin..." Arie added, not looking up from the thread she was unraveling.

I wiggled closer, eager to hear more. "What do you like about him?"

She paused so long I wanted to shake her, until finally she exhaled and the corner of her mouth twitched upward as she said, "Everything."

Chapter 6

Arie

I LEFT MY FATHER'S room the next morning. He appeared to be sleeping peacefully, but he was a shell of himself. So small and thin in his big bed; he looked like a fragile stranger. It hurt to see him like that. His mind was so scarred by King Amir's influence, that he'd disappeared somewhere inside it. The castle healers told me he hadn't stirred in almost two days. Rena stayed with him—her presence sometimes brought back hints of him—but I could tell it was losing effect.

Kadin had vowed to search for help, sending his crew across the kingdoms on my behalf, while Gideon searched for a Jinni cure.

I paused by a window to rub my tired eyes. I couldn't let myself think about Kadin, or I'd begin to question my choices regarding him.

It was for the best. I lifted my chin and moved down the hallway, not sure where I was going, just knowing that I needed to keep moving. Kadin might not understand, but if King Amir or other kingdoms looking to prey on Hodafez found any weakness in me, they would exploit it. *Besides,* I told myself as I slipped inside my chambers and made my way out to the private balcony, *I doubt Kadin will wait around for me. He's probably already moved on.*

Being on the balcony only reminded me of meeting Gideon there, a few days after my coronation. He'd taken the small green lamp I'd owed him, bowing over it as he promised to help: "Whatever I'm able to do, it will be done."

I wasn't entirely certain what that meant. Or how much time he truly had to spare while still on his urgent mission.

Frustrated, I left the balcony and made my way to the throne room instead, needing something to do. Something to take my mind off these morbid thoughts.

Entering the throne room, I made my way to the smaller room at the back where my father used to spend his days. After an hour or so of pacing, Rena poked her head through the door and slipped inside to join me.

For some reason, Rena had latched onto me during her first week on land and I had yet to shake her. Most of the time, though, I didn't mind. Her idle chatter took my mind off everything else I was dealing with. A kingdom that hated me— hated my Gift. No one wanted to even be in proximity of the Queen who could *read their minds.*

I would've liked to reveal that I could only hear the thoughts centered around me, which would've been true only a short month prior. But lately I could hear more and more. Every thought laid bare, no matter how simple or complex, how kind or cruel.

The line for me to listen to the townsfolks' requests was nonexistent.

But Rena, the tiny girl from the sea, didn't mind my company at all. She dropped into a chair by the window, happy to watch another rainy day as if it was a play.

As a Meremaid, she was immune to my Gift, a surprising relief. The pocket of silence surrounding her gave me a much-needed reprieve from the chaos swirling around my mind in everyone else's company.

Today, she listened to me debate what to do about King Amir's letters, chiming in with an "I don't know," or a "not sure," every so often.

Yesterday's letter from King Amir asking to meet had not been the first. And staring out at the empty throne room again today, I finally made my decision. Better to deal with the kingdom of Sagh while my father was still alive. I felt a twinge of grief at the thought—but once he was gone there was no guarantee they would still want peace.

Striding into the hall, I called for someone to send a scribe. Once he was seated in the back room with inkwell and parchment before him, I began.

"To King Amir of Sagh. I'm sure you can understand why your presence is unacceptable in Hodafez at this time."

Though the scribe paled, he began to write. I knew it was unusual. But I couldn't be bothered with the appropriate political phrasing and circling around the truth. For a moment, the only sound was the scratching of the quill on parchment and my footsteps as I paced.

When it stopped, I continued, "I'll allow you to send ambassadors on your behalf. No more than two. And no soldiers."

Furious scribbling filled the air. Two was generous.

"Sign it."

Taking my father's seal, which rested in a drawer in his desk, yet another reminder of his condition, I waited for the scribe to drip hot wax over the fold before I pressed the top of the ring into it with the Hodafez seal.

* * *

WHEN A SERVANT KNOCKED to say the ambassadors of Sagh had arrived the next morning, I choked on my breakfast. It was almost a whole day's ride. Did they leave immediately and ride all night? I shook my head as I dressed in a hurry, making my way down to the throne room to officially greet them.

When I entered the throne room, the two ambassadors of Sagh, dressed in the dark purple and blue royal colors, stood to face me. They were surrounded by flashy gifts from King Amir, most of them made of gold, although I felt confident it was only a thin veneer over wood or other materials. The politics of those gifts alone was enough to overwhelm me, as I tried to decipher if it meant the king truly wanted peace or if he was trying to conceal other motives—but for the first time in weeks, I also felt distracted by a heavy buzz of thoughts. There were at least two dozen citizens of Hodafez in attendance. No doubt drawn by the ambassadors passing through the streets on their way to the castle. They were willing to brave my Gift to see what the visitors had to say.

"Many blessings and favor to the lovely Queen of Hodafez," the ambassadors began before I'd even sat down. "The king of Sagh wishes to extend his warmest thanks and also condolences for your father's condition."

Pretty phrases that meant nothing. Both men were tall and gray-haired, tipping their chins to me in a small bow, but their disrespectful gaze irked me. *Do this for the kingdom,* I reminded myself, folding my hands in my lap as I stared at them. *For father. He would want peace.*

"We look forward to discussing how our two kingdoms might align for the greater good," said the same man, the leader of the two. He pushed his spectacles higher on the bridge of his nose, turning to the other ambassador, who pulled out a small inkwell and some parchment. "Perhaps we could discuss the issues between our two kingdoms privately?" He gestured one arm in a billowy sleeve toward our small audience in the surrounding chairs.

I willed myself not to react. They hadn't even fully introduced themselves yet and already they were jumping into the negotiations? It was undeniably rude, but refusing would be equally rude. Their sly request would set me against my people, asking the few gathered here for the first time in weeks to leave, and yet I couldn't refuse either, without damaging the proceedings before they'd even begun.

"Of course." I nodded, turning to the small group of people seated around the room. "Thank you all for coming." I made an effort to smile at each of them. "I will have the castle staff feed you a warm meal before you go as a thank you for your attendance and support during this hard time."

They stood with some shuffling, mumbling to each other as they slowly made their way out of the room. I cleared my throat and called after them as they streamed out the main door, "As soon as we are able to share the results of the negotiations with the public, I'll let you all know."

The room grew quiet as the two ambassadors shifted. The second man cleared his throat, staring pointedly at Rena, who still lounged on the side of the room. "Your majesty," he spoke up, "we must insist on speaking solely with the crown of Hodafez…"

"Yes, of course," I said on a sigh. "Rena, could you check on my father again while I speak to these gentlemen?"

The two men stood before my throne, eerily still, as they waited for Rena to leave the room. Something prickled on the back of my neck. I swallowed and looked away, watching Rena's back instead as she stepped through the wide double doors at the far end of the throne room.

With a deep breath, I returned my gaze to the men and gasped. The air shimmered around them and as I watched, they changed from regular human men to something unmistakably other: *Jinni.*

I panicked.

"Don't do anything rash," the first Jinni said as I opened my mouth to yell for help. I found myself gasping for air instead, unable to move from my throne. *What are they doing to me?* I clawed at my throat, eyes wide.

One of the men—or rather, Jinni—stepped forward. Fear and lack of oxygen blurred my vision but when the tightness in my throat eased up, I coughed and blinked away tears, until he became visible.

It was Enoch.

I'd know his purple eyes anywhere. What was he doing here with the other Jinni?

Still unable to speak, I tried to imagine myself open to them and their thoughts, to let my Gift help me. But there was only dead air around them. The Jinni knew how to protect themselves from other Gifts. If only I'd learned to do the same! If only Rena would come back and help me!

Enoch took his glasses off and put them in his pocket. "As I was saying, we come before the Queen of Hodafez as ambassadors." His voice was monotone, and his eyes dull, same as the last time I'd met him.

No. I wouldn't let this happen again. I stood, but only managed to take two steps before the air around my legs became thick as mud and solidified so that I couldn't move.

"We are not here on King Amir's behalf," Enoch continued, as if nothing had happened, "but rather the Queen of Jinn." He didn't give me time to process before he added, "You, Queen Arie, are now her happy subject."

There was a sweet melodic tenor to his voice that lulled me into contentment. Happy subject. *Of course I'm loyal to the Queen of Jinn. After all, I should align myself with other Gifted beings.* My left eye twitched. *I should go to bed early tonight; I'm not getting enough sleep.*

"You're also going to let the ambassadors from Sagh stay in your home for the next few weeks." Enoch pointed to himself and the other Jinni who stood comfortably, hands crossed, smirking at the two of us. I didn't appreciate his attitude. I might ask the Queen of Jinn to send a different ambassador in his place in the future.

I gave myself a mental shake. They were waiting on my answer. "Please do," I began, smiling at them. *Why can't I move my feet?*

"That's very kind of you," Enoch said before I could offer further hospitality. "Most importantly, however, you will do everything we tell you to do because you trust us implicitly. Do you understand?"

"Of course," I murmured, dipping my chin in agreement. "Anything you need." The air around my feet lightened and I moved back to sit in my throne, embarrassed that I'd gotten up in front of the ambassadors in the first place. A queen should always be seated in negotiations to maintain control. I pressed a hand to my temples where a headache was forming.

The second Jinni moved around Enoch, and I got a closer look at him. He was nearly as tall as Enoch, but stood more casually, making Enoch's posture, with his hands behind his back, look almost militant.

"Do you have her under your control this time, Enoch?" the second Jinni asked, climbing the short row of stairs to stand directly before my throne and peer into my face.

I frowned at how close he stood. *This seems like inappropriate behavior before a queen... What does he mean by control?*

Enoch sighed. "Ignore him," he said to me. To the other Jinni, he added, "I would, Lemuel, if you didn't undermine it."

"Just checking." Lemuel shrugged, his thin lips twisting into a smile. "I want to assure Queen Jezebel that her human kingdoms are in good hands before I return to that fool Amir. He still believes himself the Queen's favorite." Lemuel chuckled at that, but Enoch didn't join him or say a word. My head hurt. *How do I know this other Jinni? Why do I trust him?* I couldn't quite remember…

"Check in daily," Lemuel continued as he wandered around my throne, circling me as he spoke to Enoch. "I want her preparing her people for the changes, and I'll send Amir your way in just a few days' time."

Again, Enoch only nodded his agreement.

"I'll take care of her father on my way out."

My pulse skipped a beat and panic rushed through me even as another part of me stayed calm and content, listening to them.

"Keep your charge under control this time," Lemuel growled at Enoch, and then he winked out of sight.

My mind was hazy. *What's happening?*

Enoch's long face was stiff, his chin jutting out proudly, and he stood to the side of the stairs, close by but facing the windows. We waited quietly. I wasn't sure what we were waiting for, but I trusted Enoch, so I sat content. It was good he was here, I felt too tired to think straight anyway.

A bell tolled.

The thickness in my mind made it hard to remember what the bell meant. It was for big events. Weddings. Coronations. Funerals…

Enoch stepped up the stairs leading to my throne, until he stood close enough for me to see the different shades of violet in his eyes. "You are grieving your father's death," he murmured. "I'm truly sorry." His eyes dropped from my face as he swung to the side and gestured toward the main doors. "You will retire to your rooms now to be alone and mourn. I'll make sure the criers spread the word. You don't need to speak to anyone the rest of today."

Tears welled in my eyes at his words. *My father's dead?* I wished I could've seen him one more time before he passed away. My feet obeyed Enoch with a will of their own, carrying me to my room in a blur as the tears fell. Someone tugged on my arm on the way, but I ignored them.

I crawled into bed, weeping, but as time passed, the fog began to lift. *Why did I trust the Jinni?* I dried my eyes, forcing myself to get up and move toward the door. I needed to see my father's body, make sure he had a proper burial. And deal with this strange sensation that something deeper was going on.

My hand was on the doorknob when someone spoke behind me. "I'm afraid you need to stay in your rooms, your majesty."

I whirled to face the speaker. Enoch. Though his posture was stiff and tall, he brought his hands from behind his back to pat me on the arm. "It's better for everyone if you stay put."

But my memories were returning. I might not be able to leave, but I could fight back. I reached for the tall lamp and threw it at him.

He ducked easily. The glass lamp crashed into the wall behind him and shattered.

"Why are you doing this?" I yelled, backing away as I searched for another weapon in my small sitting room. I knocked a chair over between us, circling the table. "What did my father ever do to you?"

"Keep your voice soft, please," Enoch replied, and the command settled over me. I found that even though I opened my mouth, I couldn't scream. I felt like throwing up. One more word from him and I could forget everything.

"You killed my father," I cried, quietly now. I couldn't leave. I couldn't call for help. I spied the letter opener on my small writing desk and sidled toward it.

"I'm not a murderer," Enoch replied. For some reason, he didn't take away my free will completely.

I stopped in front of the desk, feeling along the surface of it behind me until I found the small metal object with the sharp tip. "Then why is my father dead?"

"That wasn't me. There are some things that are out of my control."

"Aren't you the Jinni here?" I asked. Then, not waiting for him to answer, I hurled the letter opener at him.

My aim was off. It nicked his shoulder before bouncing off the wall behind him.

Enoch grimaced at the small rip in his sleeve that revealed hard muscle underneath. A small cut from the letter opener bled lightly. "We're done here," he said, his voice returning to an indifferent monotone as he strode toward me. He captured my gaze as he added, "You don't want to see anyone for the rest of the day. You're mourning your father's passing. If anyone tries to help you, you'll turn them in to me immediately. Understand?"

I nodded, tears filling my eyes at the mention of my father. "I understand."

Chapter 7

Rena

INSTEAD OF GOING TO the king as Arie had asked, I'd scurried up the stairs to the throne room's balcony seating. A low railing surrounded the opening into the throne room on three sides. Without shame, I dropped to my knees and crawled forward to eavesdrop, shoving the annoying human dress out of the way, until I neared the wall. Slowly, I lifted myself up to catch a glimpse of the room below.

Peering over the edge, I was just in time to catch the ambassadors of King Amir shifting into Jinni.

My forehead wrinkled in confusion. *Are they friends of Gideon? If so, why did they come in disguise?*

The room's perfect acoustics made their words echo and reach me easily. It all happened so fast. By the time I recognized the purple-eyed Jinni from two weeks prior, he was already vanishing after his friend and Arie was exiting the throne room crying as a bell rang.

I raced down the stairs and long hallway after her. "Arie, what happened? Are you okay?"

She didn't answer.

I put a hand on her arm, but it didn't slow her in the slightest. Glancing around, I waited until the nearby servants were out of hearing distance before I added, "You don't actually believe what those Jinni were saying, do you?"

It was as if she couldn't hear me.

"Come. We need to leave." I would help her keep her head. I held out my hand the way I would to a little-Mere, but she didn't take it, continuing to walk down the hall.

"You can't stay here," I said in a sing-song tone, comforting her the way I would my little nieces and nephews in the ocean. "Trust in Rena, come with Rena, Rena will keep you safe," I crooned, tugging her arm. She dug in her heels and stopped. As soon as I let go, she returned to her original path toward her rooms.

"What's wrong? Why aren't you listening to me?"

I followed her all the way to her room, where she shut the door in my face. The strange vacant expression as she did worried me more than anything else. The lock clicked into place on the other side. She'd ignored me before, but this was different. The Jinni's magic must be stronger than I'd thought. I hadn't felt a thing, but Arie was completely at their mercy, like a human puppet. At least she didn't seem to be in any immediate danger.

Though I hesitated to leave Arie like this, I didn't know what to do. The other Jinni being in the castle made me nervous.

I hurried out to the stables and stopped the first servant I saw, a quiet man brushing down one of the looming beasts that Arie admired so much.

"I need a horse saddled immediately," I told the man, out of breath. I couldn't remember his name—human names were so odd—but he recognized me and nodded, which was all that mattered. "And hurry," I added, in case *immediately* wasn't enough. "There's no time to waste."

He nodded and bowed, showing me the balding spot on the top of his gray head as he scurried out of the stall to do as I asked.

I'd yet to feel comfortable riding, but I'd learned just enough balance to keep my seat and had to admit I didn't mind the view. From the ground, though, the beasts were a different story. I always preferred to keep my distance until it was time to mount.

Tapping my lip, I glanced around the stables. *No telling how long I'll be on my own. I should plan ahead for a few days, just in case.* There certainly wasn't anything edible in the stables, and it was too risky to stop by the kitchen on my way out…

I scanned the stables again, picking up anything metal I saw lying around. The humans seemed to find metal valuable. I could use it to buy food.

Filling two saddlebags, I nodded to myself, satisfied with their weight. Now for my next problem: the guards. It wouldn't be wise to let the Jinni know I was leaving, but my red hair was such a vibrant color, even on land, that it would undoubtedly draw attention.

Hanging on the wall were an assortment of brown and gray riding cloaks, simple and worn. I snatched one off the wall and pulled up the hood, tying it in place. That should help.

A throat cleared behind me. "Excuse me, miss?"

I turned to find the stable hand waiting.

"Your horse is ready, as requested."

"Tides be with you," I recited the traditional Mere blessing automatically. Pointing at the saddlebags I'd filled, I added, "Could you strap those on as well, please? I'll saddle up in the usual spot."

He nodded, not questioning me. He knew the spot I referred to. To the side of the stables, they'd set up a series of sturdy wooden boxes for me to use as steps. Arie and the other humans could swing onto the enormous beasts from the ground, but to my everlasting embarrassment, the creatures and I couldn't seem to figure it out.

It took three tries, but once I put the correct foot into the stirrup and gained enough confidence to crawl into the saddle, I held onto the pommel for dear life.

"Don't tell anyone where I went," I commanded the man who'd helped me, even as the beast lurched into motion below me. I squealed a little, embarrassing myself, and panicked as the horse headed toward the main gate on its own before I finally remembered to pick up the reins.

Glancing up at the guards stationed along the outer wall, I hoped they wouldn't pay me any extra attention in the stream of travelers entering and exiting Hodafez. They paced along the walls, studying the crowd, but none of their gazes lingered on me.

I took a deep breath and blew it out. Now, if I could just find Kadin and his crew; they could help save Arie and allow me to closer to finding Gideon, all in one. *But where exactly did Arie say they were staying?* The city of Hodafez stretched out before me like a maze. This might take longer than I'd thought.

The horse and I slipped down the mountainside through the city of Hodafez, sometimes literally. *Why did I ever leave the ocean?*

This is for Gideon, I reminded myself, for the thousandth time. *And for me.* After all, there was only one acceptable way for this deal with Yuliya to end: I had to win.

Chapter 8

Kadin

THE CRIERS RAN THROUGH town yelling the news. Arie's father was dead. She'd been mourning him for weeks now as he'd slowly faded, but today the whole kingdom let out their grief, wailing outside the city walls as they prepared for his funeral to take place the following day.

I passed a woman with rich black hair that made me do a double-take. But, of course, it wasn't her. Despite my best efforts, I saw Arie everywhere. Even in the honey-colored slant of the shop-keeper's brown eyes when she handed me the lunch I'd purchased. At night, the men would ask if I'd seen her, even though my report was always the same: I wasn't looking for her. Just looking for work. They'd nod, exchanging disbelieving glances, and we'd return to our food. Even in my dreams, I couldn't get away from her.

We hadn't seen each other in two weeks. Not because I hadn't wanted to, but because she'd asked me not to. Though I'd occasionally found quiet places in the courtyard to watch for her or stole inside the castle itself on occasion, I'd respected her wishes. But if there was ever a time to go see her, it was now. She needed someone to comfort her; she shouldn't be alone. My feet carried me in the direction of the castle with a will of their own.

The streets were subdued. Everyone worried what would happen to Hodafez now that its king was gone, and his daughter, Arie, the Queen Regent, was now officially their Queen.

At the castle gates, I was told the Queen was not receiving visitors. I didn't let that deter me. If she still wanted my visits to be a secret, I knew another way in.

It didn't take me long to sneak into the stables, find the entrance to the secret tunnels, and creep through the pitch-black space until I reached her rooms. I hesitated. Perhaps I was assuming too much that she would want to see me. I couldn't bear making her grief worse.

Pressing my ear against the entrance, an enormous mirror that swung open on silent hinges, it was difficult to hear anything at first. Then, sobbing. Heartbreaking gasps between crying. That decided it for me. I pressed the latch that would let the mirror swing open and stepped through.

At first, she didn't know I was there.

When I stepped forward on silent feet, she sniffed and turned to wipe her face, pausing as I came into her line of view.

Her face lit up. "Kadin!" She stood, wiping away the tears that kept falling. I covered the rest of the distance, pulling her gently into my arms.

She started crying again. "He's gone. He's dead." Her tears seeped through the shoulder of my shirt, but I didn't mind.

I squeezed tighter, wishing there was something I could do. "I know," was all I could say. "I know."

I waited until her tears slowed, before I pulled back. "I'm sure he died peacefully."

She sniffed, wiping her face with the back of her hand as her forehead wrinkled. "I... I can't remember..."

"Were you not there?"

"I don't think so... Kadin, something isn't right," Arie's voice trembled. I'd never seen her so vulnerable. "I don't know why I can't remember, but... I'm scared."

"It's okay," I murmured. "Let me help you."

At my words, a blank expression stole over her features. She stepped back and yelled, "Guards!"

I froze. "Arie, what happened?" I stretched my hands toward her, not quite touching her. "What did I do? I just wanted to make sure you were alright—"

"Guards!" Arie screamed again. She stood, fists clenched at her sides, but something flickered over her face and she stopped yelling.

I swallowed whatever words I'd been about to say, holding up my hands in protest. "I'll go, if that's what you want. It wasn't my intention to upset you. I'm sorry."

Turning back to the mirror, I stepped through the secret entrance, hand on the clasp to pull it closed behind me. I couldn't quite believe her reaction; something made me stay. "If you ever do want to talk, I'm here for you," I offered.

"I'll have you thrown in the dungeons." Her voice wavered.

It hurt. More than I would've expected.

A key turned audibly in the lock and her outer door slammed open. Heavy footsteps, at least a dozen, pounded into the front room. If they came through the door while I was still here, I couldn't say what might happen.

In a hurry, I yanked the mirror closed behind me. Even though it was pitch black, I ran. Hands on the walls on both sides to keep me balanced and on track, I slowed when I came near the stairs, but still nearly tripped down them. I didn't dare waste time lighting a candle.

I ran on.

Listening hard for the sound of pursuit behind me, all I could hear was my heavy panting and the scrape of my hands along the walls. They were uneven and occasionally rough, sending tiny spikes of pain along my fingers at the rough spots, but I didn't slow, not even when I reached the courtyard.

I wouldn't stop until I left the castle far behind—or until someone stopped me.

Chapter 9

Arie

THE GUARD'S ARRIVED ONLY moments after Kadin disappeared behind the mirror-door. They poured into my room, ready to fight whatever I asked them to.

I wanted to tell them where Kadin had gone, but something stopped me.

The first guard strode up to me. "What is it, my Queen? Why did you call?"

"There was an intruder!"

He gestured to the other men, and they immediately began a search of the room. "How did he get in?" he asked, his hand hovering over the sword at his waist.

One of his men called from the side, "We were in the halls and didn't see anyone."

"Maybe over the balcony, then?" The guard pointed in that direction and two of his men strode toward it.

My mouth opened, but no words came out. Wrestling against the strange protectiveness I felt toward someone who'd just trespassed, I raised a finger and pointed toward the mirror. Still the words wouldn't come to explain how Kadin had come in through the secret entrance. Frustrated with myself, I pointed more aggressively.

The guard frowned, following the direction to my reflection in the mirror. "Your intruder is..." he trailed off, growing uneasy, "is *you*, your highness?" He cleared his throat, glancing around at his men, who'd all slowed in their search. "Ahh..." It was *his* turn to struggle to find words. "If you feel that way about yourself, perhaps a friend or mentor could help. The guard isn't her majesty's best solution in this case, I'm afraid."

He waved for his men to exit the room, which they did, hastily. Bowing as he backed toward the door, the head guard made more excuses before leaving on a far too obvious sigh of relief.

"What's going on?" I muttered as I found my voice. I didn't want any help. And I didn't want to see anyone, especially Kadin. I wanted to avoid him at all costs.

Didn't I?

✳ ✳ ✳

THEY POSTED A FEMALE guard inside my room, at the door to my balcony, and another just outside my rooms in the hall. Just in case the "intruder" came back, although I could tell they questioned my sanity.

At first, I paced up to the mirror and away again—each time something kept stopping me from actually opening the secret passageway and revealing the truth to the watching guard. Though she tried not to think about me, her thoughts were less than flattering. Her worries varied between her queen losing her mind and what she would do if the intruder was a ghost or a Jinni.

Hours passed, and over time, an awareness slowly came over me with the same tingling sensation as when a sleeping limb woke up. As it did, the guard's presence began to feel intrusive. I moved into my sitting room to be alone, trying to get space to think.

Memories of the Jinni arriving in Hodafez floated through my mind. They didn't mesh with the other memories already there, as if somehow two scenarios had happened simultaneously.

In one, I happily invited the Jinni ambassadors into my home without question. In the other, the one returning to me, I'd fought them with every inch of my being. That was the part of me that had saved Kadin, although just barely. *Did he make it out of the castle safely? I have to find a way to stop this...* I trailed off. Enoch could make me forget again at any moment; I needed to do *something*.

Sitting down at my desk, I dipped a quill in ink and hurriedly scribbled a note to myself with everything I could remember. Though the ink spattered and some of it smeared on my hand, I didn't stop until I was done. Waving it rapidly, I blew on the ink, desperate for it to dry.

Multiple footsteps sounded in the hall, drawing closer. Even though the ink wasn't fully dry, I hid the note in the folds of my skirts as I re-entered my bedchamber. Ignoring the guard by the balcony, I headed toward the lavatory. Locking myself inside, I searched the small bath for a hiding place. Inside the tub was too easy to spot. The mirror stood on a stand and was too open as well. There was little else in the room besides a rug on the floor to dry wet feet and the shelves for towels.

Outside, the door to my bedchambers opened. I ran to the towels and buried the note underneath the one furthest back and least likely to be moved by a well-meaning servant—for a few days anyway. I bit my lip. *How will I know to look there later if I lose my memories again?*

Too late.

"Queen Arie," Enoch purred, his voice slightly muffled through the door, but the compulsion I'd learned to recognize was clear. "Please come speak with me as soon as you're able. We have much to discuss about this intruder. I think you're hiding something, but I am confident you'll tell me whatever it is."

My stomach sank as my feet carried me toward the door to open it and obey, numbness taking over. Unfortunately, I felt confident that if he asked the right questions, he was right. I *would* give Kadin away.

Chapter 10

Kadin

WHEN I REACHED THE Khov Inn in Hodafez less than a half hour later, I was still confused. *What had possessed Arie?*

I found a table in the common room and sat, leaning my head back against the wall with a sigh. A few small groups sat around the room eating breakfast or lounging, but most tables were unoccupied while travelers went about their day.

That left me alone in the corner with my thoughts. Ever since we'd come to Hodafez to help Arie evade her forced marriage, things had changed. Our group felt like it had splintered into pieces. Illium had left us completely. Naveed, Ryo, and Daichi were all off in different kingdoms, still searching for a solution for Arie's father. They didn't know yet that he'd passed away.

The only one who'd come back so far was Bosh. He was on the other side of the room, playing cards with a few gentlemen, but I didn't really feel like talking to him. The only person I wanted to talk to right now besides Arie was Naveed. Maybe he would know what foolishness had caused Arie to react like that. Sure, she'd told me to leave her alone after her coronation a few weeks ago, but I'd thought she simply needed time, not that she hated me. Maybe I'd been wrong.

I found a splinter along the side of my wooden chair and rubbed my finger across it, feeling the pain and doing it anyway. If you never forgot how pain felt, then it couldn't surprise you when it happened again.

It felt like I'd lost my crew, and now Arie. And I'd lost someone before. The day my brother died still felt as fresh to me as the day it happened four years ago. Whether I should blame Prince Dev or his horse, it didn't matter to me anymore. It was my baby brother. He'd been only five years old. I'd knelt in his blood, trying to save him, but there'd been nothing I could do. And nothing I could do when Prince Dev made the rest of my family disappear, either.

I'd wasted years gathering my crew, searching for a Jinni who would bear witness to the prince's crimes and bring justice. I'd thought Gideon's punishment would be what I needed. To finally fix what Prince Dev had done to my family. But it hadn't solved anything. Not even close.

So here I was, leaning against the wall of some small village pub, drinking alone, more aimless than I'd ever been in my entire life. I picked up a toothpick, trying to ignore the niggling thought. *Why was I still here?* Maybe I should leave Arie alone like she asked.

My men hadn't complained, but there wasn't a single job here, besides Arie's castle, of course. Arie—or should I say, the Queen of Hodafez—had gifted each of us a horse, along with a grand assortment of jewels from the castle keep after we helped stop her wedding, remarking that it was probably easier for her to just give the jewels directly to us—referencing our chosen occupation. As if I would ever stoop to robbing her.

Still. Job or no job, if I wasn't welcome here, I should just leave.

I stepped outside for some fresh air, taking just a few steps when I spied a familiar red-headed girl bopping down the street on a horse. Already past our inn, she turned the corner down another street.

Frowning, I walked around the inn to the street behind it and waited, until she rounded the corner. She was so focused on staying in the saddle that she didn't see me until the horse almost ran me over. "Kadin!"

"Stopping by for a visit?" I teased, but stopped at the way she said my name. "What's wrong?"

"It's Arie—something's wrong with her, and these Jinni came—"

"Not here," I cut her off, glancing around to see if anyone had been close enough to overhear. "Come inside."

I helped her out of the saddle, leaving the horse and some coin with the stable boy, and led the girl, who's name escaped me, toward the front door.

"Arie's not in her right mind," the girl blurted as we walked. "I was—"

I held a finger to my lips. "Wait til we're alone." I flung open the door. Bosh still sat at one of the tables with a group of men in town playing cards. He swiveled around in his chair as the door crashed into the wall and grinned. "Rena! What're you doing here?"

That was her name. I made a mental note to remember this time.

"It's a long story," Rena told him, opening her mouth as if she might spill it right in front of all the men at the table.

"Not here," I reminded her under my breath. Strolling over to the table, I stopped to pick at a bit of dirt under my nails. "Just got wind of a job."

Bosh immediately scooped up his small pile of winnings, and shoved them into his bag in one big swipe. "I'm out, fellas." He nodded to the men around the table. "Probably better I go now anyway, while I still have my horse." His wink and jovial smile, and probably the fact that they still had a good chunk of his reward, kept them from complaining.

I didn't let either of them speak until we reached the room I shared with Bosh, and the door was closed. Moving to sit on one of the beds, I gestured for Rena to take the chair. "Go ahead."

She threw up her hands as she sat, struggling to explain. "Something's wrong with Arie. Do you remember that Jinni at Arie's coronation with the purple eyes?"

I nodded.

"This morning, he and another Jinni came to the castle in disguise, and they told Arie ridiculous things, and she just… she *believed* them. He has her completely under his control! I think if he'd told her she was a Mere, she would've jumped right into the—"

"I understand," I interrupted, glancing at Bosh. "I've seen it before." With King Amir. It explained a lot. No wonder Arie had acted so strangely. The Jinni might have their code of unbreakable laws to protect the humans, but so far the only Jinni I'd ever met who honored the code was Gideon.

I stood to gather my things. "We need to help her. The tunnels might be compromised, but Bosh and I can find another way in, and we can help Arie get out of there."

"And then what? Let the Jinni take over her kingdom while she runs away?" Rena mocked. "I'm sure she'll appreciate that. Or, more likely, they'll just capture you too."

"What else do you expect me to do?" My voice rose, though I hadn't meant it to. "Leave her there for them to kill her?"

"They're not going to kill her," Rena argued, shaking her head. "I heard them. They said something about needing her to prepare the people for changes, and um…" She squeezed her eyes shut trying to recall. "Also they mentioned King Amir coming in a few days." She opened her eyes and smiled at me. "See? We have at least a few days before anything happens. Arie will be fine while we get help."

"Help," I repeated in a monotone.

She rolled her eyes. "Unless you have secret Jinni Gifts like Arie, you're not going to be able to take them on your own. And I don't know anything about Jinni. We need someone who *will* know what to do. We need Gideon."

I blinked. Staring at her as I mulled it over, I had to admit, she had a point. If the Jinni caught me trying to get Arie out of the castle, I would be completely helpless. And I doubted Arie would be okay leaving her kingdom behind.

"There's one flaw in your plan," I told Rena after I'd gone through all the angles. "We don't have any way to get in contact with Gideon."

"I do," she said with a proud smile. "I just need to figure out how to use it."

I opened my mouth to question her when a fist pounded on the door to our room. "Were you expecting anyone?" I hissed at Bosh.

He shook his head, eyes darting to the door.

"Open up in the name of the Queen!" a male voice yelled.

Arie sent guards? This was worse than I'd thought. My mind raced as I ran to the window to see if there was a way out. We were on the second story. The jump to the roof below was too far.

"What's going on?" Bosh whispered.

"Arie might've sent guards after me," I glanced around the room. There was nowhere else to hide besides a tiny wardrobe or under the bed. The first places they would look. I waved them toward the window. "Quick, get on the roof!"

Bosh stepped through the wide window without question, holding out a hand for Rena from the other side. I followed, pulling the window shut softly. The roof wasn't too steep, but it wasn't very wide either. Bosh and Rena stepped to one side, out of sight, and I stepped to the other as the door slammed open inside. I pressed myself against the side of the inn. This was a poor plan. They only needed to poke their head out the window and our hiding place would be revealed.

Drawers opened and slammed closed, followed by multiple footsteps, as the owner of the inn complained loudly outside. Rena's lips were moving inaudibly as she held her necklace of shells in one hand.

When the window burst open, I froze.

A guard's head appeared, surveying the sharp drop down to the street.

"No one's here," a voice called from inside.

Grunting, the first guard turned to close the window. When his gaze hit me, my breath stopped. But there was no light of recognition. The window clicked shut. Footsteps tromped around inside, fading, and the door slammed shut behind them.

I stared at Rena as she let go of her shell necklace. *Had she done that?*

There wasn't time to question it.

Pushing the window open, I hopped back inside to throw the rest of my supplies together. "Pack your bags," I told Bosh over my shoulder. "We're leaving."

We hauled our bags over our shoulders and slipped down the back staircase.

Picking up my pace, I ran to the stables, tossing another round of coins to get the stable boys to help saddle our horses.

Rena and Bosh were quiet, glancing at each other, and at me, but I didn't say anything, and they didn't ask.

Once outside we swung onto our steeds, and waited nearly a full minute for Rena to find her way onto her own, using a nearby gate. Without a word, I kicked my gelding. Hooves pounded the dirt road behind me as they followed, and I didn't stop or slow until we'd left the town behind us.

We slowed our horses to a walk and continued that way for at least an hour, until another town appeared ahead.

Bosh and I still had jewels from Arie, but two men and a Mere spending the Queen of Hodafez' jewels might draw a bit more attention than we wanted. I swiveled in my saddle to face Rena. "Did you happen to bring any money?"

"Oh, lots." Rena's smile was genuine, stretching lazily across her face in confidence. She patted the saddlebags on both sides of her horse. I relaxed. With Rena's money, we'd be fine.

"I know how attached you humans are to your metal," she added, when I didn't say anything.

I choked a little. Coughing, I managed to catch my breath and said, "What? Show me." My gut told me I was going to regret asking.

Bosh and I drew closer, letting our horses set the pace as we flanked Rena. She struggled to open the leather saddlebags with one hand.

She pulled out horse shoes. Dozens and dozens of horse shoes. With a few bridles mixed in.

I rubbed a hand across my face and sighed.

Bosh broke out laughing, which made Rena scowl.

My lips twitched. I couldn't help myself and joined him. Rena, however dense she might be about the human world, was smart enough to realize she'd made some sort of mistake, but it was equally clear she had no idea what she'd done wrong.

Bosh reached over to take one of the horse shoes from her hand, pretending to study it, though it wasn't like there was much of a price range for horse shoes. "Hmm." He nodded, handing it back to her. "If you sell all of those, you might get enough to buy everyone dinner."

"That's it?" Rena frowned at the metal. "I thought for sure we'd be set for weeks."

Chapter 11

Rena

I FLOPPED AROUND ON horseback like a fish on land, which I supposed, described me perfectly. Kadin rolled his eyes at my complaints, but I was certain my poor backside swelled with bruises within minutes of mounting. Even though we'd slowed to a walk ten minutes down the road, my legs ached from gripping the saddle.

"Honestly," I told Bosh for the hundredth time, "I don't think these creatures were meant to be ridden. I feel quite certain."

He just laughed. I'd met him a few weeks ago, and though we hadn't spent much time together, I liked making him laugh.

"How much further do we have to go?" I whined. My legs were numb.

Kadin glanced over his shoulder. "I'm thinking a half day's ride should be far enough. Just over the border into the kingdom of Piruz. We can't help Arie if the Hodafez guard puts us in the dungeons." He sat on his steed as if he and the horse were one, flowing with the dark animal's movements, patting its black mane, not even bothering to keep one hand on the saddle horn. A complete natural *or* a complete fool, depending on who was watching.

I had a few protection spells from the sea to hide us and fend off at least a few men, but I didn't say that. I needed to keep my family's secrets, even if I didn't keep my tail.

Hoof beats pounded the road behind us. A small contingent of four guards from Arie's castle approached. I reluctantly loosed one hand from the pommel where I'd held on tight. I needed it for the spell. I reached a hand to my neck, tugging at the necklaces there, searching for a particular shell. I found the shell, clutching it in my hand and whispering over it.

The guards came roaring down the road.

Bosh paled. His hands shook, and I was almost tempted to tell him what I'd done, but in just a few short seconds the men galloped up to us and passed, without a second glance.

Bosh and Kadin both watched them go. "That was… lucky?" Bosh said, squinting at them in the distance.

"Mmmhmm," I agreed. "They must be on a different errand."

Though a frown wrinkled Bosh's forehead still, he nodded to himself, mumbling, "That must be it."

"I'm sure," Kadin said, not sounding remotely convinced. His eyes narrowed as he studied me. "Did I imagine it or did you do something like that back at the inn too?"

"I don't know what you mean," I said, squinting back at him. My horse tripped over nothing yet again. "Oof! This beast is determined to kill me! How much further do we have to go?"

The reminder of our hasty escape closed the door on Kadin's questions like a final shove. His brows drew together. "We should pick up the pace." But then he glanced back at me over his shoulder and added, "Whatever you were doing before, keep doing it."

Bosh and I chatted, but Kadin didn't say another word until we'd ridden for a few more hours. His forehead wrinkled in concern, probably still thinking about Arie. My legs were so sore and stiff, I could hardly think about anything, much less my plan to find Gideon and make him fall in love with me *while* saving Arie.

I shifted in the saddle and winced. "Please tell me we're getting close."

Kadin slowed his horse. "We crossed over the border into Piruz about a mile back."

I'd yet to figure out how to stop my beast, and it continued on a few paces before slowing too. Thank goodness they were pack animals.

"The guards were headed this way as well though," Kadin said, mostly to himself. "We should probably camp in the woods for one night, just to be safe. Bosh, you and Rena go make camp out of sight of the road. I'll go into town for some food and bring it back here."

"Deal." Bosh turned my horse and his own, heading for the trees as Kadin kicked his horse forward again.

"Wait!" I called after Kadin. Both men stopped their horses to look at me. I struggled to lift the saddlebags I'd filled with metal. "Don't forget the money!"

"Right." Kadin coughed. He cantered back toward us, scooping up the saddlebags to sling them over his own saddle instead. "Thank you."

"Good luck, boss," Bosh said with a laugh.

Kadin only rolled his eyes as he turned to leave.

I didn't even bother trying to understand their code.

Chapter 12

Kadin

BOSH HAD BUILT A roaring fire in the little clearing by the time I got back with food from town. We'd come far enough from Hodafez that I felt confident we'd be safe. At least for the night.

Even though Arie was only a half day's ride from here, I felt so helpless riding in the opposite direction. Too much time had passed already.

Rena watched me out of the corner of her eye as Bosh and I cooked dinner. I pretended not to notice, still trying to decide what to think of her.

We'd yet to be discovered, despite two close calls, which should have been a relief, but instead I couldn't stop worrying over what this Mere girl could do. Was she as dangerous as the Jinn? Worse? Those soldiers had passed by earlier as if we hadn't existed. And they'd looked right through me at the inn. Whatever she was doing, it could be a useful talent... *if* I could trust her.

I stood, needing to do something with my hands while I considered all the angles. Gathering small branches from the surrounding area, I threw them on the fire, only dropping to sit beside it once it was a roaring flame. I leaned back against a tree trunk. This would keep us warm all night. But we still needed a plan.

"You said you had a way to contact Gideon?" I asked Rena.

She sat in front of the fire, mesmerized. Pulling her gaze away from the flames, her hand floated up to her neck, and she nodded. "I just need to figure out a few small details," she assured us. "It shouldn't take long."

I wished desperately that I still had Gideon's talisman. That would've been so much easier than trusting a near stranger. But Arie seemed to trust this Mere-girl, so maybe I should too.

Even though it was still light out, I hunkered down on the forest floor and shut my eyes. "I just wish there was a way I could see her," I said. I couldn't help myself. "To make sure she was okay."

"Well," Rena drew out the word. "There is *one* way..."

My eyes flew open, and I sat up. "How?"

Rena glanced between Bosh and I, chewing on her lower lip. She spoke cautiously, "I could cast a dream spell."

I didn't know what that was and I didn't care. "Do it."

Chapter 13

Arie

I COULDN'T REMEMBER MY day, other than the sense that I hadn't left my rooms and I was mourning something. I was left completely alone, other than the guard outside the door. When a servant brought dinner, her thoughts jarred me into awareness, but Enoch was beside her and as they left, he told me not to worry and go to sleep. I crawled into bed without anyone prepping the room for the night, blowing out the candle myself. A whisper in the back of my mind said something was wrong.

Closing my eyes, I struggled to sleep. As I drifted off, awareness finally returned.

The light outside was a strange twilight when it should be dark. My room was bright without a single candle lit.

This was a dream.

And here, in this safe protected place in my mind, everything that had happened came back to me.

Enoch and the other Jinni. Controlling me. In one fell swoop, I'd lost my kingdom. And my father—no! *Was he truly dead?* Even in my dream, my eyes welled. I sank onto the bed. Memories of what I'd done under Enoch's compulsion flooded my senses. Kadin's face as I'd called for the guards came back to me. I started to weep—I didn't mean to—I just couldn't help it.

A knock sounded on the door to my bedroom—*but wasn't this a dream?* Frowning, I moved to open it.

My subconscious must have responded to my feelings by summoning a vision of Kadin. When I swung it open, he stepped inside.

Even though he wasn't real, I threw myself into his arms with reckless abandon. They wrapped around me, warm and comforting. I buried my face in the hollow of his neck and whispered, "I wish you were really here."

His arms tightened around me. "I am."

"I mean more than just in my imagination." I sighed, not letting go. What did it matter if I was vulnerable with him, if no one would ever know?

He didn't let go either, although I supposed that made sense, since he was a creation of my mind. "Arie," he murmured into my hair, "I'm really here and I can prove it."

I pulled back, but only enough to stare up into his face, brushing away the long hair that fell in front of those golden eyes. He did seem incredibly vivid.

He wiped away one of the tears trailing down my cheek before pulling me into another hug. "Rena came to me and told me about the Jinni. She has a way of letting us speak in the dreams. I'm really here. We had to leave Hodafez when the guards came after us, but we're hiding out in—"

"Wait!" I pulled back further, studying him. "If you're truly here and I'm not just wishing it, then you shouldn't tell me anything. I can't be trusted. Enoch can…" My voice grew thick with tears, but I held them back this time. "Enoch can make me tell him."

Kadin nodded, his expression thoughtful. "So, you wished I would be here?" he said finally. The corner of his mouth tilted upward.

My cheeks grew warm. How unfair that you could still blush in a dream. I cleared my throat, ignoring the question. "I shouldn't know any details of where you are, but at least tell me you're safe?"

"Completely," he said, rubbing my arms. "Are *you* safe?"

I hesitated. "For the time being. Honestly, I think Enoch intends to use me as a puppet. I'm no good to him dead."

Kadin's jaw clenched until a muscle ticked in his cheek. His golden eyes were fierce. "We're going to get you out immediately."

I wanted to sink back into his arms and agree, but I shook my head. "It's too dangerous. Enoch would overpower you in a heartbeat and then we would both be lost." For the first time since he'd appeared in my dream, I withdrew from his arms. It hurt. "You need to let me go."

"Enough," Kadin snapped, startling me. He took my hands and continued in a gentler voice. "I don't know who you think I am, but there's no way I'm going to forget about you." He took a deep breath, staring past me for a moment, then met my eyes. "We're going to try to find Gideon. If we can, I know he'll help."

"That would be better," I admitted.

He let go of one hand and stepped back, but even as he turned toward the door where he'd entered my room, he still gripped the other, eyes on me. "Just... stay safe, okay? I'll come for you as soon as I can."

I nodded, my throat too tight to speak, and he left, closing the door behind him.

Unable to help myself, I flung it open again, but he was gone.

Still. A tiny seed of hope had been planted. Maybe I could survive this.

Chapter 14

Rena

I LAY ON TOP of the log we'd dragged—or rather Bosh and Kadin had dragged—close to the fire, while Kadin lay on the other side and Bosh kept watch. Coming out of the dream spell, I sat up. It had grown dark out while we were asleep.

I glanced up at the sky and fell backward off the log in fright. "What are those?" I shrieked, not caring if I called the guards down on us in my panic. Thousands of little white creatures hovered over us. "Are they going to attack?"

The men jumped up at my cries, ready to fight whatever was out there, but as I lay in the dirt panicking, they looked at each other and Bosh burst out laughing. Even Kadin's lip twitched in a smile.

"What?" I yelled. I didn't see what all the fuss was about. "This isn't funny!" I said when they didn't answer.

"You've never seen stars before?" Bosh asked me between chortles. "What a sad life you lead under the ocean."

Stars. I'd heard of them, but assumed they'd be bright and fierce like the sun. My heartbeat slowed its thundering pace, and I climbed back onto the log, still staring at the black sky. "Those?" I asked, "Really? They're so small."

That just made him laugh more.

"I haven't had much reason to go outside at night before," I mumbled, my face growing red. "And the few times I did, the city lights were so bright I don't remember seeing them."

As we ate bits of warmed bread and meat that Kadin had brought from town, I studied the stars and snuck a few glances at the men when they weren't looking. Strangers to me, but friends to Arie. I could trust them about as much as anyone.

It also helped that I'd seen how much Kadin cared about Arie. He didn't know anything about dream spells, or he'd have realized he and Arie weren't alone when he entered her room.

I'd peered out at them from behind a curtain, but I swear, I could've been standing beside them and they still wouldn't have noticed.

Kadin scratched the back of his neck and stood. "I need a minute." Disappearing through the trees, he left Bosh and I alone next to the crackling fire. He'd been quiet ever since seeing Arie.

"They're so silly," I said, taking another bite of the chewy, overcooked meat Kadin had bought. "They love each other, but they won't do anything about it."

Bosh coughed and the tips of his ears grew red. "I think they *are* doing something about it, in their own way."

I scoffed. "That doesn't make any sense. If they really loved each other, they'd say it. Nothing else would matter."

"Love isn't always about getting what you want," Bosh argued. "It's about putting the other person first. They think they're doing the best thing for each other."

Eyeing him, I considered that. "Have you ever been in love?"

He blushed all the way through the light stubble on his cheeks. "No. I'm only sixteen." He coughed. "Do you want more?"

I nodded immediately. He moved to warm the food and I stopped him. "That's good," I said, taking it as it was. The humans ate a lot of hot food. I still wasn't used to it.

"Did you know your eyes reflect light in the dark like a cat?" Bosh interrupted my thoughts. "Do all Mere's eyes do that?"

"They do?" I lifted a hand to my eyes, startled. "I honestly don't know. The bottom of the ocean doesn't have any light to reflect."

"I like it," he said with a grin, turning back to the fire.

I smiled too and found myself studying Bosh's eyes in return. If mine were like a cat, his were like nothing I'd ever seen before. I was captivated by the way two tiny flames from the fire could leap into a human being like that—did they do so for a Mere as well? I instinctively lifted a hand to my own eyes to protect them at the thought. The Mere had few weaknesses, but fire was one of them. It hurt us more than it hurt humans and the recovery took far longer. I made sure to keep my distance from the flames, just to be safe.

Kadin returned to our little circle, dumping a handful of brush into the fire and standing over it to warm his hands. "Okay, explain to me how we're going to find Gideon?"

I scooted back to avoid any runaway sparks, while Bosh leaned in. Both of their faces were eerily lit up by the orange flames.

"Okay." I swallowed and wiped the crumbs from my hands so I could pull out the Key. It felt wrong to show it to humans. But they didn't need to know everything it could do. "It's not a big deal." I shrugged, holding it up so they could see the intricate designs and the crescent moon shape at the top, along with what I now knew were little stars tied to it with seaweed, right below the metal moon. The little stars were really tiny shells from the ocean that dangled and danced in the breeze. "I just need to figure out how to make it call to Gideon."

"It doesn't call to Jinni already?" Kadin frowned. "Are you sure it's actually an artifact?"

"Oh, it's definitely a Jinni artifact," I assured them. "It's just hidden right now, kind of in disguise—" The word reminded me of the Jinni visiting the castle in disguise earlier. *How had they removed it?* That shimmering effect. It was like stripping the outer shell that cloaked them, and once it was removed, they were visible. I studied the Key as an idea came to me, but I couldn't do it here. There was no privacy.

"Can we go into town?" I said before he could ask more questions. "I've heard stories about humans drinking in a pub and I've always wanted to try it."

* * *

IT TOOK SOME CONVINCING. But the night was still young. When I refused to explain until I had a drink, Kadin gave in, and we rode toward the nearest town.

As soon as we stepped inside the tavern, I excused myself.

The lavatories weren't as clean as back at the castle. It was just one outhouse out back, with a man exiting it. Nose wrinkling at the smell, I decided to go around behind it instead. That should be privacy enough. In the moonlight, I pulled the Key out from under my dress, touching the tiny star-shells that hung from the crescent moon at the top. Carefully, I unwrapped them, until I had one long strand of seaweed and stars in one hand and the Key in the other.

I waited.

Nothing happened.

Perhaps the Jinn couldn't sense the Key over the smell of the outhouse. I moved further outside under the blanket of the night sky, pocketing the strand of star-shells as I did. Still, no one came for the Key.

Though I waited another minute, I started to feel antsy. Maybe I'd been wrong. Maybe the Jinni Key wasn't an artifact after all, and I was wasting the little time I had left.

Frustrated, I tucked the Key back under my dress and made my way inside. A drink would be a good distraction.

* * *

"I HAVE FIVE SISTERS," I told Bosh and gulped another swallow of my third drink. My nose wrinkled. I was still waiting for it to taste as good as everyone else's faces said it did. Maybe Mere taste buds were different?

"What are they like?" Bosh laughed and shook his head at the way my mouth puckered after each sip, taking another swig of his own drink.

"My sisters?" I blinked. "Well, they're…" My mind was fuzzy as I pondered how to describe them. "Every day is a fight." I shrugged. "*Do this for me, Rena. Don't do that, Rena.* Even when I left, they were trying to scare me. *Keep your abilities hidden, Rena, the humans won't like them.*"

"Abilities? As in more than one? What can you do besides the dream spell?"

I hadn't meant to say that last bit. How was Bosh able to pay such close attention to the words that swam around us like little minnows? I could hardly keep track of the ones that had come out of my own mouth.

"It's okay," Bosh said with a casual shrug, setting his drink on the bar to ask for more. "I have abilities too."

My eyes grew wide as I stared at him. *I never would've guessed*. I'd known about Arie's Gift, but I'd thought humans like her were rare.

He began to blur into two before me. He and his double lifted their cups, hiding some expression, and chuckled to themselves.

I narrowed my eyes at the two of them. "Another joke?" My voice slurred, and I shook my head a little to clear it.

"Mmmhmm, good catch." He winked at me. "You're missing out," he called over his shoulder to what I assumed was Kadin. I didn't bother to check because every time I looked away from Bosh, a wave of dizziness swept over me. "This is the most entertainment I've had all month!"

Ignoring him, I asked, "If it's just a joke, then why are there two of you?"

Both him and his double burst out laughing.

One of the other travelers in the inn sat down at the bar with us in time to hear my words. "Maybe you should take a little break," he muttered under his breath.

"Or," the woman on the other side of the bar nudged another cup my way, "you could drink more! Maybe after this cup you'll see three of him!"

I grinned in delight, picking up the mug to drink it all. I barely even tasted it now, but the warmth burned down my throat and spread through my whole body. It made me forget the cool metal key that lay on my breastbone out of sight, burning a hole in my thoughts ever since I'd unveiled it nearly an hour ago. *Why was it taking so long?* It probably wasn't even working. I hadn't told any of them what I'd done. If it wasn't going to work, there wasn't much point.

I jumped out of my chair—the man on the other side of us caught me as I swayed. "I have an idea! Someone teach me to dance!"

"Gladly!" Bosh stood, holding out a hand to me, palm up. I imitated him, placing my palm face up in the air like his.

"No." He laughed, taking my extended hand and placing it on top of his own. "Like this."

Bosh took my hand and put his other hand on the small of my back just two steps into the dance, and though we whirled away and around, we kept coming back to that same stance.

I could see why the Mere were so disdainful of dancing in stories. It was so full of emotion and teasing. And complicated. I kept stepping on Bosh's toes. He didn't seem to mind.

The human drink had gone to my head. This close to Bosh, I couldn't help but notice the shadow of a beard on his chin, a dimple in one cheek when he smiled, the laugh lines around his eyes from a life of choosing to smile. He seemed to be a genuinely nice human. I decided through the drunken haze in my mind that we could be friends.

"So, tell me," he said between breaths as we leapt and twirled around the wooden dance floor with a few other couples. I bumped into one and we both offered a distracted apology before spinning away. "How long are you going to stay in the human world?"

Better not to tell him. "I'm not sure," I began to answer when his face was in front of mine. Then he flicked his wrist, and my body, loose from drink, obeyed the command, flying away from him with complete trust and abandon, snapping to a halt at the end of our arms. He flicked his wrist again to bring me back.

Two spins and I smacked into his chest, knocking the air out of both of us. His arms wrapped around me again.

"What was the question again?" I asked.

His warm breath was on my neck as he laughed, and I joined him.

Another spin out and back to the easy steps of the dance, but I was starting to fumble, even with Bosh leading the way.

"I was just curious, you know, if I'd see you after we save Arie and all that. Or if you have to go home?"

When I didn't say anything, he slowed a little, distracted from dancing, and we bumped into another couple. "What's wrong?" he asked, moving away without so much as an excuse to the pair.

"Oh, nothing." I stopped in the middle of the dance floor, pulling my hands away to rub my eyes. My head was starting to pound. "I don't want to dance anymore," I said without explanation.

I hadn't let myself think about what would happen if I didn't find Gideon and had to go home. I'd left the ocean with all my spells and high hopes, and I'd never made a backup plan because I hadn't thought I needed one.

Moving away from the dance floor, I found a group of men around a table playing cards. Dropping into an empty seat, I fixed my skirts, which made me miss my tail. I pushed away the dark thoughts and smiled at the men. "I want to play!"

Bosh was right behind me. "Rena, you don't have any money." He glanced up at the men around the table. "Maybe we could play for pebbles?"

"That's not any fun," the man with the smallest pile of coins grumbled, and the rest of them sat back as if already losing interest.

That annoyed me. "I have some things of value," I argued, pulling one of my necklaces from around my neck. A cord of seaweed, soft but stronger than most ropes when braided together like this, with over a dozen different shells, all small and delicate. The shells knocked together as I held it up. Or maybe it was because my hand was unsteady. I shook my head to clear it, but that just made me dizzy.

"Maybe those things are currency in your world." The first man laughed, shaking his head. "But here, they're about as good as pebbles."

"No, silly. These aren't just shells. They're all spelled." I held it out in front of me, pointing out one shell at a time as I explained. "This one here," I touched the tiny conch shell, barely the size of my thumbnail, where it dangled from the thin cord, "is a fighting conch shell. Which is ironic, since it's what I use to hide when I don't want to be seen."

They perked up, interested now, leaning forward to peer at the shells more closely.

"This," I slid my fingers to the round shell next to it, only slightly larger, "is a keyhole limpet. It's spelled to help you open any door." Their eyes lit up at that. I swayed a little, bumping into Bosh as I shrugged. "Well, not a *door* exactly. In the ocean, it's less used for locks than it is for sand dunes blocking the way, so it packs a bit of a punch. Not the best for a quiet entrance." They leaned back in disappointment, which made me want to find something else they'd like.

Flipping past the horn snail and the shark's eye, I stopped at the second largest shell on the cord. It was a smooth pearly white with a curl to it that made it look almost like an ear. "This is called a baby's ear." I blushed as I thought of the last time I'd used it. "And it can help you hear... well, let's just say you can hear almost anything you want to."

"If we used it now, would we hear those two lovebirds outside necking?" one man asked, elbowing his neighbor as they cackled. Even Bosh cracked a smile.

"I'm not familiar with that term." I frowned, tugging the shell away from the others, wrapping my fingers around it and closing my eyes. "But we can test it if you want—"

"No!" Bosh caught my hand between his own, startling me into opening my eyes. "Um, that's okay," he said, laughing nervously, still cupping my hands between his own. "We'll take your word for it."

I gathered 'necking' must be something embarrassing. Bosh's hands on mine were warm and when he pulled back, I missed it. I thought maybe I was cold, and crossed my arms to hug myself, but it wasn't the same. *Strange*.

"What do the others do?" the men asked, eyeing them curiously.

I picked up the necklace once more, choosing a shell that was almost the length of my pinky finger, and the same size around. "This is a rare cerith," I said, holding it up to the light so they could see the beautiful brown striping that swirled around the outside of the otherwise tan shell. I pulled it back, curling my fingers around it. "But I can't part with this one."

"Why not?" Bosh asked. The tavern's candlelight danced in his wide eyes. "Can't you get more? Are they hard to make?"

"Not that hard." I enjoyed being the center of attention; their eyes were fixed on me. "But most of the ingredients are closer to home, where the ocean grows too deep for humans to swim. So, if I lost this one," I tapped the cerith lightly, "I'd be in trouble. This is what gives me legs."

They stared at it with new eyes. The way it came to a point like a tail, yet had two distinct colors, forming two separate winding paths. The way they stared at the shells made me uncomfortable. Belatedly, I remembered my sister's admonition not to share my secrets.

"I don't really want to part with any of them," I said into the silence, pulling them close. "So, I guess I can't play after all."

"Yeah," Bosh said. "You don't want to lose those. Especially not the one for your tail. I don't want you to have to go home early."

"What would it do for a human?" one of the men asked, before I could answer Bosh. "Would it make one of us grow a tail?"

"I don't know," I lied, shrugging. "Maybe it would split your two legs into four." I held it out to him, pretending it was nothing. "Want to find out?"

He was quick to shake his head. I hoped this might be enough to make them lose interest in the shells, if they thought they only worked correctly for the Mere. I tucked them underneath my dress and out of sight, standing to leave the table.

"I know this doesn't mean a whole lot coming from thieves," Bosh whispered in my ear as I did. "But we won't take them. I promise."

"Oh, I'm not worried." I said, loud enough for the others at the table to hear, waving a hand at that as I shrugged. "It's very hard to steal from a Mere." The insinuation was that the shells couldn't be taken from me. But I still determined to keep them hidden away from now on. Because that was a lie.

Chapter 15

Kadin

FROM THE DOORWAY TO the common room, I watched everyone having a good time. Rena was unaware of her volume, yelling through her conversation with everyone, while the rest of travelers in the common room laughed at her. Even Bosh's volume had risen and his long limbs were sprawled loosely over the bar and stool.

I couldn't get rid of my own tension so easily. There was so much joy in the room; if I tried to join in, I'd only drag them down.

Something in the corner of my eye made me shift to look past them as the room fell silent.

A dark-haired man stood in front of Rena. His translucent blue-tinted skin made me think it was Gideon for a brief moment. But it couldn't be. Even from his back I could tell he was too short and he didn't have a cane. He glanced around the room before stalking toward Rena. Foolish girl that she was, she only smiled up at him.

Whatever she said was too quiet for me to hear. I pushed through the tables and groups of people, hurrying to join them just in time to see the strange Jinni frown. His eyes were an eerie shade of dark red. So much for Arie's promise when we'd first met that all Jinni had blue eyes. *How much of what we thought we knew of the Jinn was inherently false?*

"How are you immune to my Gifts, girl?" the Jinni asked Rena without really asking her, facing someone else in the far corner of the room who'd gone unnoticed until now.

A woman. Another Jinni.

Her glossy black hair waved softly over her shoulders and down her back with an other-worldly shine, and her eyes held the light-blue hue that I'd grown used to seeing on Gideon, though hers were lined heavily in charcoal and slanted in concentration.

The way she stretched her hands toward Rena then growled made me think she'd tried to use a Gift as well. They didn't know they faced a Mere. Could Rena protect herself from them? Could she protect *us* if the Jinni grew angry? My mind flashed back to the way she'd hidden us in the inn and along the road. I should've asked more questions. I'd been a fool to let her have her privacy. Now we were at the mercy of two strange Jinni, who didn't strike me as particularly friendly.

"You know why we're here," the woman said in a smooth tone with a smile that didn't reach her eyes.

Rena nodded, but shrugged. "You can't have it." *It?* My mind stumbled over the unknown before the image of the crescent-moon key that she claimed was a Jinni artifact came to me. Rena had said the key was in disguise. Normally I would have thought through all the angles before taking her word on it, but I'd been too focused on Arie. And Rena kept so many secrets. She hadn't even bothered to tell me she'd found a way to unveil it.

I didn't have time to chastise her as the two Jinni approached, circling her like wolves stalking their prey. I pushed through the people backing up, trying to get closer, though I had no idea what I planned to do.

"It's no use," Rena began, smiling at them and growing more confident, if that were possible. Must be the alcohol in her system. "Your Gifts won't work on—"

The woman lifted a glass bottle from a table and smashed Rena across the back of her head. Hard. Her red head hit the floor, and before I could blink, the woman reached down and yanked the leather string from Rena's neck. The crescent key dangled in the air.

She nodded to the other Jinni as we all stood with mouths gaping open, and with a movement I could only describe as leaning into nothing, the raven-haired woman shifted from a human form to an actual raven. The man followed, transforming into a bat. Just a few flaps of their wings overhead as everyone ducked and screamed, and they were gone. One woman in the corner fainted.

I finally got through the crowd and reached Rena, where she lay crumpled on the ground. Bosh already knelt by her side.

"Wake up," Bosh said, shaking her by the shoulders.

"Gentle," I said, as he lifted her off the floor. His worried eyes met mine. There was no blood; only a small bump forming on the back of her head. "Try to wake her up. I'll get us a room." Rena would have a headache, but she should be fine. I wasn't nearly as certain about us, or Arie, now that we didn't have that key.

Chapter 16

Rena

I GROANED, KEEPING MY eyes shut to stop the pounding in my head. Someone lifted me and hugged me so tight I gasped. "Can't breathe!" My eyes flew open to find everyone kneeling around me on the floor.

Bosh was the one who'd been hugging the air out of me. "Sorry," he said and let go. I fell backward at the sudden lack of support and he caught me just in time to keep my head from hitting the ground. "Sorry!" he said again.

I winced. "Is this what a hangover feels like? You made it sound like a minor headache," I accused him. "This feels like running head first into a tidal wave."

"You don't remember?" Kadin asked. He stepped through the watching crowd as they whispered. "There were two Jinni—they knocked you out and took your key."

That wasn't possible.

I touched my throat, feeling for the cord that hung there with the Key ever since I'd left home.

It was gone.

No.

"They shouldn't have been able to touch me!" *My protection spells hadn't worked?*

Bosh held a finger to his lips. "Rena, you're shouting."

"But I don't understand," I hissed. It hit me then. *They hadn't attacked me with their magic.*

"They were shapeshifters," Kadin said, drawing my attention back to his solemn eyes. "I'd heard some Jinni possess this Gift, but never seen one use it."

"Can all Jinni do that?" Bosh asked.

"Do what?" I whined. "I missed everything!"

"They turned into a bird and a bat," Bosh told me, wiggling his eyebrows. "It was kind of cool." That made the onlookers shake their heads and grumble. The barkeep muttered something about broken glass. Most of them returned to their food and drinks, and the volume in the room slowly returned to normal, though some people still watched us out of the corner of their eyes.

"I don't think they all can," Kadin answered Bosh with a shrug. "If the stories can be trusted, every Jinni's Gift or assortment of Gifts is different."

"That would've been nice to know," I grumbled, sitting up and sliding awkwardly out of Bosh's arms. His face flushed a rosy pink color that made me stare at him, which only made the color grow more visible.

When I glanced over at Kadin, his gaze had lowered to his hands.

"It'll be okay," Bosh reassured him. "We can still save Arie."

Kadin took a deep breath and stood, not looking at us as he started pacing. "I know. We just need a new plan."

"I already know the first step," I said, then regretted it when hope skipped across his face. "Going to bed," I finished awkwardly. Trying to stand, I winced, touching the back of my head. There was an enormous bump under my hair. It wasn't bleeding, but it was tender.

"This way," Kadin said, waving to us from the door. "I've got us a room."

Bosh scooped me up, letting me lean on him, and we followed Kadin toward the stairs. The whole room made a show of *not* watching us leave. As we walked, cold metal settled onto my chest, underneath my dress. I stiffened.

"Are you okay?" Bosh paused to glance down. His face was so close I could feel his breath on my cheek.

"Mmmhmm." I nodded, which caused a stabbing pain in the back of my head. I winced again.

"No, you're not." Bosh shook his head, focusing on the stairs. He half-carried me into the tiny room that held a bunk bed on each side with only a small table and chair between them. A stubby candle burned cheerily on top.

Bosh lowered me carefully onto the bottom bunk. *Was he blushing?* If my head didn't hurt so bad, I might've teased him. "You can have the bottom," he told Kadin, gesturing to the lower bunk as he climbed onto the top.

"I just need some time to think," Kadin said into the space, turning to leave. "I'll be back in a while."

After he left, I crawled under the covers. Bosh was in the opposite bunk, on top and out of sight. My head ached too much to sleep, but it also hurt too much to get out of bed and blow out the candle. I lay there, dizzy, watching the tiny flame dance.

The drink had left a shiny haze on my mind, but I was alert enough to wait until Bosh started snoring before I sat up, lifting a hand to my neck. A moment of dizziness forced me to stop and close my eyes until it passed. *Why did I drink so much?* Never again.

Once the pulsing stopped, I tugged at the chain around my neck. It had taken longer to return than usual—maybe because the Jinni had flown away so fast—but the Key had come back. It always did.

I pulled the little star-shells out of my pocket and wrapped them around the top of the Key once more.

It was so simple. Like all our magic, it involved a little bit of the ocean—in this case seaweed and shells—wrapped around the object. Making it completely invisible again. They shouldn't be able to sense it now.

I sighed in relief. Falling back into bed, I was so tired that not even my pulsing headache could keep me from dozing off. No Jinni would come searching for the Key and interrupt my dreams tonight.

A smile curled over my lips as I drifted to sleep. Dancing with Bosh had been fun. I liked this group. I didn't want my impending deadline to ruin this feeling, but I couldn't help it. There was less than two weeks left now before my deal with Yuliya ended. I took a deep breath and tried to focus on sleep. No more drinking and goofing around. I needed to find Gideon as soon as possible. First thing tomorrow morning, I'd unveil the Key again.

With the way my head felt, I didn't want to meet Gideon right now anyway.

Chapter 17

Arie

ENOCH LEFT ME ALONE throughout the day in long stretches. I knew because it was long enough for me to slowly come back to myself and find that hours had passed.

But it took longer each time. Without overhearing someone's thoughts, there was nothing to tether me to reality.

Ever since Enoch had learned of Kadin's visit, I'd been terrified that Enoch would find him and bring me down to the throne room to pass judgment. *What if he already found him and just hasn't told me?* I couldn't decide which was worse.

I needed to get out of my room, but the guards were also under Enoch's compulsion. No matter how hard I listened, they didn't think a single thing—no doubt thanks to Enoch—

and whenever I tried to leave my quarters without permission or step out onto the balcony, they stopped me. Even the secret passageway wasn't an option, since the guard standing at the entrance to the balcony would see.

I paced my room. Pieces of memory floated back to me. My father's funeral. There'd been hundreds of people gathered in the courtyards, but I'd never gone outside. The speaker had announced that I was now the rightful queen, his voice carrying. From the upper windows, I'd watched them weep as father's body was lain to rest. Proof that they hadn't been lying after all. Enoch had let me see it, let me grieve, before sending me back to my rooms to forget once more.

Tears slipped down my face at the memory.

I promised myself that I wouldn't let them win. Taking a small inkwell and quill from my desk, I hid them in the lavatory behind the towels as well as extra parchment paper, adding to my notes every chance I had.

Father is dead.

The script was smudged by my tears.

Enoch keeps the guards unaware.

Kadin is coming. He'll find a way.

The cryptic notes weren't much, but I didn't know what else to say. At least I had a record of the truth versus the lies Enoch was feeding me.

No doubt the guards wondered why I spent so much time in the lavatory, but they didn't say a word.

On my foot, out of sight beneath my skirts and the safest place I could think of to write a message, I'd also written: *lavatory, towels.* Whenever I sat on the toilet, my skirts lifted just enough to reveal the hidden message to myself.

Hours blurred together, and each time I saw the note on my foot, I would panic and rip through the towels, drinking in the words I'd left behind like a potion to cure my insanity.

I didn't know how my father had survived this mind control for so long. Though Enoch never touched me, it felt as if my mind was being reshaped each time he forced his will over mine, making me question my every thought and decision. I didn't know which memories were even mine anymore.

I lay down, hoping to sleep and see Kadin again. But instead, my mind kept playing another scene over and over.

Walking through the castle gates, with men on each side. They surrounded me. Obeying Enoch's orders. Or was it King Amir? *Who was even behind all of this?* I vaguely remembered mention of the Queen of Jinn, though what she would want with a human kingdom was beyond me.

Dragging me to the hanging post, they read the list of my crimes to our people. The rope around my neck was so heavy that its scratchy threads dug into my shoulders.

Each time my vision reached this point, I would shake my head to clear it, and try to forget. And then it would start all over again, the way nightmares always do.

I tried to think about Kadin's face instead. His golden eyes, and the dark shadow of a beard forming on his jaw, which only made him more handsome and drew my eyes to his lips. He would figure this out. I tried not to listen to the dark thought that whispered, *It's already too late.*

Chapter 18

Rena

WHEN THE SUN ROSE it woke me before everyone else. I had yet to get used to the changing light. Back home, we marked time with the feel of the tides; the light always remained the same. Blinking in irritation, I threw off the covers and scowled at the men who lay in the other bunk beds, both happily unconscious.

But my annoyance didn't last long. Remembering how the Key had come back to me last night, I lifted it out from under my dress again to see it in the light and reassure myself. There was a good chance I could meet Gideon today, if the second attempt at unveiling the Key went better than the first.

After all, he came back to this area often to visit Arie. He could be nearby even now.

Climbing out of bed, I paused. That moment we'd shared a year ago had kept me going, but now it felt impossibly long ago. With less than two weeks until my deal with Yuliya ended, the threat of failure loomed over me.

I shook my head to clear it. I could only hope Gideon would feel a strong connection to the one who'd dragged him from the bottom of the sea and saved him. If it was even half as strong as what I felt, it would be enough. There *had* to be a chance that he could love me. Because if he couldn't, who could?

Bosh rolled over in his sleep, and the turn brought back the memory of dancing with him the night before. I would love to dance with Gideon. Or maybe he could show me the human world and what he'd been searching for this last year. The first step was finding him. After that, anything was possible.

Moving the small wooden chair over to the corner, I sat by the small window. Light streamed in with a soft touch, warming my skin. This I didn't mind at all. I curled up in the chair and pulled the Key out from under my dress to stare at it. Slowly, I unwrapped the strand of seaweed and star-shells that kept it hidden, placing them in my pocket again for safe-keeping.

I imagined the Key calling to the Jinn, like a whistle only dogs could hear. Was Gideon close enough to sense it?

I almost expected him to show up right at that very moment. Or, if not him, another Jinni like last night. Instead, I sat in the quiet room, listening to the soft breathing of the two men, waiting. Nothing happened. Minutes passed. Last night it had taken a while. My stomach growled. Maybe I'd slip out and get some breakfast.

Down the dark stairwell on silent feet, I found the common room empty. A vast difference from last night. Just one woman in the back, preparing for the breakfast crowd. *Everyone else must still be asleep.*

The woman offered me porridge, murmuring that breakfast was a part of our stay, and asked if I wanted warm milk to go with it. I shook my head and waited until her back was turned to curl my lip at the meal. Warm everything. What I wouldn't give for a little bit of cold fish. And a seaweed wrap. And a few other nibbles that apparently humans couldn't or wouldn't stomach.

With a sigh, I moved to a quiet spot in the common room and spooned a lump of porridge into my mouth, forcing down one bite at a time to quiet my poor belly.

"Who *are* you?" a soft voice spoke behind me.

Whirling on the bench, I nearly fell off. His black hair, his pale blue eyes, and that long nose and face staring back at me. All familiar. Yet completely different from what I remembered. His presence held an intensity this time that hadn't been there before.

"Hello, Gideon," I whispered in awe.

✳ ✳ ✳

HIS THICK BROWS ROSE at my use of his name. "Have we met?"

My gills fluttered shyly in response as I opened my mouth to answer, to pour out the story of our beginning, but he held up a hand and cut me off.

"No. Not important. I can sense an extremely valuable Jinni artifact on your person, one I haven't sensed in decades. I don't know how you made it appear and then disappear before, but you must do so again immediately," Gideon demanded. He gestured to me with a cane. I didn't remember him having a cane before. *Had he been injured?* I worried over him, wanting to ask what had happened.

"Did you hear me?" His tone was sharp. Nothing like the husky quality of one barely aware, as it had been the last time we'd met. The only other time, actually. In my mind, we'd had many conversations since then. It stood out to me with stark clarity how little I knew him. I could predict what the Gideon of my imagination would do in this moment. But somehow, I doubted this real-life version of him would do anything I expected.

"Of course I hear you." I lifted my chin, feeling defensive. *Would he take the Key from me like the others?* No, I assured myself. *Not Gideon. That's not the Jinni I've watched this last year.*

Pulling out the cord around my neck for the second time that morning, I revealed the Key. Flustered, I focused on the task so I wouldn't have to meet Gideon's eyes, taking the strand of seaweed and star-shells from my pocket and gently tying them around the Key once more. I'd imagined our second meeting so many times, so many different ways, yet I'd never seen it going quite like this.

He breathed a sharp sigh of relief as I finished veiling the Key. Surprised, I dared to look at him. "You felt that? The difference?"

If possible, he grew more stiff. When he nodded, it was just one short dip of his chin. "Along with anyone else in this kingdom or those surrounding. The call is strong. I'm surprised no one else found you first."

"They did," I told him, shrugging. "It's just not that easy to steal." That made his frown deepen, when I'd thought he'd be pleased.

"What's wrong?" I asked, hopeful. *Did he recognize me?* In my dreams, he'd always known me immediately, but a slow awareness could create even deeper gratitude. An even stronger bond. I smiled up at him, but his features didn't change. No response. My smile faded a bit in the awkward silence.

"Is this a joke to you?" he said, after studying me for a moment. "Who are you," he repeated his earlier question, and my hopes rose again, until he added, "to be holding such an object?"

I swallowed. Should I reveal that I was the daughter of the Sea King and Queen? Certainly not in line for the throne, so it wasn't terribly relevant, but I still wanted him to see me for me, instead of as a Mere princess.

"A Jinni Key," he murmured to himself, staring at the little piece of metal in my hand, "and you don't even know what you possess."

Indignant, I closed my mouth. Who did he think I was? Did he think this Key had somehow just *fallen* into my possession? My irritation grew.

"Of course I know what it is," I snapped, shoving it back under my collar and out of sight, daring him with my eyes to ask for it now. *How rude.* I stood to move past him. "I'll go fetch Kadin," I said as I crossed the room. "He needs to speak with you urgently."

He sputtered. He actually sputtered. "I don't know what in the name of Jinn is going on here," he said, "But I'm not letting you out of my sight!"

Chapter 19

Kadin

THE DOOR TO OUR room burst open, waking me instantly. Panicked, I sat up and threw off the covers, imagining the worst.

Rena entered the room. Flounced in, really, arms crossed, frowning, not bothering to say hello or apologize for waking us. I hadn't seen her angry before, but something had her riled up. "Gideon's here," she muttered as she fell into the chair by the window, and it took me a second for her words to sink in.

"My apologies," a male voice said from the doorway.

Deep black hair down to his shoulders and neatly brushed back, stiff posture, thin but muscled, and the ornate cane: I recognized Gideon immediately. He'd found us after all, just like Rena had promised. So why didn't she seem happy about it?

"Come in, Gideon. You don't need to stand in the doorway." Climbing out of bed, I moved to wake Bosh, but he'd already left the room.

Gideon took a few steps inside and stopped in the middle of the small room.

"How did you find us?" I asked, glancing between Gideon and Rena, who still stared out the window at the street below.

Gideon didn't answer right away, moving to close the door before he spoke. "I followed the Key the Mere girl possesses," he said slowly, after an almost imperceptible pause. I stood between them now, and his eyes seemed almost to look past me to Rena for a moment.

"But it was stolen…" I said, swiveling back and forth trying to see both their faces at once. "I'd thought it was like a light in a dark room, but it sounds more as if you're tracking it like a hound on a trail?"

"The 'girl's' name is Rena," she interrupted, as if I wasn't in the room. While Gideon's blue eyes were passive, Rena's green eyes danced and sparked. But when she stopped glaring at him long enough to look at me, her expression turned sheepish. "And I was going to tell you. The Key came back."

"Came back," I repeated stupidly. "When?"

"Last night," she mumbled.

"The Jinni Key cannot be stolen," Gideon spoke up from the other side of the room. "The last time I knew of its existence, it belonged to different members of the royal family of Jinn. And they made sure it was spelled to always return to the owner unless given freely."

"Wait," I rubbed my forehead, dropping onto the bed so I didn't have to twist my head back and forth to look at them both. "Does that mean… Rena, did you *know* it would come back?"

Now she definitely looked ashamed, ducking her head and playing with the wavy ends of her red hair as if lining them up was of extreme importance.

That answered my question. "You should be ashamed," I snapped. All my emotions building up from the night before spilled over. "I've been sick with worry over Arie and what might happen to her." My voice rose, "This so-called Jinni Key was her only hope and you let me believe that it was gone forever. You're so selfish!"

The silence following my words felt as heavy as if an actual storm had begun, soaking each of us, weighing us down. Rena's red cheeks grew pale. "How dare you speak to me that way," she hissed.

Though Gideon had all the strength of his Jinni heritage, he was still a man in the same room with an outraged woman. He swallowed, moving to the other side of the room on silent feet, keeping his gaze on the wall, as if to remove himself from the quarrel.

"I want you to leave," I said without thinking. I was shaking. I clenched my hand into a fist so they wouldn't see my fingers tremble. "Get your things and get out. I need to speak with Gideon alone."

At this, Rena's mouth fell open and she looked truly worried for the first time. "I didn't mean to... you can't do that!"

"You're dismissed," I said in a hard tone.

Though Rena looked to Gideon as if he might back her up, he was engrossed in the designs of his cane, making his stance in the whole conversation quite clear.

Rena released the breath she'd been holding, and in the quiet space, I heard the hitch of held-back tears.

She lifted her chin. "Good tides then," she said in a tight voice as she opened the door and walked out, not bothering to shut it behind her.

Chapter 20

Rena

I FELT SMUG. I'D only said 'good tides,' instead of "tides be with you," which was the traditional way to bless someone when leaving. A slap in the face as far as my people were concerned. Although, Kadin probably didn't know that.

He slammed the door behind me, right on my heels, and I jumped. If I'd remembered how doors made such effective tools of communication, I would've done it myself. That would've been very satisfying. I contemplated opening it just so I could slam it again, but decided against it. Instead, I wandered down the dark hall past other rooms where guests of the inn still slept, making my way toward the stairs. I sat down at the top, unsure what to do.

This wasn't right. Gideon was supposed to stop, mouth falling open, and stare at me. Then, when he finally spoke, he would say in a breathy voice, "You're the girl I've been looking for." In some versions, he even kissed me.

I clutched the Key. He was close enough that I should be able to sense his greatest desire. I whispered, *Gideon.*

The inky vision appeared on the dark wooden wall before me in the quiet stairwell. There he stood, handsome as ever. Proud forehead and long nose with those distinctive blue Jinni eyes, too vivid to be human. This time, he stood at a gate to what I assumed was Jinn, but he held out a crescent moon shaped Key—*my* Key—as an offering to get in. The gate slowly opened before him, allowing him inside. I sighed and dropped the Key, letting the vision fade as I put my head in my hands.

Nothing was going according to plan. I'd been certain that once I found Gideon the most difficult piece would be over. I'd never once dreamt it would go like this.

And how dare Kadin dismiss me. I crossed my arms, sulking. So I hadn't told him immediately when the Key came back. I'd still gotten Gideon here, hadn't I? Although Gideon had been no help at all.

He and I would need to have a private conversation about backing each other up. Well, as soon as we had a private conversation where I reminded him that I was the girl who had saved him.

It baffled me that he could have forgotten, but I supposed that a brief glimpse of a girl in the middle of the ocean might be difficult to line up with another redhead on dry land. I couldn't fault him too much.

Taking a deep breath in, I blew it out. This was just a small setback. Once he remembered who I was, everything would go back to how I'd planned. We still had almost two weeks to get to know each other. I hugged myself tighter. Back in the ocean, I would've thought that was more than enough time. Now, I wasn't so sure.

Standing, I moved down the staircase to return to breakfast. I wasn't going anywhere. Kadin couldn't make me leave.

When I saw Bosh at the table toward the back, I wove around the other empty tables to meet him, grinning as my solution came to me.

"Good morning." I settled on the bench beside him. "You'll never believe our good fortune! The Key came back to me!"

He swiveled to face me, his arm brushing mine as he did. "No way! Did they bring it back? I knew the Jinni wouldn't break their code."

"Not exactly…" I hesitated. How could I get him on my side? "I wasn't myself last night—I blame the drinks. I completely forgot the Key always comes back when stolen. It can only be given."

"Wow," Bosh said on a breath, shaking his head. "That's lucky. Now we just need to hope that the next time we use it to call Gideon he's close enough to find us before any other Jinni. Their law says they can't use their Gifts to harm, but some of them don't seem to care."

I bit the inside of my cheek to keep from saying anything. The Mere had always known the Jinn weren't as righteous as they claimed to be. But it wouldn't do to scare poor Bosh. Humans couldn't do much about it; better they didn't know too much.

I cleared my throat and focused on winning Bosh over completely. "That's the good news I came to tell you. Gideon is already here. I used the Key again this morning, and he must've been the closest because he showed up. He's talking to Kadin right now." I left out the rest. No need for Bosh to know.

"Well, that worked out nicely," Bosh said, grinning wider. His shoulders dropped in relief and he picked up his bowl to eat. "Makes me think this whole little errand will be a breeze."

I beamed at him. "Absolutely." In a show of solidarity, I got up to get a second bowl of the mushy breakfast and eat with him. I'd make sure of one thing before Kadin and Gideon came downstairs: Bosh would be on my side. And I wouldn't be going anywhere.

Chapter 21

Kadin

A DOZEN EMOTIONS CROSSED Gideon's face as I explained what had happened in his absence.

"I understand your predicament," he told me when I'd finished. "But I'm not sure what I can do."

"We watched you fight Enoch in the castle before," I argued, "and you chased him off. Why couldn't you do that again?"

Gideon sighed and tapped his cane lightly on the floor, just once, but for him it might as well have been wild fidgeting. "That was quite lucky, to be truthful with you. I'm not sure I would have survived that fight if he'd gained the advantage, and I simply cannot risk it again. My mission is far too important."

"What is your mission?" I asked, always strategizing. "Maybe if you help us, we can help you in return. What do you need? Money? Resources? Soldiers? If you help Arie take back her throne, I guarantee she will give you all those things and more."

He shook his head. "No."

"What then? I'll do whatever it takes." I never begged like this. It showed your hand too much. But then again, this was Gideon; he could read my mind, so I'd probably never had the upper hand to begin with. "Just tell me what you need. Gideon, it's Arie!"

He stared at me, unblinking. If it had been anyone else, I'd have thought he didn't care, but I knew better. Gideon cared almost as much as I did.

The silence stretched long enough for me to hear the village outside waking up and people beginning to fill the streets, calling to each other, bargaining over market items. I held my breath.

"In Jinn, we don't have multiple kingdoms," Gideon spoke finally, and I frowned, trying to figure out how this was an answer. "We only have one. One King, or one Queen. And *one* heir." He finally pulled up the chair and sat. "The heir to the throne of Jinn, the crown prince, went missing a little more than a year ago. It's my duty to find him."

Only one ruler for the entire realm? And why was it Gideon's duty? I mulled that over for a moment. "Well then. We'll help you find him. My crew can find anyone. We found you, didn't we?"

"I believe he's still somewhere in Jinn."

"Oh." My gaze dropped to my hands. I stood and moved to look outside.

"I've spent the last year since his disappearance, trying to return to Jinn to find him," Gideon said softly.

When I glanced over at him, it felt like looking at a map I'd been following, but I'd just realized the directions were all wrong. "You can't get back?"

For a long moment, Gideon didn't say anything, just rubbed his jaw in thought. I began to think he wouldn't answer at all. He expelled a long breath of air, as if releasing years of pent up secrets, and softly said, "I cannot."

"Okay." I shrugged. "In return for helping us defeat Enoch, I solemnly swear to help you return home to Jinn. On my honor and deathbed, I so swear." A small voice inside me asked why I was doing this for the girl who kept pushing me away. But I didn't need to answer it. I knew why. "Tell me whatever you need right now, and we'll help you the best we can."

He thought it over carefully, as he always did, and I was surprised when he nodded. "There is one thing," he told me. "I want that girl's Key. It's one of a kind and extremely valuable to a Jinni, especially the royal family. I think there's a strong chance I could trade it for entrance to Jinn."

I sighed. Once again, saving Arie hinged on the unpredictable Meremaid. *Would she agree to this plan?* I probably shouldn't have snapped at her earlier—that hadn't helped. With any luck, she was still in the inn. I could only hope she cared enough about Arie to consider this trade. "I'll see what I can do. Let's go find Rena. We don't have a lot of time."

Chapter 22

Rena

BOSH AND I SLIPPED out of the inn for a quick jaunt through town, searching for a vendor selling raw fish. It was proving difficult. Those who had any were either selling it in bulk or it'd already been cooked.

"Just a taste," I'd pleaded with the last one, but he hadn't been a fan of that idea.

"I really don't think you'd like it, you know, in your… current form," Bosh stumbled over his words. He'd seen my gills from the first day and been fascinated with the Mere ever since. Except when it came to my desire for a meal from home. His nose scrunched up in disgust at the thought of cold, raw fish.

"Trust me, it's delicious." I tilted my head back and closed my eyes as we walked, trying to forget the poor start with Gideon. I focused instead on the way the sun kissed my face with warmth, something I'd never get sick of.

"I'll take your word for it," Bosh said. He grasped my elbow, gently guiding me back on track.

I let him, keeping my eyes closed for another moment. It was moments like this that I felt torn between two worlds. In love with my own, but falling hard for this one. The real reason I'd asked Bosh if we could get out of the inn for a bit, was partly to solidify my place in this group and partly to make a new plan. All my previous strategies had hinged on Gideon remembering me, and that clearly wasn't the case.

And if nothing works? If I was wrong all this time?

I stopped in the middle of the street to look at Bosh. "Show me something human," I said fiercely, taking his arm and squeezing. "Something I can remember—forever." I'd almost said *when I go back home.* But I didn't want to go back home. Certainly not under Yuliya's conditions. I couldn't give up yet. There was still a chance. After all, Gideon was *here*, now. That was half the battle.

"Hmm, human things..." Bosh looked around the nearby vendors, squinting in thought. "What about cold cream?" He licked his lips. "It's so good. It's mostly milk and sugar."

"Sugar?" I didn't recognize the word.

"Mmmhmm, and milk."

"Milk…" I thought of the warm milk they'd tried to give me at breakfast with the porridge and grimaced at the memory. Gross. Cold cream sounded awful. "No, thank you."

"Um, let's see." We wandered further down the street as Bosh thought. "We could go see the castle," he said, eyes lighting up. "This town is only a few miles from the Piruz castle. It has beautiful architecture, very unusual—"

"I doubt it compares to back home." I waved a hand in dismissal. "When your kings learn how to grow a living castle from the coral reef, smoothed by the current into delicate spires, and use its flow for movement within and protection without. Well, I'll wait to see one of those." I smiled over at him, feeling proud of my elegant home, which was at least ten times as large as any human castle—it stretched from the depths of the ocean nearly to the surface. If only he could see it. It could rival a human sunset.

"Oh. Okay." He didn't meet my eye. Was he hurt? Belatedly, I realized I'd insulted his idea. Belittled it even. I felt oddly guilty. I didn't like it.

"On the other hand," I tapped my chin as if reconsidering, "it does qualify as a human thing I could never find back home, in which case, it's perfect. You're a genius!" To make him feel better, I gave the poor human a kiss on the cheek. The fuzz on his face tickled my lips, and I pulled back quickly. He blushed. My cheeks heated too.

Ignoring the awkward moment, I skipped on ahead as if truly excited. "Aren't you coming?"

He laughed, catching up to me and pulling me away from one street toward another. "Actually, it's this way."

Chapter 23

Kadin

"HAVE YOU SEEN RENA?" I asked the innkeeper. Gideon followed me into the room, and we stopped between the long wooden tables. At one of them, travelers lounged eating breakfast. The innkeeper shrugged. He didn't bother to look up, moving around the bar, cleaning.

"If you mean the redhead from last night, she asked that kid to go for a walk," a man spoke up from a table where he was playing cards with a small group.

"A walk *where*?" I asked through clenched teeth as I forced what I hoped resembled a friendly smile. Time was precious right now, and they were going sightseeing?

"Um…" The man shrugged, looking to his friend, who spoke without looking up, playing another card.

"For fish."

"Ah, yes," the first man nodded, then shook his head at the memory. "She wanted raw fish. Strange girl."

I thanked the man, turning to Gideon and tilting my head toward the door. "Let's check the marketplace."

Gideon nodded, and we set out, exiting the tavern in a hurry, seeking the redhead with the indispensable Key.

I expected we would spread out, but Gideon stayed with me. "How long have you known this Mere-girl?" he asked.

"Not long," I told him. "We met her just a few weeks ago."

"And you trust her already?"

I opened my mouth to say yes, that she was the reason I'd escaped Hodafez with my head still attached to my shoulders. Something held me back. Usually, I trusted my instincts in these situations, so after a slight pause, I shrugged. "I'm not quite sure, to be honest."

There was a small pool of silence around Gideon. I didn't expect him to respond, but when I glanced over at him, I was surprised to find him scowling. "I can't tell either," he murmured, tapping his cane to the ground as we walked, not leaning on it at all. "But the Mere are not to be trusted. It's been this way for centuries."

Now it was my turn to frown. The Jinn weren't all they said they were, so maybe I shouldn't be surprised to find that the Mere weren't either. Right now, all I cared about was rescuing Arie. Everything else was irrelevant.

I followed my nose and found the meat market quickly. Not just one, but all the fish vendors remembered Rena. Something about how she wanted them to describe their catch. The last one at the far end of the market pointed down a side road when I asked where they went, and said simply, "That way."

I picked up my pace, more determined than ever to find Rena. On the road ahead, I spied the pair of them. Bosh's head thrown back with laughter and Rena's long red hair swinging back and forth as she shook her head at something. They seemed to be having a grand time.

I broke into a jog to catch up to them. They heard my footsteps pounding on the road and turned.

"Kadin," Bosh greeted me with a smile, not deterred by the scowl on my face in the slightest. "Come join us! We're going to see a castle!"

Sure enough, I spied the tips of the Piruz castle towers in the distance. I stopped where we stood, forcing them to stop with me. I pinched the bridge of my nose, trying to find the right words. "You can't just wander off." My voice rose louder than I intended in my frustration. "We have to figure out how to help Arie. Have you completely forgotten about her?"

Rena was small, barely five feet tall and skinny. I loomed over her without even trying, but she placed her hands on her hips, not intimidated in the slightest, glaring fiercely. "Of course not!"

"Arie is alone!" I shouted back. "She's completely helpless while you're going off on a little adventure." I shoved my hands into my pockets to keep from strangling both of them, lowering my voice, forcing it to steady though it came out strained. "Gideon is willing to help us." I waved behind me at the tall Jinni who stood further back on the road, waiting. "He only asks that you give him your Key. So tell me, what do you want for it?" Everyone had a price.

"Nothing," she snapped, crossing her arms and turning to walk away. She yelled over her shoulder, "This Key is priceless. I'm not giving it to anyone."

I kicked at the dust on the road. The last four years of thieving made my fingers twitch; I could just steal it. But if the Key really was spelled to return to the owner when stolen, there was no point. I couldn't give it to Gideon, unless Rena gave it to *me*. Willingly.

Bosh spread his hands and shrugged apologetically. "Women, huh?" he said. Leaning in, he lowered his voice and added, "You just gotta be a little nicer. Let me talk to her."

Rolling my eyes, I let him jog to catch up with her while I remained a few paces behind.

Bosh was a good kid. Orphaned at a young age, he'd been thin as a reed when he'd joined my crew. He was still young, but he'd filled out and grown into those wiry muscles. Sometimes I let myself pretend this is what my youngest brother would be like, if he were still alive.

So, I let him try his way, even though I was impatient. The sooner we gave this Key to Gideon, the sooner he'd help us save Arie.

Chapter 24

Rena

BOSH CAME TO ARGUE his case, so I let him speak, let him feel he'd swayed me, though I'd already made up my mind to go back. I just hated being told what to do.

"Arie needs our help," he began.

I nodded along. I'd never said I wouldn't help her.

"And I guess Gideon wants your Key? I don't know if you'd be willing to give it to him, but he was offering to help us in exchange for you using the Key to help him. And I was thinking you'd said something about that yesterday, so maybe you'd be open to it?"

Throughout his speech, I continued to nod. I already knew Gideon wanted it. What he didn't realize is that he didn't actually need the Key at all. He simply needed me to unlock his deepest desire to return to Jinn, and he would be back home. Though, I had to admit, the price was guaranteed to be steep and extremely painful.

Perhaps, I *could* give him the Key—then Yuliya couldn't have it. *Would that work? Or would it go to her instead since I technically gave it to her first?* The possibilities flooded in, but one stopped me. *If I give him the Key, he'll leave.* And I wasn't ready to give up hope just yet.

Bosh chattered on, steps slowing as he reasoned with me, until we came to a stop in the middle of the road.

I sighed. I would help Gideon. And Arie. And Bosh and Kadin. *When I'm ready.*

Off to the side, Kadin and Gideon waited, though I didn't deign to look at them.

"So, what do you say?" Bosh asked, out of breath from the rapid speech. "Will you give us the Key?"

As Gideon stepped forward, unconsciously showing his hand, I made my decision. I *would* give Gideon the Key, but *only* after he was so smitten with me that he begged me to stay and fulfilled the other part of my deal with my sister.

I pulled the cord over my head to loosen the Key, holding it out toward Gideon. Ignoring the others, I stepped up to him, letting the Key dangle in the air between us. "I'd like to offer you a deal," I said with a pleasant smile. "Spend the day with me, and I'll give you the Key. As long as you help us save Arie, of course," I amended. That should give me even more time with him. The plan was perfect.

His own hand, already halfway extended toward mine, hovered in the air so close that I could practically taste his impatience on my tongue. He pulled back and straightened. To have what he'd been searching for just inches from his grasp, yet completely out of reach.

"Just one day," I baited him. "How bad could it be?"

Bosh was quiet. He seemed uncomfortable with tension. He'd never do well in the sea courts back home. I'd learned a long time ago not to care what someone thought of me, to mind my own business. As my father liked to say, life was simpler that way.

"You'd delay us an entire day?" Kadin's voice shook as he stepped closer until I could no longer overlook him. "What about Arie?"

I shook my head, still smiling, though not even Bosh would smile back now. "Arie is perfectly safe while Enoch is controlling her. It will be far more dangerous for her when we return. I think it would be quite wise to have an extra day to prepare a strategy, don't you? Unless you already have a plan I'm not aware of?"

That made him pause. I pressed my advantage, curling my fingers around the Key slowly, drawing it back to my body and effectively out of sight.

The reaction from Gideon was instantaneous. "I agree."

Though Kadin and Bosh seemed less convinced, they nodded as well.

We set out down the road back to the tavern, spread out, tense and mute.

I let myself embrace a silent victory.

Chapter 25

Kadin

***I TOLD YOU THE** Mere couldn't be trusted*, Gideon spoke into my mind as we returned to the village.

The others were oblivious to our silent conversation.

Though I struggled to think about anything other than Arie, my lip twitched and I almost smiled at the Jinni. *I think...* I hesitated over what I wanted to say. I wasn't completely sure.

I'd told Rena to leave, yet found her more ingratiated with Bosh than ever. Maybe she'd cast a spell over him—or all of us—so that we would allow her to stay. As much as I wanted to blame her for the delay, I found myself agreeing with her suggestion that we take our time and make a plan of attack, rather than race back and hope to figure it out when we arrived.

Normally, Gideon was patient, but this time when I didn't finish the thought, he spoke to my mind again. *Tell me what you think. What is the purpose of this ploy to spend time with me?*

I shook off the direction of my thoughts, deciding to simply tell Gideon the truth. *I think… it's not so much a ploy as it is that… she may have a bit of a crush on you.*

I could almost feel the stunned mental silence as Gideon processed this. The crunch of dirt under our feet was the only sound as we neared the village.

A crush… truly?

I hadn't known a thought could hold such a *tone,* but I found myself holding back a laugh at his complete and utter shock. A Jinni male was no different from a human male when it came to reading women, it would seem.

Why else do you think she wants to spend an entire day with you? I countered, glancing over at him with a small smile. If all the men, Mere, and Jinni I knew were lumped together, Gideon would be one of those I trusted most. I'd come to think of him as a true friend.

We walked back to town, entering the busy streets once more, as Gideon seemed to ponder my words. He nodded to himself so slightly I doubted the others noticed, then threw a quick thought to me. *Might as well get it over with, then.*

Even as the thought reached me, Gideon strode ahead to join Bosh and Rena. "How would you like our day together to begin?" he asked Rena politely, and, ever the gentleman, he nodded to Bosh as well, "You're welcome to join us if you'd like."

Bosh opened his mouth to answer, but was saved from the awkwardness by Rena shaking her head adamantly. "Not if you want the day together to count. It has to be just you and me."

Gideon didn't say a word, but the stiffness in his spine and stride spoke volumes. I covered my mouth, stifling a laugh.

Chapter 26

Rena

GIDEON WAS A PERFECT gentleman, just as I'd always believed him to be. Except it was nothing like I'd imagined. It was absolutely boring.

"What do you desire to eat?"

"Where would you like to go?"

"As you wish."

No apparent thoughts or opinions of his own! The conversation felt stilted and one-sided as I babbled about back home, trying to let him get to know me, to see if he would finally remember that we'd met.

No luck.

He just listened absently, as if with half his attention, always able to repeat back to me what I said, but I got the distinct feeling he didn't care at all.

We sat on a grassy hilltop looking down on the village from above with hands still sticky from our lunch. Well, mine anyway. Gideon had stretched out a hand, pulling a soft blue handkerchief out of thin air and wiped his hands clean, but hadn't offered it to me. I hated being dirty. The sensation was unfamiliar and I didn't know how humans could live like this.

I'd yet to carry my own handkerchief and if it were anyone else I'd simply ask to use his, but something gave me the sense he would find it far too intimate, like touching tails.

So, while he stretched out his hand and the handkerchief vanished into whatever secret place he kept his things, I wiped my fingers on the grass when he wasn't looking.

The awkward silence stretched over us as we stared down at the little people below. For the third time, the urge to ask him to show me something human rose in me, but I tamped it down. That would be offensive, and as silly as if he asked that of me.

Then, my mind prompted me to ask him to show me something Jinn instead. How would he take that? If he'd said more than two words strung together, I might've taken the chance. But I couldn't get my mother's voice out of my head. *The Jinn are not to be trusted. The Jinn are evil. Never trust the words of a Jinni.*

Frustrated, I pulled my knees up to my chest and crossed my arms over them, as I searched for a safe question, staring with longing at the castle towers peeking out of the forest in the distance, wishing I was there with Bosh instead. Humans were so much easier to deal with.

My eyes wandered, landing on Gideon's cane. Impulsively, I reached out to pick it up. "This is beautiful," I began, a question forming in my mind as I wrapped my fingers around the cool metal.

In a heartbeat, he held me by the wrist in an almost painful grip. "Please don't touch that," he said softly.

To my surprise, my protection spells released, throwing out a wave of energy that hit him square in the chest, knocking him flat on his back.

I dropped the cane. Hurrying to his side, I knelt by him. It felt almost like when we'd first met, as I leaned over him. I half expected his eyes to be closed, and placed my hand on his chest without thought, licking my lips at the memory.

Instead, his eyes were open, and his chest rose up and down as he struggled to catch his breath.

"I'm so sorry," I said. "You startled me. I didn't mean to." And I didn't, but I could tell without a word from him that he was angry. "I'm sorry," I apologized again. "Truly."

He only gave a curt nod. Pulling himself up, he moved more warily now, lifting the cane from between us to set it on the opposite side, out of my reach.

"I was only curious," my voice came out in a thin whisper. Something clogged my throat and a tinge of wetness came to my eyes. "I was going to ask what happened that you need a cane." The question came out flat. At this point, I didn't really expect him to answer.

I'd ruined everything.

Blinking rapidly, I tried to clear my eyes of the watery cloud. Tears were so much easier to hide in the ocean.

But Gideon surprised me after a long moment by loosening his rigid posture, leaning back with a sigh. "It's an old injury," he said in that quiet voice of his. "From something that happened almost a year ago now."

Hope rose and I lifted my gaze. He focused on the village below. This time when I blinked the wetness away, it didn't come back. I kept my body facing the village, like his, but watched his face closely, catching the way his lips tightened at the memory and the creases in the corner of his eyes deepened.

"It must have been painful," I said in a soft tone as well.

"At the time," he agreed with a small nod. "It's nothing now, but I keep this," he touched the cane, without looking at it, "to remind myself of that day. Of what can happen when you let your guard down."

A million questions rose to my mind at that tiny piece of information. *What happened? Will he get offended all over again if I ask?* I didn't want to risk it. Instead, I basked in the happy feeling of being gifted a tiny secret. Maybe he just needed more time. After all, I'd had a year to think of him, while he may not remember that day at all.

The thought reminded me of his words. "You say the injury happened a year ago?" I asked, before it occurred to me that even this might be an invasion of his privacy. Such a fine line to walk!

He nodded though.

This was my moment.

I took a deep breath. *Where to start?*

One simple question would work: *was it when you fell from the sky?*

And then he would say, *how did you know about that?*

Oh, I would tell him in a casual tone, as if it was nothing, *I was the one who saved you from drowning. Did you truly think you'd landed on a rock in the middle of the ocean without help—or somehow survived a landing like that without a broken skull?*

I opened my mouth to speak.

"I'd rather not talk about that day," Gideon said. "If you don't mind."

I deflated.

With my plans to begin with our first meeting thwarted, I debated just telling him anyway, or asking about something else. Maybe I could circle back around to it.

"Do you have family?" I asked, thinking of my five sisters. That was a safe topic, right?

But Gideon grew even more grim, if that were possible, and still as death. "Not anymore."

Ah. Another taboo subject.

Then again, he hadn't said he didn't want to talk about it—yet. I refused to give up hope that I could find a crack in his fierce façade. "What happened to them?"

Gideon sighed, a long drawn out sigh that reminded me of my mother. "My parents passed away a few decades ago. And I didn't have any siblings, but I have a bond-brother who went missing a year ago, and I fear he may be dead as well."

Another event that happened a year ago? This was too juicy to pass up. Like when a school of fish swam right into your hands.

"Was that related to why you fell from the sky?" I asked.

For the first time all morning, Gideon's sharp gaze fixed on me, direct and focused. "How did you know about that?" he asked, as I'd known he would.

I smiled. "Well, I know you didn't want to talk about it…" I trailed off, enjoying the fact that I finally had his full attention.

"Tell me." His tone was flat. He didn't fully trust me yet. Maybe he thought I was playing him. But he would see.

"I know," I said, still smiling as if this were a pleasant conversation, because I so hoped it would be, "because I saw you fall. I'm the one who dragged you from the bottom of the ocean onto that rock."

The sun glinted in his pale blue eyes, but he didn't turn away. His thick brows lifted in surprise, but other than that he didn't react to my big reveal at all.

"We held a full conversation, actually," I continued, feeling odd telling him about his own experience. "Well, a short one. You told me why you… fell."

"Did I?" his soft voice held an undercurrent of tension. "And why was that?"

Was this a test? I questioned my memory. What if I'd heard him wrong? Or misunderstood?

I swallowed, forcing myself to hold his gaze, though I felt more and more nervous. Especially after learning the other events of that fateful day, and realizing how much of the story I didn't know.

"Well," I said, swallowing yet again and lifting my chin to appear confident. "According to you, it was because you were banished."

Gideon flinched.

I opened my mouth to say something else, but nothing came to mind. The revelation was no longer about our history, but centered around that word.

Banished.

"I realize our kind don't really get along," I said. He probably hated that I knew this secret about him, that a weakness was exposed to a natural adversary. But I needed him to know I wasn't the enemy. "I won't tell anyone, I swear. I could've told Arie or the others, but I haven't. You can ask them." Well, that would defeat the purpose of the secret, but at least I could offer.

All this time, Gideon hadn't moved. His eyes were squeezed shut as if that might somehow block the truth, or maybe block me. I tried not to be hurt.

"We can talk about something else," I offered after another long moment. There were a lot of those in this conversation. I hated silence.

"Did I tell you anything else?" he asked, pinching the bridge of his nose, eyes still shut.

"Um, well," I blushed at that question. "Besides your name, only one other thing…"

Now those blue eyes blinked open, fixed on me. "Yes?"

I know I'd told myself I'd be honest with him, and I wanted him to trust me, but after everything that had happened, I felt certain if I admitted the last bit to him he would only sneer and call me a liar. "I'd rather not say."

"Was it about the queen?" he asked. At some point his body had angled to face mine, and I'd done the same. He looked worried.

"The queen?" I asked, curiosity piqued. "What about her?" This felt like back in my mother's chatter room with the Mere-ladies gossiping. I gasped. "Is she the one who banished you?" It made sense, now that I thought about it. Who else would have that kind of power? Well, I supposed I didn't know much about the Jinn, so I couldn't be sure.

"I shouldn't have said that," he muttered, confirming my suspicions.

"What did you do that was horrible enough to be banished?" I asked thoughtlessly.

"Nothing!" For the first time since I'd met him, Gideon raised his voice, which for him, was essentially yelling.

"You're very touchy, you know that?" I snapped. I was over tiptoeing around him. It was far too much work. "If you didn't do anything, then you've no need to get so worked up. It's not like I'm going to banish you again." Well, at least not from the human world. Technically, he was already not allowed in Rusalka. But now was probably not the best time to mention that. "Obviously the queen thinks you did something. But if you didn't, then we can prove your innocence!"

"I cannot." Gideon stood and began to pace. I'd never seen him so physically upset. After a moment, I stood too, feeling silly to be sitting on the ground so far beneath him.

He shook his head, stopping in front of me. "I haven't discussed this with anyone before, do you understand?"

I smiled up at him. He was trusting me with his secrets? "I won't tell a soul."

Instead of reassuring him, that seemed to make him pause. "I wish I could be sure of that."

I held up a finger for him to wait. Pulling another cord from around my neck, I drew up one of my necklaces. Unlike the Key, which I'd kept hidden, this jewelry lay on the outside, with a beautiful strand of seashells from the depths of the ocean. In the sunlight, their colors faded from dark purples, blues, and pinks, into softer pastel hues.

Carefully, I untied a shell and handed it to Gideon, serious now. "This is spelled for promises," I said as I placed it in his hand.

At the word, he tried to hand it back to me, "I don't want anything spelled," he said, "I know how the Mere work. How do I know it won't do something else?"

I frowned. "You don't even know what it *does* do yet. Could you not have even an *ounce* of trust for the one who saved your life?"

He stopped protesting, properly chastised.

"This," I continued, pointing to the shell, "means I must keep your secret, for as long as you have it, until or if you decide to give it back to me." I shrugged, crossing my arms. "But if you think it's nothing, then you might as well give it back."

His fingers curled around it at that. I nodded, satisfied. Dropping to the ground with a sigh, I gave in to the warmth of the sun, leaning back to lay in the soft grass and close my eyes. "Anyway, tell me or don't tell me. I don't care."

The best reaction to gossip, my mother always said, was pretending it meant nothing. This almost always prompted a desire to prove the information was valuable.

Gideon settled back down next to me. Peeking at him, I was disappointed to find he'd kept his distance. Still. It was something. I closed my eyes and waited.

"The queen banished me," Gideon began after one of his agonizing pauses that I was growing used to, "because I was searching for my bond-brother. And I'd discovered something she didn't want anyone to know."

The mystery was too exciting for me to feign indifference now. I rolled onto my stomach, propping my head in my hands to stare at him. "What did you find?" I whispered reverently.

Gideon didn't play with the grass or his cane or do anything so obvious to expose his anxiety, but I was beginning to recognize it was his utter stillness that gave him away as he spoke. "You know how I mentioned my bond-brother disappeared?"

I nodded.

Gideon didn't move a muscle, didn't even blink. "I believe the queen was behind it."

Oh, the intrigue! "Why would she do such a thing?" I asked, almost breathless with curiosity. "Did he do something wrong?"

Gideon was a statue now. Staring at my shell in the palm of his hand. I waited with hinged breath, but I never would've guessed what he said next.

"In a way. We have a tradition that every 50 years, the ruling monarch will defer the throne of Jinn to their offspring. The Crowning Ceremony is meant to be this year. His crime was being her son."

Chapter 27

Rena

GIDEON AND I HAD only spent half a morning together and had already run out of things to say. The revelation about the Jinni prince was probably to blame for that. I wanted to ask what happened when the only heir to the throne was missing, but even I could sense that information was for Jinni ears only. The currents in my mind were strong, dragging me from one possibility to the next. Clearly the queen had somehow removed her son so she could keep her throne. The lifetime of a Jinni rivaled that of the Mere, and we had our suspicions they might live quite a bit longer than even we knew.

All of this I could only assume, because for the millionth time that morning, we sat in utter silence.

"What would you like to do for the rest of our day together?" Gideon asked at the hour mark, as he had the last three times.

This time, boredom won.

"You can travel anywhere you want?" I asked.

That got me a sidelong glance and one of those thick brows raised in silent question.

"Could you take me to see an elephant? I've always wanted to see one."

Gideon's lip twitched at first. Then he surprised me by throwing his head back and laughing. An actual belly laugh. "You're quite unpredictable, you know that?" he said when he caught his breath.

I smirked.

"Alright, as you wish," Gideon stood, dusting off his pants, though of course they were impeccable. He held out a hand to help me up, and my heart fluttered as I took it. One moment I was staring up into his pale blue eyes, then the next moment he flashed away and was gone.

"Wait! Come back!" I shouted, but he already had. He grasped my arms more firmly, disappearing a second time and leaving me alone once more. Reappearing once again, he frowned at me, as if his leaving me behind was somehow my fault.

"What's going on?" he demanded, gesturing toward me in frustration. "It's as if you're rooted into the ground. You're anchored so deep I can't move you from this spot."

"Oh!" I'd completely forgotten. I reached up to my neck to grasp the limpet shell, murmuring to remove the protection spell that prevented Jinni Gifts from working on the Mere. "Sorry. Try it now."

Gideon's brows arched skeptically, but this time when he took my hand and tried to travel, I felt myself shift with him. The world altered in an instant.

* * *

"WE'VE BEEN WAITING FOR ages," I whispered to
Gideon. We lay in the tall grass on a hill above a small pool of
water that Gideon called a 'watering hole.'

The flash of traveling from one place to another felt like
slipping from beneath the water to the surface. So close
together, yet so far apart. According to Gideon, we were about
a full day's travel south from where we'd spent the morning.
He also refused to guarantee we'd even see elephants, which I
refused to accept. "What's the point of traveling all this way if
we're not going to stay until we see one?"

He only shook his head at my logic. Those thick
eyebrows of his were so expressive. Even without words the
meaningful lift and twitch of a smile lifted my spirits. I found
myself saying things just to get a reaction from him.

"My sisters have never seen an elephant before," I told
him, wiggling my brows as well. "They're going to be so
terribly jealous when they find out." And when I told them the
story, I'd leave out all this ridiculous staring at a shallow pool.

He just laughed. His eyes only landed on me for a
moment, but the depths of blue made my heart sing. Such a
gentleness behind those eyes. And so much pain. I could tell
I'd only brushed the surface this morning. If I could make him
laugh again, that would make this day a success, I decided.

"What kind of noise does an elephant make?" I asked,
thinking of whales and their deep bellows or the higher trills
of smaller mammals. So many options. I thought through them
quick and mimicked the chirrup of a dolphin calling to a lover.
Though I highly doubted Gideon knew the meaning of the
sound, I blushed.

"Shhh," he waved a hand at me, and I stopped,
disappointed. "First of all," he deadpanned, "they sound
nothing like a dolphin."

My blush deepened. Did he know more than I'd thought?

"And second, if they hear that, I guarantee they'll run the other way, and then you'll never get a chance to see them."

I sighed at his logic. I didn't want to scare them away.

Settling back into watching, I rested my head in my hands and let my eyes drift aimlessly across the grassland and the trees on the other side.

Then, movement. So far in the distance I almost missed it. Gray shifting through the green of the trees. When it finally emerged near the edge of the watering hole on the far side, I frowned. "It's so small," I said, thinking of the great sperm whales back home. This creature didn't even look to stand as tall as my horse.

This earned me an unexpected smile and a soft laugh that made me nearly forget the elephant. I stared at him adoringly. "That's a youngling," he explained, still grinning.

"Ahh," I turned back with interest. So, this was a baby elephant. The creature waddled closer, splashing into the water, enormous ears flapping. Then, out of nowhere, he raised his trunk and sprayed a bucket's worth of water over his back! I clapped my hands over my mouth to keep in my squeal of excitement.

"How strange!" I hissed to Gideon. When I turned to catch his reaction, I found him watching me. My heart stopped. It only lasted for the space of a breath, before he returned his gaze to the baby elephant, but I studied his profile. I liked his long nose and strong jaw, such Jinni qualities. Thin lips too. They quirked in the tiniest smile that told me he was aware of being watched.

"Look," he pointed, whispering softly, "there's the mother."

I spun to face the watering hole. At first I didn't see her. Then at the edge of the trees, bits of gray and movement.

I gasped. "She's huge," I murmured, jaw dropping. The mother stood over two times as tall as the baby, looming over it. My eyes grew as wide and round as a squid's. Her head alone was larger than me.

"That's incredible," I said, admiring the wrinkled gray skin and the way her trunk swung back and forth as she walked. Even from here, I could swear I felt the earth shake a bit with each step. My respect for the land whales increased quite a bit. They might not be as large, but they were clearly powerful. "Are those its teeth?"

Another laugh. I could never get one intentionally, but seemed to come by quite of few of them by accident. "Those are called tusks," he explained. "I believe they're for protection, but for the most part they're quite gentle creatures."

When the baby rose from the water, dripping, and returned to his mother, it was my turn to chortle through my fingers, trying to be quiet. "Look at that tail," I said with tears of laughter in my eyes. It was absolutely ridiculous! Swishing back and forth, the tail looked like a tiny stick on the animal's massive rear end with a tiny tuft of hair at the tip. Any creature in the ocean with a tail like that wouldn't last a day. Of course, since we weren't in the ocean, I supposed it wasn't that funny to Gideon, but I couldn't help giggling over it. Another juicy detail to share with my sisters when I returned home—I caught myself. *If I returned home…*

I brushed the thought aside and grinned at Gideon again. "This is everything I'd hoped it would be," I told him. "Thank you!"

He nodded. "My pleasure."

I pressed my lips together in a smile, wishing it was more than a pleasantry. While I'd grown up with everyone saying exactly what they thought, the Jinni culture of secrets and constant civility left those words empty and meaningless.

A quiet minute passed, comfortable this time, while we watched the mother elephant with her baby. I giggled when the little one sprayed her with water and she blasted him with twice as much in return. When he kicked up his feet and ran, big ears flapping in the wind, I laughed out loud. And when he returned to his mother and wrapped his little trunk gently around hers, my heart squeezed at the sight and I sighed. "They're so beautiful."

"They are," Gideon agreed quietly. The moment felt like coming to an understanding with him. We were worlds apart, and unfriendly worlds at that, yet in this, we felt the same. I let my hand fall to the earth between us, an open invitation.

"Do you know," he said, and I held my breath, hoping for another breakthrough. "In some parts of the world, humans ride these beasts."

Not what I was hoping for, yet it piqued my interest. "How?" I asked, eyeing the large animals. "You'd have to climb a tree to even mount them." I thought of my little pedestal back at the castle for mounting a horse.

"Do you want to see something?" Gideon asked.

His playful expression surprised me so much that I just blinked, then nodded.

Just like that, he vanished.

In front of my eyes one moment, then the next Gideon was gone and I was staring into the grass behind him.

I whirled to face the elephants just as the mother lifted her trunk in fright and trumpeted.

Gideon stood on her back. As she panicked, he lost his balance and quickly flashed into a seated position on her neck instead. With a hand on her giant head, he soothed her somehow, while the baby came waddling up to them curiously.

I stood and hurried down the hill, slowing as I came closer and saw the mother's enormity for myself. She'd calmed under Gideon's control, while the baby was fearless, shuffling toward me as I came near. I held out my palm, the way I would to feed a tiny seahorse, and his little trunk—not so little up close, since it was larger than my arm—stretched toward me. I startled. He was sniffing me; that water-hose on his face was also how he smelled. The little hairs on the end tickled my palm and his hide was surprisingly soft and gentle as he ran it down my arm, wrapping around. I jumped back, nervous, imagining him gripping me like a squid, but the little one let go of me immediately.

"It's okay," Gideon said from atop the larger beast. I had to tilt my head back to look at him, shading my eyes against the sun, only seeing his silhouette. "They won't hurt you."

"I'm not scared," I said smugly. I'd encountered sharks and swam with whales. This little guy wasn't nearly as terrifying as that. Besides, I'd worked on my protection spells so that they'd kick in immediately if anything really dangerous happened.

I regretted my words, as the warmth between Gideon and I again grew cold. In an effort to move past it, I stepped closer to the baby elephant, reaching out my hand once more. This time, he was more hesitant, but I stepped forward boldly, until I could touch his forehead.

I'd moved too quickly in my pride. His tiny trunk swung upward in fright at the foreign feeling on his hide. Though smaller than his mother's, it was still larger than both my scrawny arms together. It knocked me flat on my back.

This time when Gideon laughed, I didn't enjoy it. I might have even yelled at him if I could catch my breath. The little guy was a few feet away now, hiding behind his mother.

With another flash between unknown spaces, Gideon appeared in front of me, kneeling to take my hand and help me up. I was lighter than he'd expected, and as I tried to help pull myself up on my own, the combination of our strength pulled me directly into his arms, crashing into his chest. He steadied me at the waist, and my hands naturally gripped his shirt. I forced my fingers to loosen, slowly flattening my palms on his chest.

Lifting my gaze from his chest to peer up into those cool blue eyes, I licked my lips. Gideon's hands on my waist made me shiver. This was my moment. I'd waited over a year for this. I would confess my love to him, and he would return it.

"This day has been a dream," I began breathlessly. His eyes stared into mine, so unreadable. I couldn't remember what I'd rehearsed to say next.

In the space of a blink, he let go of my waist and stepped back. My hands slipped down his chest and fell away. "It hasn't been all bad," he said in response, indifferent. "I suppose the Mere have some redeeming qualities."

A high compliment I supposed, in his mind, but far from the passion I'd dreamed of for so many months. It felt too unbalanced to continue with my plans. I dug deep to find a smile, trying to be grateful that at least he was speaking to me.

"We still have a few more hours," he added. "Any other strange creatures you'd like to see?"

I could wallow in my disappointment... or I could take advantage of the Jinni in front of me, offering a unique, once in a lifetime tour.

"There is one more creature I've heard of," I said, nodding, a new wave of excitement sweeping over me at the hope he might agree. It was no small request.

"Tell me."

I took a deep breath. "I'd like to see a dragon."

Chapter 28

Arie

"THIS IS WHY I'VE decided to invite King Amir to return to Hodafez," I finished my speech, startling myself with the words. I stood in the middle of the castle courtyard with the late morning sun beating down on me. The sole audience member for my speech was the town crier, memorizing my words to carry them out into the city. Enoch hovered nearby.

Normally, I would have delivered such an important announcement to the public myself. Stranger still, my gut reaction to inviting the King of Sagh back to Hodafez seemed almost akin to terror. My pulse raced and my skin felt clammy, but I couldn't pin down why.

What else had I said? My memory was fuzzy. Anxiety swirled in my stomach. My mouth moved on its own. "Thank you, that will be all for today." The crier nodded, making his final notes, while my feet carried me out of the square and back inside the castle. He would carry the gist of my announcement throughout the rest of my kingdom until everyone had heard. But who would tell *me*?

I found myself in my chambers minutes later with no memory of getting there. I couldn't understand how I was losing time like this. Was it something to do with my Gift? That didn't make any sense. My breathing started coming faster as I remembered what I'd said about King Amir—I would *never* in my right mind have invited him back here! Something was deeply wrong. I wanted to talk to my father about it, but then I remembered he was in a coma. No. Wait... As scenes from his funeral flashed before my eyes, I crumpled, unable to stand, rocking back and forth as my body shook with sobs.

Nothing made sense. My eyes were swollen and I had no idea how much time had passed, when a hint of ink on my foot caught my attention.

Lavatory, towels.

I jumped out of bed, practically running across the room.

Right where I'd written it would be, there was a parchment with hurried scribbles in my own hand. I didn't remember writing them. The inescapable feeling that I was somehow lost within my own mind terrified me.

My eyes flew through the words. *Enoch. Using his Gift—* I took deep breaths, feeling equal parts relieved that I wasn't going crazy, while at the same time more anxious now that I knew what was going on. The short lines about my father were almost illegible, as if I'd been shaking. Tears blurred my eyes once more, but I forced myself to read everything.

Another small line further down the page, added later: *Kadin is working on finding Gideon. He will save me.*

I didn't remember writing that either. Though there was a vague memory of a dream...

For some reason, just knowing Kadin was aware of my dilemma made me feel better.

I wrote myself another short note about how I'd invited King Amir into the castle—just in case I forgot again. I wanted to add instructions for myself, for what I should *do*, but my hand only hovered over the page. I prided myself on always finding a way out of difficult situations, but no matter how long I stood there, nothing came to mind.

Striding out into the bedroom, I ignored the guard stationed by the balcony and moved through the front room to the door to the hall.

I opened it to leave, but the two guards stationed outside stopped me. "I'm sorry your majesty, you need to stay in your rooms right now."

The tiniest flicker of a memory told me this had happened before. Maybe more than once.

I closed the door without a word, moving instead to the corner of my front sitting room that held my desk and writing tools. At least here I was alone and unsupervised.

I ripped off the top of the inkwell, dipping the quill in, not caring if I dripped spatters on the page or not, as long as the letter was legible.

Kadin,

I'm afraid it's more urgent than I'd first realized.

King Amir is returning to Hodafez—I'm not sure how soon, it could be as early as tomorrow.

I paused. A tear dripped onto the page, surprising me. I swiped the back of my hand across my eyes and forced myself to keep going. I didn't know how much time I had. Taking a deep breath, I wrote what I'd never expected to say to him:

I'm so scared and I don't know what to do. I'm sorry for everything I've said in the past... I need you here. I wish I'd never told you to leave.

I bit my lip. Dipping the quill into the inkwell again until it was soaking, I drenched the last few lines, crossing them out until they were one large smear of ink, no longer readable.

Anyone could intercept the letter, after all.

Swallowing hard, I rewrote a new last line.

Please hurry.

-     *A*

Blowing on the ink until it was dry, I quickly folded the note and sealed it with the wax from a nearby candle.

Now was the difficult part. I held the letter behind my back as I opened my front door to speak with the two guards outside. "Could you please send Havah or Farideh up to see me?" My ladies-in-waiting were loyal. They would be most likely to keep a secret.

"The Jinni told us they were needed in the kitchen," the guard on the right replied. "They're not supposed to see you right now."

Under his helmet, I recognized Soroush by his dark brown eyes and graying beard. His thoughts were strangely silent, which meant he most likely wasn't aware of the mind control any more than I had been.

"Of course he did," I muttered, thinking fast. "What else did Enoch say?"

"He said you can't leave. You're not feeling well," the second guard replied in a monotone. He was younger and unfamiliar to me; most likely he'd never been on rotation inside the castle before.

I cleared my throat and decided to work with what they knew. "That's true," I agreed, "I'm not well and need to stay in my rooms, so I was hoping you'd be able to deliver a note for me? To someone in town?"

Soroush's thoughts slipped to worries about his queen not feeling well, as if he was hearing the news for the first time. Meanwhile the other guard started thinking about his fiancée in town and how he could use this errand as an excuse to see her.

If there was ever a time to take advantage of my Gift, it was now. Pulling the letter out from behind my back, I stepped out into the corridor to take his hand and place the letter into it firmly. "Give this to a man named Kadin," I said, describing the inn where Kadin had last been staying. Hopefully someone would know how to get it to him. I winked at the young guard as I added, "Take as much time as you need to see your girl."

He grinned, and with a nod to Soroush, he set off down the hallway with my letter in hand. It was a long shot. I had no way of knowing if Kadin would even get it. But it was better than doing nothing.

Soroush started to wonder what was in my letter. I needed to distract him. "I know you can't leave your post," I said, hoping he wouldn't until the other guard had returned, "but I'd like a pot of tea if you can send someone on an errand. I think it might help me feel better."

"Of course, your majesty," Soroush replied immediately, returning to his original thoughts about my health.

I coughed for good effect as I closed the door.

Now all I could do was wait.

＊ ＊ ＊

HOURS PASSED, AGONIZINGLY SLOW.

When a knock sounded on the door, I jumped up eagerly. Maybe the guard had found Kadin after all.

The door swung open to reveal Enoch standing on the other side. He stepped past me without waiting for an invitation, closing the door with a soft click behind him.

He held something up, showing it to me. My heart sank at the letter with a name I recognized scribbled on the front. It'd never reached Kadin.

"What were you hoping to accomplish by this?" Enoch asked as he held it up. The seal was broken.

I tried to remember exactly what I'd wrote and if I'd given too much away. My heart was pounding so fast—could he hear it? "It's nothing. Just a note to a friend."

We both knew that was a lie. Enoch took me by the arm and forced me to sit in a chair, taking a seat across from me as he placed the letter on the table.

"You shouldn't be able to remember this," he said, watching me with those purple eyes.

I swallowed and didn't answer.

But he and I both knew all he needed to do was ask me directly. Helpless fury filled me, with nowhere to go, until I thought I might explode.

He sighed. "How are you able to come back to yourself so quickly?"

And I told him.

Every secret spilled out of me against my will. The note I'd left myself. The longer note in the bathroom and where I'd hidden it.

Enoch only nodded before taking my arm and walking me to the bathroom. "Wash it off," he commanded over his shoulder as he sifted through the towels and found my note exactly where I'd said it would be.

I took soap and a wash rag from the clean bowl of water, and scrubbed until the ink on my foot was just a dark smear.

Enoch waited until I was done, parchment in hand, before he left the room. I found myself following him out.

Back in my sitting room, he opened the door and spoke quietly to the guards. "Remove her writing desk from the room. Make sure every inkwell and every scrap of parchment is gone."

No.

The guards moved to obey while I stood in the center of the room, watching them remove my ability to cry for help or even remind myself of what was happening. The loss hit me like a punch to the gut. It was the smallest possible way to fight back, but it'd been all I had.

I covered my mouth to hold back sobs when the door closed behind them, leaving me alone once more. Enoch hadn't bothered to tell me to forget this time. He didn't need to. There was nowhere I could go, and nothing I could do.

I hated the tears. They made me feel weak. Clenching my fists, I let myself get angry instead, swiping at my face to clear it. There was one last resort—one last thing I could try, and Enoch couldn't stop me because he didn't know.

Even though it was only mid-afternoon, I would do my best to fall asleep and try to meet Kadin again in my dreams. I could only hope that eventually, if I stayed there long enough, he'd be there.

Chapter 29

Kadin

"HOW MUCH LONGER WILL they be gone?" Bosh grumbled. We sat in the inn's common room, with two other small groups seated at the surrounding tables. Bosh had been everyone's entertainment for the last hour or so. While I was busy trying to come up with a plan, Bosh was fodder for their drinking game. With inaudible groans, each of them took a swig. They were growing quite drunk.

The bartender had guessed the lad would complain only three or four times more before it dawned on him why they'd begun to sip so in sync. The highest guess was that it might take him as many as six, before he caught on. Here they were, still going strong. Even now, I could see another complaint on his lips.

"Should I go looking for them?" he asked me, concern knitting his forehead together.

"Is the day done?" I asked him in return, merciless. I didn't have a lot of sympathy for him right now. There was so much at stake and I had no idea how to fix it. I moved away to pace by the back wall where I could have room to think.

Bosh joined the game of Castles and Conquerors going on at the nearby table to give me space, but he was distracted by his worries for Rena.

"I thought it was only a rumor that the Mere could enchant a man with their voice," another man said, having seen Rena's gills that morning. His voice carried across the room. He played a card, somehow still winning the latest game, despite drinking as much as the rest of them. "But now I feel quite certain it must be true."

They burst out laughing, and I couldn't help a small smile, as much at the way Bosh blushed, as the jest itself.

"Is that true?" Bosh spun around to ask me, even more anxious now.

"Thanks for that," I said, shaking my head at the man.

He simply shrugged, his dark face smooth and unreadable as always. "It could be true? Who's to say?"

"Very unlikely," I reassured Bosh when it was clear the man wasn't going to take it back, coming over to the table to sit and join them. "Think about it. If she could bewitch people at will, then why are the rest of us unimpressed?"

"I think she's lovely." Bosh challenged my statement without meaning to, by remaining utterly captivated. "She's so honest. I've never met a woman who says exactly what she's thinking like Rena does."

I put a toothpick in my mouth to keep from smiling. He had a point. I tried not to think of Arie, but failed. It sobered me immediately. Thinking of all the things between us still unsaid. Or at least, by me. I could only hope it was the case for her as well. I wished there was a way to see her again, but Rena was gone. Not to mention it was the middle of the day.

With the men on both sides, casually playing the game and chatting, oblivious, I sighed.

"They've been gone a long time," Bosh said only ten minutes later.

"Okay, that's it," I said, pushing away from the table to stand. "Why don't we go get a bite to eat and take your mind off it for a while?"

He hesitated. "What if they come back while we're gone?"

"So what if they do?" I shrugged. "They can take care of themselves." Maybe the break would help me clear my mind. Normally a castle heist came to me easily, but for this one I could hardly think straight. I'd never had a heist that involved stealing a person before. Not to mention a heist that ended with staying at the castle—and not in the dungeons.

We didn't talk much until we'd wandered through the marketplace and found something to eat. Taking it with us, we made our way to the beach to sit. The food settled like a rock in my stomach. "If only we could come up with something foolproof to get the Jinni out of the castle," I muttered, forcing myself to swallow the last bite. Everything we'd come up with hinged on Gideon beating Enoch, and King Amir not being present.

"I was thinking," Bosh said, fiddling with the few coins he hadn't lost in the game, "that Rena might be more helpful than we've given her credit for. Maybe even the tipping point to our success."

"How so?" My voice dripped with sarcasm. All she'd been so far was trouble. I rubbed my hand over my face. *That wasn't totally fair.* She'd helped us find Gideon. She seemed capable enough of helping us, the question was, did she *want* to?

"Think about it," Bosh insisted, waving his food in the air excitedly. "If she comes with us, maybe she could distract Enoch long enough for Gideon to stop him? The Jinni Gifts don't work on her, so she'd be perfectly safe and he wouldn't see it coming!"

My hopes lifted as he spoke. For the first time all day, it felt like the cloudy haze of confusion broke in my mind and a plan shone through, bright and golden. "You know what," I murmured, more to myself than Bosh. "That just might work."

Chapter 30

Rena

"A DRAGON?" GIDEON'S BROWS came together, then lifted in astonishment.

"Mmmhmm," I said. "I know it's dangerous, but I've always wanted to know what they look like, and I figure if anything happens, we'll be okay."

"How so?" He crossed his arms over his vest.

"Well," I shrugged, "between my protection spells, and your ability to travel at any moment, we should be the two most difficult targets a dragon will ever face, don't you think?"

He gave a sardonic chuckle, shaking his head. "I can't believe I'm actually considering this."

"Consider quickly," I said in reply, shading my eyes. "I assume it'd be better to go while there's still daylight?"

Gideon tapped one finger on the head of his cane, staring at the horizon before turning back to me with a huff. "Why not," he said, and it wasn't a question, but more of a resignation. "Let's go."

I stepped up to him, trying to be ever so graceful as I placed my hand in his palm, grazing his skin softly in an effort to awaken an interest inside him that I desperately hoped was just buried.

He grasped my fingers with a firm grip and in the span of a second we shifted from the long grasses, jungle trees, and watering hole, to a barren ground charred by fire. Burnt orange cliffs rose steeply on one side, jutting out in sharp angles, so tall they disappeared into the white clouds above.

I gaped at the scene.

A haze filled the air and it smelled like smoke, but faint, like it wasn't recent.

My attention was dragged from our surroundings when it occurred to me that I still held Gideon's hand in mine. Or rather, he hadn't let go. I drew closer to him, squeezing his fingers lightly.

But he wasn't looking at me. Eyes on the horizon, Gideon was tense. "Don't let go of me," he whispered, "Dragon's eyes are sharper than an eagle, but I have us cloaked. As long as you stay with me, they can't see us."

Somewhat of a letdown, yet I would gladly take an excuse to hold his hand. I sidled in even closer, pretending to be worried. "How will we find one?" I asked, exhilarated.

"Shh," he put his finger to his lips. He went so far as to lower his head to my ear when he replied. "Dragon hearing is known to be even better than their eyesight. And I can only cloak our appearance, not our sound or smell."

"Ahh," I mouthed inaudibly, nodding my understanding. That would force me to lean in to ask him anything. What a lovely decision this had been.

I cast about for a good excuse to whisper in his ear, while we studied the skies, searching for any sign of movement. They were clear.

Then, I gasped. I hadn't meant to, it just startled me when I spied the silhouette behind the cloud and the speed with which it soared through the sky. Only a black shadow in the distance, its wingspan stretched ten times wider than the dragon himself.

Gideon covered my mouth with his hand, and I couldn't even blame him, when the flying figure dove toward the ground at such a speed that it looked like he was falling, growing steadily larger.

He was coming directly toward us.

Before he'd even fully taken shape before our eyes, the dragon landed with an enormous crash, not more than a stone's throw away. I was even more thankful for Gideon's hand over my mouth now. If it wasn't, I would've gasped again.

His scales shone like dark black pearls in the sun, glinting in the light, rippling as he moved. I'd thought nothing could compare to the size of our whales back home, but he was at least as large as an orca—with those wings stretched wide, more like three orcas. Even as I thought this, the beast gently folded them in, creating a dangerous yet beautiful arc.

I jumped a little when he snorted. Fortunately, the blast of smoke from his nostrils and the noise of his landing covered any other sound.

I'd completely forgotten Gideon.

Behind me, he stood still as a statue. I'd have turned to look, but his grip was strong, so instead I simply stared at the dragon in front of us where it stood, sniffing the air, curious, almost like the cat I'd seen in the castle stables. A very, very dangerous cat.

His yellow eyes blinked and the eyelids slipped together from the sides. Fascinating. The black iris reminded me of a cat as well, the way it stretched from top to bottom in the shape of a pointed oval. The way the beast moved, with deliberate thought, spoke of intelligence.

Without warning, it leapt across the space between us, landing with such fluid grace he could've been swimming, wings half spread for balance, falling back into place once he landed. Now he was only a dozen paces away.

I felt myself start shaking. I was right to be afraid. The deadly creature studied the empty landscape in front of him as if he knew we were there. Smoke trailed out of his nose. I knew the stories. He could breathe fire on us at any moment. Would Gideon be fast enough?

I tapped my finger against Gideon's hand soundlessly as a signal. *Let's go.*

The dragon's long neck arched, elegant and beautiful, as he put one powerful claw in front of the other.

I began to shake Gideon's hand, then his whole arm, trying to get my message across. We need to *go!* Still Gideon didn't move. His hand still covered my mouth and I debated biting it, but didn't want to startle him. *Besides,* I reminded myself, *he knows what he's doing. Doesn't he?*

As these thoughts raced through my head, the enormous beast dropped back to rest on his haunches. Its colossal wings folded in fully, but even folded, they stretched from just a foot above the ground to the tip of his head. His ears flicked and twisted. Perfect for hearing the softest noises, even a breath close by. I tried to hold mine.

Finally, I wrenched my head out of Gideon's grasp, turning to face him and ask to leave with my eyes. If it were possible, the Jinni was even more pale than I'd ever seen him, and his eyes were glued to the dragon, not even seeing me.

I shook him harder by the shoulder, tempted to slap him out of it. Keeping my grip on his hand so the dragon wouldn't see us, I felt the tickle of fear on my spine and whirled to face the beast again, only to find those big yellow eyes staring right in our direction.

No longer on his haunches, the dragon was slowly moving toward us, head lowering.

Stalking us.

Panicking, I backed up into Gideon, shaking with terror. Without thinking, I elbowed him in the gut in desperation, hard.

The oomph of Gideon's breath leaving his lungs was so slight, but even that was too much. I'd just doomed us to death. The dragon roared—a terrifying, deep, thunderous cry that shook the earth around us and his chest lit up with internal fire.

We were about to become charred statues.

I stopped worrying about making noise now, and screamed, one last final ditch effort, "*Gideon!*"

As Gideon came to himself and his fingers clenched tighter, the fire growing in the dragon's throat… stopped.

With a flash between spaces that I'd come to recognize now, the terrible beast faded from in front of us, replaced by a familiar view of a village and a grassy hilltop that still held the indents from where we'd sat just that morning.

I cried out, falling to the ground in relief. I ripped my hand out of Gideon's and screamed at him. "How could you? That thing nearly killed us!" The shrieks tore out of my throat so painfully, it felt raw. Stumbling backward, I put more space between us, irrationally afraid he'd take me back there. "What *happened* to you?"

Still pale, Gideon stood staring at nothing, in the same position he had been when he'd stared at the dragon. He looked lost.

"I don't understand," he murmured, more to himself than to me. "It doesn't make sense."

"*What* doesn't make sense?" I demanded, standing and dusting myself off, trying to quell the shaking that still hadn't subsided. "The part where we almost didn't make it out of there alive, or the part where you froze? Because that doesn't make sense to me either!"

Gideon blinked as if not really hearing me. "There was something about him, something that reminded me of the connection I have with my bond-brother. But he doesn't have the Gift of Shapeshifting." He sighed, and the hope in his eyes faded. "It was wishful thinking. After searching for so long, I tricked myself into believing it. I've heard legends of what dragons can make you feel, but I'd never experienced it before."

"They can manipulate people too? Makes sense to me." I threw up my hands. "Jinni might as well be dragons in human form. Both of you are beautiful and dangerous."

My fits of yelling seemed to slowly bring Gideon back to himself, especially that last bit. "Beautiful?" he questioned, one of those expressive brows mocking me.

I felt a blush rising in my cheeks. "You said it first," I mumbled.

Now he crossed his arms in disbelief and his brows rose so high they practically asked me out loud to prove it.

"*You* said it to me, after I pulled you out of the ocean and I laid you on that rock," I quoted him in a half mocking tone, "'You're so beautiful.' And then you said, 'I must be dreaming.' Which I assume meant you were truly in awe of my good looks." I blushed as I said this, but I put my hands on my hips and stood my ground.

"*I* said that?" Gideon asked. "I said *that?*"

I nodded, feeling insulted. "You don't believe me?"

"I'm not sure what to believe," was Gideon's only reply.

"Anyway," I mumbled, crossing my arms. I began walking toward the village, calling over my shoulder. "You're just lucky the beast stopped. You aren't nearly as fast as you claim to be."

Gideon caught up to me, and the fact that I'd forced him to jog made me unwarrantably smug. "Wait." He touched my arm for me to slow, holding out his elbow like a gentleman for a lady. If I wasn't so irked by him, I'd be utterly pleased by the attention. I took his elbow, but kept my gaze forward, snubbing him, and continued on, forcing him to keep up.

"I wonder," he murmured, as we entered the town. "Why did the dragon stop?"

Maybe because what looked like an empty stretch of land suddenly screamed?

"I don't know," I spoke up, "but if you still want your precious Key then you've got a lot of making up to me to do before now and the end of the night."

Chapter 31

Kadin

WHEN RENA AND GIDEON walked into the tavern common room and sat down at our table, the last thing I expected to find was Rena sulking while Gideon was in a visibly good mood.

I searched my mind for the last time I'd seen Gideon smile, and couldn't think of it. Yet, when the waitress brought him a plate for dinner, he graced her with an actual grin. Rena didn't even thank the woman, just picked up her wooden spoon, poking at the food.

"What did you do all day?" Bosh was quick to ask. "You were gone for ages!"

Though we all knew he wanted to hear the answer from Rena, she didn't lift her sullen gaze from her plate, and Gideon, ever the well-mannered gentleman, replied instead. "We just now came from seeing a dragon, actually. It was quite an experience."

Bosh and I exchanged glances.

A man who'd clearly been eavesdropping choked on his food. "Here?" he said, panicking "Is it coming? What do we do?"

Rena waved a tired hand at him, barely looking up. "It was far away, don't be afraid." Then in a sharp tone to Gideon, she pointed at the man and said, "That. That is the reaction you're supposed to have to a dragon."

"Excuse me," Gideon's tone was not quite as polite this time. He set his spoon down with careful precision, whipping the cloth napkin open with a snap that gave away the frustration behind his respectful manners. "I do believe seeing the dragon was *your* idea."

That made Rena sit back in a huff, dropping her own spoon into the bowl with a clatter.

The two of them made me wish I'd spent the dinner hour alone, instead of here. An uncomfortable witness to a bizarre fight.

I could tell everyone else in the room felt as uncomfortable as I, yet Bosh seemed completely unfazed. "A dragon," he breathed. "That's incredible."

Rena shrugged, non-committal.

"What was it like?" he asked. "How big was it? Did it breathe fire? Did it fly?"

The barrage of questions seemed to simultaneously annoy Gideon, while Rena's spirits lifted. "It was faster than anything I've ever seen," she began, describing the meeting, from the moment they spotted it far away in the sky, to the moment it almost incinerated them. "I still can't believe we're standing here in front of you," she finished, shaking her head at Gideon, red hair swishing in disbelief.

Gideon only smiled, stretching out his hand, palm up. "I do believe it's time for you to hand over the Key."

"No." Rena's lips flattened into a stubborn line. "It wasn't a full day. You can try again tomorrow."

"I'm tired of your games," Gideon barked. "You owe me a Key. How did one of the Mere come to possess the Jinni Key anyway? Is it even the real thing?"

Gideon snapped his fingers and the Key from Rena's neck appeared in his hand. His blue eyes were dark and stormy.

Rena crossed her arms and lifted her chin, though it trembled with rage. "It *is*. You'll see soon enough."

Gideon only curled his long fingers around it, staring back at her. We waited in the tension; no one wanted to break it.

When Gideon broke their stare, it was only to glance down, startled, at his empty hand. Our heads swiveled to Rena, who tugged on the cord around her neck, lifting the Key into sight just long enough to prove herself before hiding it once more.

"How?" Gideon said dully. "How does a Mere have the Key?"

Rena shrugged, crossing her arms once more. "It was given to the Mere royalty as a peace offering. Right after the feuding ended in the Silent War, during the Treaty of Contempt."

"I think I would've heard rumor of a member of an outside race being given the Key," Gideon replied with a scowl.

Rena only shrugged.

During their silent standoff, I exchanged glances with Bosh.

"I don't know the full details," Rena said, breaking the silence first.

"How did you come to be in possession of it then?" Gideon challenged, leaning forward. His frustration was evident in the darkening of his eyes. "No one can steal the Key. You just proved it to be true now."

She bit her lip. "I'm actually part of the royal family. And, if we're being technical, it was given specifically to me."

"You're a royal?" Gideon's surprise echoed my own. He stood without warning. "How dare you?"

I'd be the first to admit Rena's revelation startled me, but it felt like Gideon was overreacting.

His raised voice brought the entire room to a screeching halt. Every superstitious person who'd ever heard of what a Jinni could do had likely been keeping one eye on Gideon ever since he'd entered the room, and now at the sound of his outrage, they froze. The waitress who'd come for his plate began trembling and the spoon clattered loudly against the plate as she shook.

"You purposefully kept this secret from me? I told you multiple things about the Jinn that could be used against us— this is unforgiveable."

At this point, we were a show for the entire room, and I wisely shrank back. When Bosh opened his mouth to intervene, I silenced him with a finger to my lips, shaking my head. *Not our fight.*

Gideon stormed out of the room in a temper. I'd never seen him this upset before. Rena had quite the effect on him. Meanwhile, the poor girl burst into tears and fled the room in the other direction, toward the stairs and the bedroom.

The rest of the room took a deep breath together in the silence they left behind. Slowly the volume began to return to normal, though everyone was understandably still a bit wary of our table, casting a glance between us and the door every now and then.

"That was odd," Bosh was the first to speak.

"That is why you *never* upset a Jinni," the vocal man behind us said in that deep voice of his, shaking his head at the entire spectacle.

Before any of us could answer, a hush fell over the room once more. I turned to face the door. Gideon had returned. He strode toward our table, holding something, which he placed resolutely on top of the wooden table. "Give this back to the girl," he said. "I want nothing to do with her." Everyone gaped at him, mouths hanging open.

Bosh picked up the object. "I can give it to her," he said into the silence as everyone looked on, holding the item to the light. It was a small shell.

Before Gideon could leave, I pushed back from the table to stand, lowering my voice. "Can we talk outside?"

He nodded, spinning on his heel to lead the way. I waited to speak until we were alone under the night sky with only cicadas chirping in the silence. "I'll find a way to convince Rena to give you the Key, but we need to move forward in saving Arie. These little bargains are wasting time. We *will* help you get into Jinn, I give you my word. But Arie needs us *now*. Can I count on you?"

Though his lips thinned, Gideon nodded his agreement. "Of course. Though I do need that Key desperately, there was never a question."

"Thank you," I choked out, and meant it. "I know you won't enter the castle uninvited, but go to Hodafez and keep tabs on Arie, could you? Just to make sure she's still safe?"

"Of course," Gideon said again. "It will be a relief to not be here."

"Speaking of not being here, I also need you to find my men. They should be staying at the Khov Inn. Though they may not all be back yet. Are you able to find them and bring them together?"

"I am."

"Good. Because I need them ready to go at noon tomorrow. I have a plan."

Chapter 32

Arie

IT WAS GETTING DARK on my second full day of imprisonment. I'd dozed on and off all day. It was so difficult to sleep when my stomach twisted with worry. But I wasn't allowed to leave my rooms until King Amir arrived, which Enoch hinted could be as soon as tomorrow since he'd been preparing to come here from the start. I'd spent the entire day in bed, dreading the next day, drifting in and out of wakefulness, and hoping Kadin would appear.

He didn't.

When I couldn't sleep any longer, I moved into my sitting room so I didn't hear the lack of thoughts from the guard posted on my balcony.

Pacing the small, dark room, I stopped by one wall and knelt to pick up the letter opener I'd thrown at Enoch's head. It was the only remnant left of my writing desk.

Holding it made me feel more present. It was like a tether to reality. Adrenaline raced through my veins as my body responded to memories returning, which triggered more awareness, until the fog slowly lifted.

A knock sounded on my door and this time Enoch didn't even bother for me to come open it before he entered, delivering my dinner tray himself. I tucked the letter opener into the pocket of my dress.

"You're going to meet with Amir tomorrow," he murmured as he set the tray on the table.

I didn't sit.

"Please, Queen Arie, you should eat and keep up your strength." He waved me toward the table. "Forget everything from earlier today. You shouldn't waste your time worrying over that."

I sensed his Gift sweeping over me with those last words. I smoothed my face and made my way to the table to sit, but I slipped my hand into my dress pocket as I did, squeezing the letter opener. I felt the reassuring weight of it and the burst of awareness that followed. I didn't forget.

Lifting the spoon to my mouth, I ate mindlessly. Enoch watched, his expression unreadable. Once I finished, he moved to pick up the tray and leave.

"I want you to go to bed now and get a good night's sleep," he said.

After the slightest pause, I obeyed, if only so that he wouldn't know I'd found a way not to.

* * *

ONCE I FELL ASLEEP, time was fluid. I didn't know how long I'd been waiting in my dreams when I heard a knock on the door and let Kadin in.

This time, as much as I wanted to jump into his arms again, I held back.

He did too, stepping inside, letting me lead.

I closed the door, turning to him, and couldn't help myself. The words came out as compulsively as if Enoch had told me to say them. "Kadin... I'm scared."

In a second his arms were around me and he murmured in my hair, "It's going to be okay."

I squeezed my eyes shut as tight as I could so the tears wouldn't escape, but my trembling gave me away. "Do you ever think about where we'd be right now if Amir and Enoch weren't a problem?" I whispered.

"All the time," Kadin replied immediately.

I kept my head on his shoulder, but peeked up at his strong chin and the dark stubble there.

"Your father would still be alive. But then, also, we'd never have met."

I hadn't considered that.

He cleared his throat and stepped back so he could meet my eyes. "Listen. We need to talk about the plan."

I made sure the tears weren't as close to the surface before I took a deep breath and nodded. "If you sneak inside the castle walls, you should use the tunnels and avoid the servants. We can't trust them since there's no way to know if Enoch has spoken to them."

Kadin nodded. "We'll send Rena in first. His Gifts can't touch her. She'll distract him, so he won't see Gideon approaching from behind."

His plan depended on so many small factors. It was a lot to trust. But we didn't have a choice—*I* didn't have a choice. "After Gideon takes Enoch down, it should bring me back to myself," I offered, "and then I should be able to call the guards to remove King Amir from our borders."

"How can we be sure?"

My lips quirked at the way he tried to make the plan airtight. The familiarity was comforting.

"I have one other way, if I need it." I reached into my pocket for the letter opener, but in the dream, it wasn't there. "It should work, but if for some reason it doesn't, you need to find a way."

Kadin nodded, taking my hand and squeezing it gently. "I will."

I didn't say anything else. The only time my mind was truly clear was in these dreams, and every time I was aware of the depths of the mind control, it made me think of my father. He hadn't survived it. Though I knew this wasn't the time or place to dwell on that, something in the back of my mind whispered, *What if I don't either?*

"That's our only plan, so far," Kadin said, bringing me back to the present. "And I don't like how bare it is."

"What if Enoch can't be overpowered?" I wrapped my arms around myself, struggling to breathe. "We need a backup plan with an escape route, in case all of you have to run."

"Arie," Kadin's voice was soft, gentle. He waited until I finally met his eyes. "We're not going to abandon you. We'll find a way."

"I guess we'll see," I mumbled.

"I'll make a deal with you," he said, grinning when he saw that caught my attention. "When I'm right, and we've successfully removed Enoch and rescued you, you'll owe me."

"Owe you, hmm?" I felt my lips curve slightly. I knew he was trying to distract me, and it was working. I opened my mouth to ask what, exactly, he had in mind, when I flickered.

"What's going on?" Kadin asked, taking my other hand, holding onto me as if he could keep me here.

I gripped his hands as if he was my anchor. "I'm not sure—I think—I might be waking up."

The flickering happened again and before I could say anything else, he vanished. My eyes fluttered and when I opened them, my room was dark instead of light, and I lay in bed instead of standing.

The guard outside coughed again. As much as I tried to ignore the noise of her shuffling outside on the balcony and the crashing waves, I couldn't find sleep again. After spending the whole day in bed, I was wide awake.

Chapter 33

Rena

AFTER HELPING KADIN TALK to Arie in his dreams, I lay in bed too frustrated to sleep. I'd watched them together, feeling a surge of jealousy. Where was Gideon? Where was my romantic story? How come Arie and Kadin could find a way to make it work despite everything pulling them apart, while Gideon couldn't see the perfect match right in front of him?

Tugging on my overdress and taking a blanket from the bed, I waited for one of the men to wake up and ask me where I was going while it was still the middle of the night, but they only snored.

Kadin's words came back to haunt me from our last real conversation. *You're so selfish.*

It hurt. Was it true?

I stood at the door, fingers on the handle, biting my lip. Clearing my throat, I said softly, "I'm going outside to watch the stars if anyone needs me."

No one replied.

I closed the door softly, tucking the room key in my pocket, shuffling down the stairs in the pitch-black. It should've been a comforting reminder of home, but for the first time since I'd arrived in the human world, I didn't like it. Tonight, the darkness was a reminder of my looming deadline, of all that still needed to fall into place. I found my feet traveling along the path to the hill where I'd sat that morning. With Gideon.

It was impossible *not* to think of him. I lay back on the grass, comfortable on the warm summer night, staring up at the stars. He was right. I shouldn't have kept my heritage from him. As daughter of the sea king and queen, I could use his secrets against him, just as he feared. I wouldn't, though. Never. That's why I'd given him the shell, as a token of faith.

I sighed, closing my eyes. Those pesky tears came again, tickling my face and falling into my ears. I rolled onto my side, sniffling.

Soft footsteps swished softly through the grass behind me and a second later a hand appeared with a handkerchief for my tears. It was a different handkerchief than the one Gideon had used earlier, a simple white one. He must have dozens.

I took it and Gideon sat down behind me. I appreciated that he didn't speak and I stayed facing the other direction so he wouldn't see my puffy eyes and face as I sniffed and wiped away the tears.

"I'm glad you're here," I whispered. "I've been wanting to apologize."

He stayed quiet, which I took to mean he'd give me a chance to explain.

"I didn't want you to know who I was, about my parents, because I wanted you to get to know me for who I am," I began.

He cleared his throat, shifting as if uncomfortable.

"Please," I begged, clutching the handkerchief, too embarrassed to look at him. "Just let me finish."

Now that the moment of truth was finally here, I felt so ready. "I think I've loved you since the day I met you," I told him. I wished I could see his face in that moment, but in some ways, facing away made it easier to be honest, to tell the whole story. "I swam to the surface so many days since the day we met, trying to find you." He deserved the whole truth, I reminded myself. "Very few of the Mere really believe in love, but I do. I hope you don't think I'm silly."

I waited for his reaction, but instead received one of his characteristic silences. I tried not to sigh. "It's okay," I said after a long pause, "you don't have to say anything." I wanted him to say something, so badly, but I wouldn't force it. He would need time to process the idea. He hadn't had an entire year, like I had.

Still, the hush that came over us was agony.

Finally, after my heart began to grow heavy with dread that maybe he didn't feel as I did after all, I felt his hand reach out to cover mine where I still clutched the handkerchief. Gently, almost timidly, he turned it over and placed another small item in my palm.

It was the shell I'd given him that morning. He was trusting me enough to respond with faith of his own. My heart swelled.

"Thank you," I whispered, reaching out to take his hand before he could pull it back, placing the shell back inside. "I want you to keep it. As a way to remember that you can always trust me. Always." I cupped both my hands around his, closing his fingers over it, so he couldn't help but take it. When he curled his fingers tighter, I knew he was accepting it, in his own quiet way.

As he slipped his hands out of my grip, I closed my eyes before a tear of joy leaked out, savoring the feeling. I'd been right. Of course, it was too early for him to say the words back, but the gesture meant almost more than words, really.

I smiled to myself. We may have had a fight, but we'd worked it out, and everything was back in line with the current of my plan. I felt almost like I was floating downstream, as if the weight of my desires had pressed me down for so long, and now that I'd let them loose, I was so light and happy.

After a peaceful minute had passed, I opened my eyes and rolled over to finally face him, only to find that he was gone. I spied his dark form all the way down at the bottom of the hill, a small dot in the distance making his way back to the tavern.

I could join him, but instead I lay back down with a huge smile. I wanted to savor this moment of victory. Everything was finally working out. Just like I'd told my sister it would. Just like I'd hoped.

* * *

"WHERE'S GIDEON?" I ASKED from where I sat atop my horse. The sun wasn't even up yet. The air felt cool and damp in the predawn air, reminding me of home. Reminding me of the alarming number of days left in my deadline. Only ten now.

We'd already eaten breakfast, packed, and checked out of the tavern, and I still hadn't seen Gideon. Bosh had helped me mount when I first came outside, and despite my desire to go back in and find Gideon, I didn't want to go through that again if I could avoid it. So, I waited, horse tied to the hitching post, while Bosh and Kadin roamed around me, packing the saddlebags in a hurry.

"He's going to meet us," Kadin said in passing, walking toward the inn and disappearing inside before I could ask questions.

"Don't worry," Bosh said quietly. He was in a strange mood today. "I'm sure he'll be back before you know it." He untied my horse to lead it, swinging up onto his own with ease, while I kept both hands on the pommel.

When Kadin came back out, he spoke quickly. "We have almost half a day's ride back to Hodafez, and we need to get there before noon." Without another word, he swung up onto his horse and we set off down the dirt road. I understood him wanting to get back to Arie, but shouldn't Gideon go with us? Didn't he still want the Key?

"Rena," Bosh spoke up again after a few minutes of silence, pulling his horse back until it was side-by-side with mine. He fiddled with the reins in his hands. "Kadin and I were talking yesterday, and… we'd hoped you might play a role in the rescue. That you might be willing to distract Enoch long enough for Gideon to have an opening." He cleared his throat. "Gideon says Enoch is strong, and he isn't sure he can defeat him without an advantage. We're afraid we won't be able to save Arie without your help."

Gideon needed me? I perked up. "Of course I'll help."

Kadin didn't turn around, but he sank back in his saddle, visibly relieved.

I smiled at the thought of helping Gideon. This might help bring us closer together.

Bosh's horse moved ahead of mine, and Kadin rode in front of him, so I took the opportunity to pull the Key out from around my neck and whisper my own name over it. The inky vision floated in the air, moving along the road with us.

Gideon stood before me, relaxed, smiling. "Hold this, could you?" he asked, handing me his cane as he sat to pull his boots off. We were in a small, cozy home, reclining in the common room. "It's been a long day. I have so much to tell you. But first, happy anniversary, my dear."

In the vision, he kissed my cheek and I smiled. For some reason, watching it made tears prick my eyes.

"How many years has it been?" he asked absently as he took my hand.

"Ten," I told him. "And only just beginning."

The vision ended and I let it fade away. My throat felt tight. The long road passed without my seeing it; the vision playing over and over in my mind instead. I wanted to prove Yuliya wrong, yes. But even more, I desperately wanted this desire to come true. I would do *anything.*

I tried to stay quiet and not to bother them anymore, but my unanswered question bothered me more than a jellyfish sting. "So, where *did* Gideon go?"

"He's just scouting ahead." Bosh sighed. He wouldn't meet my eyes. If the Mere were as bad at lying as the humans, we'd be extinct by now. "Know any good road games?"

"Road games," I repeated flatly. He was trying to distract me. The road stretched on for miles, and Gideon was nowhere in sight. Maybe a game wouldn't be so bad. "Okay, teach me."

Bosh only half-smiled, but he cheered up as the game went on. The first one involved naming as many plants and animals as you could spot while we moved at a snail's pace. I quickly grew bored. Not only because there were only a handful of foliage and creatures around, but because it soon became clear I didn't know the majority of their names. If we'd played this game in the sea, the tables would've been turned, and I made sure he knew it.

"Alright, alright." Bosh laughed finally. "Let's try another. Why don't we make you a better rider?"

I was skeptical that this was really a lesson masquerading as a game, but I agreed. Soon we were both laughing at the different competitions that I felt quite certain Bosh was making up as he went along. Who could ride the furthest distance without touching the pommel? Bosh. Who could do so without touching the horse's mane either? Ha! Bosh, of course. Who could hold on, but ride with their eyes closed? I lasted longer than I expected, but eventually my horse tripped again and I couldn't help myself. Still, I was proud of my progress.

Bosh waved his hands as he chattered, holding the reins for my steed in one hand as he led us along, leaving his own reins hanging over the pommel. He didn't even seem to notice that at any moment his horse could run away with him and there was nothing he'd be able to do about it. I just shook my head.

"See," he was saying, as he did something invisible with his body and his horse began to veer to the right. "It's all in the knees, you just have to apply a little pressure."

I snorted. "Can't we play a game that I can win?" I complained, rubbing my legs, which were still saddle sore from the last time we'd ridden. "I guarantee that I'll never use this information again in my life if I have anything to say about it."

Bosh laughed. Kadin rode too far ahead of us to hear our conversation, seeming to want space. But Bosh seemed perfectly content to ride beside me. It was a pleasant way to pass a long day of travel. He smiled over at me when he found me staring. I smiled back, then faced forward, shaking off the strange fluttery feeling.

"Ok, I've got it," he said, pulling me from my thoughts. "Let's play a guessing game."

I clapped my hands together in excitement. "I love guessing games."

"Okay," Bosh said, puffing out his chest and grinning. "I call this one, 'Guess Who.' To win, you just have to listen to my story and guess who it's about."

"I will definitely win this." I shifted in my saddle, trying to face him more. "I'm ready. Begin!"

Bosh tapped his lip thoughtfully. "Hmm, okay. Once there was... a child who grew up an orphan."

"That's it?" I asked when he stopped. "Well, I know it's not Arie." I tapped my lip just like Bosh had a moment ago, mocking him. "I'll guess Kadin," I threw out my decision. "Because he definitely seems like he grew up unloved."

When I glanced over at Bosh to see if I'd guessed correctly, I caught him wincing instead. "What's wrong?"

"Oh, nothing," Bosh said, stretching his lips in a smile. But it wasn't one of his real smiles. I could tell.

"What is it?" I asked again. "What did I say? You have to tell me. I'm so tired of the way humans tiptoe around what they really mean." *And Jinn,* I added to myself.

"Um, well..." Bosh fiddled with my horse's reins. "I was just trying to trick you, you see, by starting with someone you wouldn't think to guess." He didn't look up. "The orphan was me."

Oh. I reviewed my words in light of this new information. *Grew up unloved.* I cringed. Swallowing hard, I leaned across the space between us, clinging tightly to the pommel though I still nearly slipped from my saddle, and tapped him lightly on the knee to get his attention. "Bosh." I never humbled myself like this, but I knew I needed to say the words. "I'm sorry. Truly, I am. I didn't mean it."

"That's okay," he said, shrugging with another smile, but it still wasn't quite his real one.

"May I ask what happened to your parents?" I tried to be careful, seeing the irony as I tiptoed around his feelings just like I'd mocked the humans for doing earlier. But some people were worth tiptoeing for.

"I don't really know what happened to them," Bosh said. "It used to bother me. I guess someone found me wandering in the woods when I was really young. They dropped me off in a village nearby and then moved on. No one wanted responsibility for a brat that wasn't theirs when they had mouths to feed in their own household and barely enough to go around. So, the villagers took turns. 'Who will take the kid tonight?'" Bosh huffed a laugh as he mimicked the villagers. "'Not me,' they'd say, 'You take him.'"

"That's awful." An angry lump settled in my stomach at the thought of villagers who couldn't take this kind boy in and love him.

"Thanks," he said in a sarcastic tone.

"It's not your fault, you know," I said, ignoring the way his shoulders hunched, as if he didn't want to talk about it. "Those humans were selfish and cruel." The words flowed out of my mouth without a thought, but I heard Kadin's voice from just the day before, speaking similar words, and paused. Was I really selfish like those people? Would the Mere have been any more likely to take him in? No. They would've been even less likely. I blinked, trying to shake the feeling that I'd just seen myself in a new way, and I didn't like it.

"Okay, I've got one," I said in a cheerful voice, changing the subject for both of us. "Once there was… a Gifted child."

"That's easy," Bosh said, perking up quickly. Now, when he grinned over at me, I beamed back, feeling successful. That smile was real. "You're talking about Arie."

"Ha!" I pointed a victorious finger at him. "I meant Gideon. You lose!"

"That seems a bit like cheating," Bosh said, "since a child makes me think of a human, not a Jinni. But I'll give it to you."

I smiled smugly.

Bosh cleared his throat. "Speaking of Gideon, I wanted to talk to you about him…"

Instantly, I felt defensive. Shading my eyes from the sun, I stared at the road ahead. I hoped Gideon would return soon. Maybe he would flash in and walk beside us the rest of the way. Or maybe he could share my horse with me. I pictured him seated behind me, arms wrapped around me. Bosh wouldn't have to hold the reins then. Because no doubt Gideon could ride better than all of them, even Arie.

"Rena?" Bosh said, when I didn't answer. I'd gotten lost daydreaming.

"Yes? What about Gideon?" I couldn't help the sharp edge in my tone, wary of yet another person telling me to let it go.

Sure enough. "I don't know if Gideon's… feelings for you are quite what you hope." Bosh struggled to get the words out, fiddling with some small object in his hands instead of looking at me.

How did Bosh even know I had feelings? Was I that obvious? I thought of the night before. The moment Gideon and I had shared. *I don't care what anyone says, there's something between us.* I shook my head, trying to be kind as I told him, "I don't mean to offend, but you don't really know him. I've known Gideon for a long time. We met over a year ago." It was technically true. "I think he finds it hard to open up, but I'm patient. I can wait." At least, for another week.

He opened his mouth, but then closed it. Glancing away from me, he stared into his hands for a moment, then pocketed the item he'd been playing with. "I guess you're right," he said, a small smile that I couldn't quite read playing across his lips. "I don't really know. Can I just ask one thing?"

Curious now, I leaned toward him naturally, until I slipped in the saddle and had to right myself. "What's that?"

"Why are you in such a hurry?" Bosh avoided my eyes, staring at the road ahead, making it hard for me to tell what he was thinking.

I shrugged, patting my horse's golden mane absently. "I have… a deadline." I dared to let go of the pommel for a split second like Bosh taught me, grinning at him when I didn't fall off.

"What kind of deadline?"

I hurried to grip the saddle again. "It's nothing," I told him. "I'm confident I'll have time to get to know Gideon well enough."

Bosh didn't say anything to that.

I didn't know why I was lying to Bosh. The truth was Gideon and I had had a moment last night, but what did it mean to him? I didn't even know what it meant to me. Especially when he'd left without saying a word.

We rode in a comfortable silence for a while. I daydreamed about Gideon getting to know me better and even considered pulling out the Key to see my vision again when Bosh wasn't looking. When *would* he get back? I sighed, wanting another distraction. "Teach me a different game."

Chapter 34

Kadin

I COULDN'T REMEMBER THE last time I'd been this afraid. I tried not to let on. But I was consumed with regret for abandoning Arie. After everyone I'd lost in the past, I'd been a fool to just let her go.

When Gideon flashed into existence before me, just down the road and out of the others' sight, I kicked my horse into a canter. He was early. There was still at least an hour before noon. I couldn't tell from his expression if that was good or bad. Reaching him, I swung off the horse and hit the ground. "What news?"

"It seems Queen Arie has invited King Amir to return to Hodafez." Gideon spread his hands wide, shaking his head.

Obviously not her choice. Still, my stomach dropped.

"Naveed heard of her father's passing and was already at the inn. Daichi and Ryo were on their way back, so it didn't take long to find them."

"Perfect." I blew out a breath of relief. Things were finally going my way. "Did you tell them the plan?"

Gideon nodded. "They're already working on it."

"And you told them the time?" I asked, even though I knew I was repeating myself from the night before. "When they see the mid-afternoon sun touch the top of the castle?"

"Of course." Gideon smiled patiently. "We're going to save her."

"I know," I lied, lifting my chin. There was no other option. "Let the men know I'd be there if I could. I don't want to risk entering Hodafez too soon." If I was caught, I couldn't help Arie.

"I'm sure they understand," Gideon reassured me.

I nodded, unable to find words.

"Gideon, you're here!" Rena interrupted as she and Bosh rode up. She twisted in her saddle like she might actually try to dismount and greet him.

"Only for a moment," he said, mouth twisting down. "To bring news."

"Keep going," I told Bosh, waving them forward. "I'll catch up."

Rena wouldn't have obeyed, but Bosh led her horse and it followed his, out of her control. She glanced back more than once, staring at us without shame.

"One last thing." I cleared my throat, needing to know the answer, but afraid of what it might be. "Is it possible for Enoch to permanently damage Arie's mind?"

"It's unlikely." Gideon shook his head, and I blew out a breath of relief. "Enoch is much more capable with his Gift than Amir ever was or ever will be. He's over two centuries old and has served Queen Jezebel for more than half that time.

His skills are unparalleled. Depending on how severely Enoch is enforcing his control, however, she may need a few days to recover."

My forehead wrinkled, and I didn't bother to hide my concern from Gideon, rubbing my eyes, exhausted. "Thank you for being honest with me."

Gideon clapped a hand on my shoulder for a moment, surprising me. "I care about her, too. We'll make sure no more harm comes to our Arie."

I reached out and clasped hands with him. The only words I could get out were, "Thank you."

"I'll check back at noon," he said. There was nothing else to plan. I nodded as he vanished, climbing back onto my horse and taking a moment to gather my thoughts before I rode after Bosh and Rena.

"Let's keep going," I called out as I reached them at an easy trot. "I want to be as close to Hodafez as possible by noon." I knew Gideon could flash us up to the city in a heartbeat, but I couldn't sit here and do nothing. And just in case anything happened to him, at least I'd be close enough.

"Is everything on schedule?" Bosh asked once I drew up to them.

"It is," I said, not adding anything further. "They just need a little more time to get everything into place."

When we reached the ocean, it was just a little past noon. We stopped near the beach to start a small fire and cook a light meal while we waited for Gideon.

"Can I try to see Arie again?" I asked Rena.

"It's the middle of the day," she said, squinting at me. "She's not going to be there."

I knew she was right, but I had to try. "Please?" I begged. "We have to wait for Gideon anyway."

She shrugged. "Good point."

I thought it'd be difficult to fall asleep so early, but with the dream spell in place, I found myself standing outside the door to Arie's dream bedroom within a few minutes. I knocked. Over and over, I knocked. But no one answered.

After trying a few more times, I turned to find Rena walking up to me in the dream hallway. "Told you. She's not asleep. It doesn't work if she's not asleep."

I startled. "How did you get here?"

She shrugged. "I'm always in here."

"You didn't think to tell me that before?" I muttered, my frustration deepening.

"It wasn't important. And I wanted to see if you loved Arie as much as she loves you."

That gave me pause. "You think... did she say that?"

"No." Rena smiled. "But neither did you."

I didn't have an answer for that.

"How come you won't say it to each other?" she asked, crossing her arms. "Gideon won't say anything either. I don't understand why everyone keeps love quiet like it's a big secret. Haven't you ever thought the other person might like to know?"

Even in the gravity of the moment, waiting for Arie to show up and worrying for her, I felt my lips twitch at Rena's uncomplicated approach. "Love isn't always simple." I shrugged, though I couldn't help but think of how obvious Gideon's feelings were, and added, "Sometimes you have to think of what the other person wants."

"That doesn't make any sense." Rena shook her head. "If you never tell Arie how you feel, how will you ever know? And how will you get your happily ever after, like in the stories?"

"You aren't listening, Rena. You can't go into love looking for what you can get. Love is about giving."

She squinted at me, taking that in.

I didn't know why I was even discussing this with her. I knocked again. Still no answer.

Rena didn't say anything else, but she was starting to fidget.

I hated to give up, but she was right. We left the dreamscape and while Rena said she wanted to go down to the beach because she missed the water, I turned to stare at the small fire. This was a living nightmare.

Chapter 35

Arie

I HAD NO MEMORY of the morning. It was the noon meal, and I was sitting down to eat with only Enoch for company. That alone was strange, as I usually dined in the main hall, not alone in the smaller dining room.

When King Amir strode in, I struggled to hide my confusion as we stood to greet him. "My apologies for not greeting you formally." I searched for the right words. "I didn't realize you'd arrived." I didn't even remember inviting him.

He didn't bother to explain, staring down his long nose at me as he flung his rich robes back in a shallow bow, moving to sit, though I was still standing.

I forced a smile in return as Enoch told Amir we were both thrilled to see him. A wave of calm washed over me as he spoke and I turned to my meal.

"There was a complete lack of fanfare," Amir complained during the second course.

Enoch murmured his response so quietly I couldn't fully make it out. Something about needing to avoid prolonged exposure to the thoughts of others. A precaution.

He caught my eye and raised his voice as he added, "Arie is so thrilled to see her old friend, the King of Sagh, after so long. Aren't you, my queen?"

"It really has been a long time," I agreed with a pleasant smile. For whatever reason, I couldn't quite place why that was. I chose not to bring it up and focused on the hot soup in front of me instead.

Enoch and Amir held up most of the conversation on their own, although Enoch liked to remind me that we were all having a wonderful time.

"Absolutely," I always replied. For once, I wasn't just keeping polite conversation, but truly meant it.

They finished their meal before I did, and pushed back their chairs.

"Queen Arie, I trust that you'll have a pleasant evening in your chambers once you're finished," Enoch said in that soft, warm tone of his that always reassured me. He tucked one hand behind his back and the other bent in front of him, in a deep Jinni bow. Amir simply stopped in the doorway, waiting for him.

"I will, thank you." I smiled and turned back to my soup.

"Your highness," Enoch's soft voice floated back to me as his footsteps echoed across the marble floor. "If I could have a word?"

King Amir grunted his agreement. I glanced back in time to catch him waving a servant out of his way. "Everyone wears such a mournful expression," he complained to Enoch. The door swung shut slowly and his voice carried from the hall. "I realize they buried their king yesterday, but I still find it rude."

The pain of his words sliced through the fog in my mind like a sharp knife.

My father was dead?

My father is dead.

The reality of my situation flooded into my mind faster than it ever had before, as if a dam had been broken.

I stood unconsciously, following them into the hall, keeping my distance.

Enoch and Amir disappeared through the door to the throne room ahead. No one else was around. I couldn't waste this opportunity. I glanced around to make sure no one saw before I trailed after them.

Slipping inside the throne room, I ducked behind a grand pillar and out of sight.

"I don't like it," Amir complained loudly as they walked. "Why would Queen Jezebel still want my kingdom to be merged with Hodafez? Why can't she use my kingdom alone?"

"That is not for you to know," Enoch answered smoothly, as they stepped through the smaller door and into the back room behind the thrones, voices fading.

I risked being seen and scurried across the wide room, ducking behind another pillar, closer to the open door, where I could hear them again.

"I understand—" Enoch was saying.

"No, you *don't* understand," Amir's strident voice interrupted. "She's a *mind reader*. I want *nothing* to do with that. She should have had a Severance long ago. You need to perform one on her immediately."

Enoch's voice was softer. I leaned closer to the door to hear. "A Severance is not so simple. There are certain elements and materials that need to be gathered for all the components of a Severance to align correctly."

"Then get them," Amir snapped. "Because the only way I'll go through with this is if her Gift is severed. End of story. Remind your queen that she promised me this kingdom. I've done my part, now you do yours."

He strode out the door without warning. I ducked behind the pillar. A few long moments later, the grand doors to the throne room creaked open and slammed closed.

Severed.

He wanted Enoch to perform a Severance.

My breathing came in short gasps. I shut my eyes and tried to hold my breath. I still sensed Enoch's presence. Did that mean he could sense me?

A chill stole over me at the thought.

Opening my eyes, I considered what to do. Sneak back to my room and effectively return to my prison. Or face Enoch… somehow.

I pulled the letter opener from my pocket. On silent feet, I tiptoed toward the door to the smaller room. When I peeked inside, Enoch's back was to me.

There wasn't time to think about it. I stepped inside, moved behind him, and placed the sharp tip of the letter opener against his throat. "Don't move."

"Queen Arie," he replied calmly, obeying. "What brings you here at this hour?"

"I finally have my mind back," I hissed. "And you need to leave."

"I wish I could," he replied. There was a touch of unexpected sadness in his voice.

I angled so I could see his face. There was that insinuation again, that he wasn't in control. "What do you mean?"

"It's not up to me." He quietly turned over his hand, palm up, and the letter opener appeared in it.

My hand at his throat was empty. I gasped.

Turning to face me, Enoch only said, "This isn't personal. But I'm afraid you're feeling faint, and you're going to pass out."

His Gift swept over me at the same time as my knees grew weak and the edges of my vision grew dark. Head spinning, I fell to the floor and everything went black.

* * *

KADIN'S WARM GOLDEN EYES met mine. He and I were in his hometown in the kingdom of Baradaan, where he'd shown me a secret oasis. Instead of dipping our toes in this time, though, I grinned at him, soaking up the sun.

Time passed the way it does in dreams, long and short at the same time, but it didn't seem very long before the space in my dream shifted. Instead of the oasis, I was in my bedroom, lying in my bed. An awareness returned, the way it had the last few times I'd met Kadin here.

A tear escaped my eye. I hadn't even realized I was crying, but more tears came until my pillow was soaked.

The whisper of something tickled my mind.

It was Kadin.

I could hear him thinking on the other side of the door—my reach had grown. Another new development for me. No longer was I limited to just one room, it seemed. At least not when the thoughts involved were his.

It took a minute for it to sink in that this was no longer a regular dream, but the dreamscape where we'd met twice before.

He was debating whether or not he should knock again. *Again? How long had he been there?*

I took a quick moment to wipe my wet face with the sheets, not wanting him to see me with puffy, red eyes.

A second later, there was only silence. I panicked. *Was he still outside? This might be my last opportunity to speak to him before it's too late!*

I threw off the covers, raced to the door, unbolted it, and swung it wide. It opened on a dark, empty hallway.

He was gone.

* * *

WHEN I WOKE, IT was because Enoch was placing me gently on a bed. But it wasn't my bed. I didn't recognize this room at all. It was small with bare stone walls. The bedposts were thick, solid wood stretching to meet a maroon canopy overhead. And there was dust on the furniture, even on the scratchy bedspread. It tickled my nose and made me sneeze as I shifted.

He turned to leave without a word, reaching the door before I'd managed to sit up.

"Wait," I called after him. "Will you really go through with it? The Severance?"

Enoch's pride kept his posture stiff, but he turned back, meeting my gaze and letting me see his shame instead of hiding it. "I can help you forget," he offered finally, taking a step closer.

"No!" I threw my hands up. "Please... don't."

He stopped. Surprising me, he obeyed my wishes and left, closing the door behind him softly. A key turned in the lock. Even so, I leapt out of bed and ran to test it. Locked. I ran through the small attached rooms, but there was only a lavatory and a closet. Neither had any outside access and the windows in the bedroom were too high to use for an escape. The view revealed where they'd put me. I was in the East wing of the castle, which had been closed for weeks since guests were few and far between. No one would hear me scream for help.

Curling up in the bed, I drew the covers over myself, shivering. It was still summer. Why was I so cold? I pulled myself into a ball, as small as possible, and wished for sleep. Maybe Kadin would come back.

Thoughts raced through my head, making sleep impossible. Every time I thought about the Severance, a spike of adrenaline would pump through my veins. I got up to pace. Was there any way to avoid a Severance? Any way to protect a Gift, so it couldn't be removed?

I'd never thought to ask Gideon. Because I'd never wanted to keep it before. In fact, before this moment, I hadn't even known how much it had come to mean to me. But it truly was a part of me. I couldn't imagine losing it.

Closing my eyes, I took deep breaths, hoping desperately to fall asleep and meet Kadin. He could ask Gideon for me if there was any way to prevent a Severance. There *had* to be a way. I refused to listen to the niggling thought that said there wasn't.

Chapter 36

Rena

I STARED OUT AT the crashing waves. There wasn't anything like this back home, far beneath the surface. Here, the ocean wasn't peaceful. It seemed angry.

Gideon hadn't left any word for me. No special greeting when he'd arrived either. If anything, he seemed almost like he held a new grudge, though I couldn't imagine what that might be now.

Gazing at the ocean, the wide-open horizon calmed me somewhat. I tilted my head to let the sun warm my face, digging my toes into the sand as the waves licked at them. The sun was beginning its descent. Kadin's plan would begin in a few hours.

I was so torn in this moment. Missing the sea, yet not wanting to go home. Especially not wanting to leave if there was even the slightest chance Gideon could love me in return.

A throat cleared. I whipped my head around to face the sound, blinking when I found the object of my thoughts only a few feet away. "You're back," I whispered, but the wind stole the words and I had to repeat myself in a louder voice. "You're back."

"Ah, yes." Gideon tucked his hands behind him, stiff, facing the ocean instead of me. "I came to report. But before I do, I felt I should find you and apologize for losing my temper yesterday."

I tilted my head, confused. "That's okay. I already forgave you. I thought you knew that when we talked last night?"

"What exactly are you referring to?"

"You know…" I stepped closer, thinking of the way I'd held his hands in mine. "After you stormed out, when you found me outside later? Looking at the stars?" I waved at the sky.

His expression didn't change. No flair of recognition. "That didn't happen," he said flatly.

I gave a short laugh, though I didn't really appreciate his joke. "Yes. It did." I took another step, so that there was only a foot of space between us, willing him to close the remaining distance. "I was there."

"Well, I wasn't."

"I have to be honest," I said, crossing my arms now. "I don't understand."

"You weren't talking to me," he said bluntly.

"Yes," I repeated more firmly, digging into my pocket to pull out the white handkerchief he'd left behind and waving it in the air. "I *was.* You gave me this, and tried to give the shell back. And then I told you that I loved you! How can you not remember that?"

"You can't be serious." Gideon's brows rose at the confession. He truly seemed surprised.

I swallowed, hurt. "Don't you remember? When you tried to give the shell back," my voice barely above a whisper, "I told you to keep it."

Gideon only squinted at me, perplexed.

My throat felt tight. "It really wasn't you?"

"I threw the shell on the table that night," Gideon replied. I winced.

He dropped his gaze as he added, "I told them to return it to you."

Them. Which one of them? In my mind, I could see immediately who would take on the task. The only one who even wanted to talk to me. Bosh. That's why he'd been trying to warn me to move slowly with Gideon. Because it'd been him in the dark, trying to return the unwanted gift, while still trying to salvage my pride. Suddenly the shifting and throat clearing made sense. The way he'd tried to bring it up again this morning.

"I understand you were angry," I said slowly, trying to move past this unfortunate revelation. "Maybe we can start over. Let the tide wash away what's happened?"

"I don't think so." Gideon crushed my hopes, shaking his head slowly. "You say that you meant to confess feelings for me?"

"That I love you," I corrected him, striving to be confident, but sounding small. "I fell in love with you a year ago when I saved you from drowning, and I hoped... I had hoped that if you got to know me you might feel the same."

"I see." He cleared his throat, staring out at the waves as he clutched his cane. He grew so still that he could've been one of the stone sentries back home.

This was not going the way I'd imagined it would at all. When Gideon finally spoke, he shifted just once to look me in the eyes. "I was in love once. A long time ago." His voice was wistful. "I've lived more than a hundred years and don't expect I'll ever find love like that again."

I forced myself to hold his gaze, though I felt like a little-Mere being scolded by an elder. I'd not realized there was such an age difference between us. Gideon still looked young enough to be just a few years my senior.

"Please understand me," he said gently. "I don't want to mislead you. I feel it's only right to let you know that not only are we from two very different worlds, but we are completely unsuited for each other. I apologize for the brutal honesty, but I do suggest you find someone else who might be able to return your affection."

At some point during his speech, I'd grown unable to hold his gaze, staring at the sand under my feet now, watching the tears drip off my nose.

"I'll leave you alone," he said, "and report to Kadin. Do we have an understanding?"

I nodded at his feet, and they moved out of my vision as he walked away, until the crunch of his boots on the sand faded into nothing.

What a fool I'd been.

Chapter 37

Kadin

"WHERE'S RENA?" BOSH ASKED.

I didn't turn away from the fire as I opened my mouth to answer, but another voice spoke first, "Down by the water."

I sat up, recognizing it immediately. Gideon stood at the edge of our little camp. He stepped forward as Bosh's back disappeared over the hill, headed toward the ocean.

"Is everything in place?"

He nodded. "They're ready. But there's still another two hours before it's time."

Two more hours until we would find out if our tenuous plan would work. If Arie could be saved. Gideon let me stew in silence, moving closer to the fire. I chewed on a toothpick until it snapped in half.

Bosh appeared over the hill, running, yelling something unintelligible. As he grew closer, the words grew clear. "Rena's leaving. Something happened. I asked her to wait, but she keeps saying she has to go!" He stopped in front of us, panting, speaking between breaths. "We have to do something."

"What? Why is she leaving?" I demanded.

"She wouldn't say." Bosh bent over, leaning on his knees, but glanced up at Gideon. "Something must've happened."

Gideon cleared his throat. "I fear it's my fault."

I tensed. "What did you do?"

"I may have… spurned her affections."

I gaped at him. "Can you take it back?"

"I'm truly sorry," Gideon said, and his shoulders were bowed as if he carried a heavy burden. "I cannot."

"This can't be happening," I whispered to myself.

Our plan depended on Rena—the girl who only did something if it benefited either her or the one person who'd just utterly scorned her.

I dropped my head into my hands, unable to think or move past this moment. I was crushed. Beaten. Broken.

I'd tried to have hope for everyone else, but if I was honest, I didn't know if our plan would work anymore. I was terrified I wouldn't be able to save Arie.

"Let me try to talk to her," Bosh spoke up. "Maybe there's some way I can convince her to stay."

"Go." Gideon moved to perch on a nearby log, looking defeated as well. If Rena had left already, then he wouldn't get the Key he wanted so desperately.

Bosh disappeared back over the hill.

"What do we do?" I asked into the shocked silence. "Can we move forward with our plan without Rena? Will you be able to overpower Enoch on your own?"

"Honestly," Gideon hesitated, "I'm not sure."

Chapter 38

Rena

I STOOD HALFWAY IN the ocean with the water surging and hitting me in the stomach, gathering the nerve to leave and face my sister. The waves drenched more and more of my clothes as I watched them break, over and over again.

I was trying to find the nerve to go home. To abandon Arie, who'd become my friend. To face my sisters and admit the truth. That they'd been right all along.

Love wasn't real.

Tears flowed down my face, falling into the sea and melding together. This was where I belonged. I lifted my hand to the shell around my neck that would change me back.

"Rena, wait!" Bosh called. He waded out next to me, ignoring how his clothing got soaked. "Please, wait," he begged, stopping only when he stood in front of me, between me and the empty horizon. "Before you go, at least hear me out." He spread his hands in a helpless gesture. "I don't know if it was ever really said out loud, but Arie needs you—we *all* need you—desperately. We can't save her without you."

"I understand." I wavered. "But I can't stay here." Not now. My fingers brushed the top of the water with one hand, while the other gripped the shell harder.

"I know. Well, I don't *know*, but I can guess what happened," he said.

Shame heated my cheeks. Now Gideon had told everyone?

"I know Gideon didn't mean to hurt you. He always tries to do what's right and he probably didn't want to lead you on, but that doesn't mean he hates you. You shouldn't give up on us so fast, you've only been here a month. Maybe… maybe there's still a chance—love takes a long time."

"Love takes a long time," I repeated. "Love is about giving," I quoted Kadin. "There certainly are a lot of rules about love and it doesn't seem all that worth it to me." I let go of the shell momentarily, turning to face him. "How do you even know I told him I loved him?"

He lowered his gaze.

"It was you, wasn't it? That night?"

Bosh nodded, twisting to pull something from his pocket, which was drenched with each new wave that crashed into us. "I'm sorry. I didn't know what to say and then you started talking, and I couldn't find a way to tell you without making it worse. And I tried to tell you again this morning, but I didn't know how." He held the object in his palm, stretching it out toward me. "I'm sorry," he repeated.

It was my shell. The one I'd given Gideon as a promise of trust. I wondered if Bosh knew the significance of his offering.

"As a way for you to always remember you can trust me," he said, repeating the words I'd thought I was saying to Gideon. *So, he did know.*

I considered his face. Softer than Gideon's. Younger. A fuzz of a dark beard coming in. Kind brown eyes, squinting in worry. He really meant it; he'd been trying to help, even if he'd only made things worse.

I took the offered shell and gazed down at it, running a finger across its ridges with the other. "This doesn't change anything."

Bosh moved unexpectedly, picking up the cerith shell from around my neck, wrapping his fingers around it. "What would happen if I took this? Will you have to keep your legs?" he asked, his voice husky as he looked ready to snap it off the necklace.

I crossed my arms, frowning. "If you put much more distance between myself and that shell, then you'll bring my tail back yourself," I warned him. He let go immediately. "Besides," I added, "even if you took it, I couldn't go back now." I'd been hurt and humiliated.

"I don't know what to do," he said and his voice broke a little. "Rena, what can I say to convince you to stay?"

"You just want me to stay so I can help rescue Arie," I accused him, though deep down I knew this was a good reason.

"It's more than that," Bosh argued, running a hand through his hair, getting it wet and slicking it back. "I want you to help, yes, but I want you to stay afterward too. Stay with us."

"Why?"

"Because I like you." Simple. Straightforward. I liked him too, but what difference did it make?

"Goodbye, Bosh." I held out my hand to shake in the human farewell.

He took it with both of his, clasping my hand in his own. It felt different than the other night. Maybe because I knew it was him. It felt warm and safe.

"At least come back and visit?" Bosh said with a weak smile that made me miss his real one.

I only stared back at him. There was no visiting. I should never have come. I could only hope that by going back now, my deal with Yuliya would be null and void.

His hand squeezed mine tighter, but I pulled it away. I waded further into the sea, not looking back, and murmured the spell over the shell in my grip.

My tail came back in sharp spasms as I sank below the surface. A few powerful kicks took me a dozen paces away before I allowed my tail to surface briefly and wave in the air, knowing Bosh would see the red scales in the sun. No doubt he would think it was beautiful. To Gideon, though, I was the enemy. I'd thought when I met him in his state of delirium that he could accept me, but now I knew better. The Jinni had never liked the Mere, and Gideon was no exception.

My tears were invisible now, merging with the ocean as they always had in the past.

I swam further out, waiting for a long minute, and then a bit longer, half-expecting Bosh to be gone by the time I finally resurfaced, just enough to see the shore. His tiny form still stood there in the distance, peering out over the water, hunched over and dejected. Guilt tore at me. I tried to ignore it.

Dropping back under the water, I swam a short distance further and found a little underwater island with coral all around. It created a colorful shelter for me to weep in peace. I wasn't ready to go home yet. I still wore the human dress, though it swirled strangely in the water. If I hadn't been in such a mood, I would've laughed at the way my tail looked sticking out from underneath.

After adding more tears to the ocean, my sobs slowly subsided and a strange depression fell over me. I'd never felt this way before.

I lay there on the ocean floor, staring at the coral around me. Two little clownfish swam in and out of a beautiful orange anemone in front of me. I'd missed these vivid colors and the constant activity of the sea.

It looked like the clownfish were bringing food for each other. I rolled over, placing my back to their relationship.

This gave me a view of a pufferfish outside carefully crafting circles in the sand for the female looking on, perfecting his design for her approval. It looked nearly complete, which meant he'd been at it for at least a week, if not longer. I'd always thought this mating ritual to be romantic. Now I fell onto my back, staring up at the ripples of sunlight on the ceiling of water above, only to find a pair of seahorses, dancing for each other.

For each other.

Not for themselves.

This time I didn't turn away, watching the way the male and female twirled and pranced. It reminded me of dancing with Bosh. One of many things he'd done for me. What had I ever done for him? For any of them? Even for Gideon? Besides offering him the shell, nothing.

I bit my lip. Rolling back onto my side, I stared out at the pufferfish as he finished his project. The female inspected it carefully. If she approved, she would give him her eggs. If not, she would find another pufferfish's circle.

I didn't know why this made me think of Bosh. It should remind me of Gideon's rejection. Instead, it felt like my eyes were opened to how I'd just done the same thing to Bosh. The boy who no one had loved. He deserved someone to love him, even if only in a small way, even if it was only staying a few extra days, helping, being there for him. He deserved someone willing to do something *for* him.

So did Arie. She'd been my friend when I didn't deserve it. If the situation were reversed, I felt confident she would've tried to help me.

I clenched my teeth. If I went home now, before the deal was finished, I would have to give Yuliya the Key. But then life would otherwise go back to the way it was before I left. Tortured occasionally, but mostly ignored. It wasn't the worst life ever. I could forget about the human world and about Gideon.

That was a lie. I would never forget.

It would be much riskier to stay in the human world—for one thing, no matter how long I stayed, I was guaranteed to lose the deal I'd made with Yuliya. Gideon had made that extremely clear.

If I stayed to help, I'd not only give up the Key but also be forced to go home as a failure.

Plus, they might have already left to rescue Arie and were probably furious with me. Bosh might never forgive me. But I had to try.

I swam without thinking any longer, picking up speed as I went, until my gills fluttered heavily, gasping for air. I leaped out of the water every few feet, taking deep breaths, and pressed on. There was no time to waste.

When the shore came into sight, I forced my weary muscles, unused to swimming for so many weeks, to carry me forward even faster.

STEPPING OUT OF THE ocean on two legs once more, suffering through the spell for the second time that day, I stood there for a moment, readjusting and recovering from the pain, dripping wet.

I leaned over to wring out my skirts as best I could, and then lurched into an awkward run, muscles trembling. If swimming had been tiring, then this was a monumental effort, especially being sore from riding. I stumbled in the sand, but pushed on, onto firmer ground, up the hill and through the grass, until I found the campfire.

It was empty.

I let out a yell of frustration. Here I was trying to do the right thing, and I was too late. Or was I? Breathing hard, I ran down the hill, through the trees, until I found the road.

Left was back the way we'd come. The quiet backroad was deserted.

To the right was the road to Hodafez. Also empty.

I threw up my hands, grabbing my wet hair, wanting to pull it out at my options.

I'd never thought I'd wish for a horse in my entire life. I almost wanted to cry for my poor legs, as I began to run once more, down the road toward Hodafez. At this pace, how would I ever make it in time?

"Wait!" A voice called before I'd even run two paces. I nearly fell over in surprise. Catching myself, I swung around to find Gideon standing there at the edge of the road.

"What are you doing here?" I asked, frowning, "Everyone else already left."

"Me?" He shook his head in disbelief. "What are *you* doing here? I was told you left."

"That's very judgmental coming from someone standing right next to me," I said, crossing my arms. "And I did. Leave, that is. But now I've come back." I could explain my epiphany to him, and any other time I would have, but this time I only lifted my chin. I didn't want to explain anything to him. Didn't even want to talk to him, really. I smiled at the realization. It was very unlikely that I was in love with him if I could hardly stand to speak to him. "What are you doing here, anyway?"

Gideon toyed with his cane as he stared at me, looking equally reluctant to explain. "I took Kadin and Bosh into Hodafez to wait for the signal. Bosh asked me to come back here to wait for you—begged, rather. Just until it was time. I agreed for his peace of mind, but was about to leave when you came barreling through the camp like a mindless fool and ran right past me."

I glared at him and he was quick to add, "I apologize. I'm in a state. I didn't mean that last bit. I'm sure you were simply in a hurry."

My lips parted. Gideon was apologizing to me? What was the catch?

The Key dangling on the cord next to my heart. Obviously.

I pulled it out. "I suppose you want this." It swung back and forth in the air.

Gideon's gaze followed the path of the Key. He closed his eyes and drew a deep breath, before meeting my gaze. "I apologize, regardless of the Key."

I considered him. Tucking it back under my collar, the corner of my mouth tilted up. "Good. Because I'm not ready to give it to you." I didn't bother to explain, turning to face the road and start walking. Over my shoulder, I added, "If you still want to get into Jinn more than anything, we can talk about it after we save Arie."

A few long strides and Gideon reached me, holding out a hand.

I considered it.

Not one part of this experience in the human world had gone the way I'd wanted it to. It probably never would. Still, these were the first beings I'd met who put others above themselves. And I found myself wanting to be like them.

I reached out a hand toward his, and accepted.

Even as he began to fade out of sight, he returned, letting go of my hand. He exhaled deeply, as if at the edge of his patience. "Rena. Your spells."

"Oh, right. Sorry," I said, hurrying to remove the protection spell so he would be able to take me with him.

The world blended together, changing in the span of a heartbeat into a quiet, shaded alley in the bustling city of Hodafez. I immediately replaced my protection spells. Kadin and Bosh stood in front of us.

They stiffened at the sight of us, but then relaxed. Bosh laughed and pulled me into a hug, squeezing so tight I grew concerned my protection spells might go off. "You came back! I knew you would!"

Kadin crossed his arms, also staring at me. "We thought you left."

Ugh. These questions again. I opened my mouth to answer, but then turned to Gideon first. "I'm going to need you to go somewhere else for a minute," I told him. "I don't want you to be here."

"Excuse me?" Gideon gave a small laugh. "I think not."

I clenched my teeth, wishing I had one of my spells that hid us from sight so I could also prevent him from hearing my words. It was embarrassing to apologize in front of him. Facing Bosh and Kadin again, I shaded my eyes, trying to block Gideon from my line of sight. "I decided to help after all," I said lightly.

"No."

Kadin's answer was swift and surprising. I glanced at Bosh, but he seemed as startled as I. "I was under the impression that you needed my help," I said slowly, "I'm sorry for the confusion earlier, but you can't possibly be willing to let a little misunderstanding keep you from saving Arie."

He flinched at that, but stared past me toward the castle. "As much as I might need your help, I can't trust you. Not after you left like that."

"I'm sorry." I threw up my hands, yelling, "I don't know what more I can do. If you want to be alone, then fine, but don't say you didn't have a choice!"

A throat cleared. We turned to find Gideon standing there, gripping his cane. "Pardon me," he said into the small pause. "Might I suggest taking this conversation somewhere more private? Or at the very least *not* drawing attention to us?"

"We don't have time to talk," Kadin replied. "The signal from the men should be coming any second now."

"Gideon," I said, "Why don't you go check on the men and whatever it is they're doing?"

Though he likely saw through my attempt to get him to leave, this time he agreed without argument, vanishing into the air, leaving me alone with them.

Kadin's stance was frigid. Bosh was glancing between us, shifting from one foot to the other. It felt like swimming in ice water as I struggled to find the right words.

"Okay, fine. You were right." I didn't bother warming up to it the way the humans did, just went straight to the heart of our problem. "I was selfish."

Kadin didn't say anything right away, thrown off by my admission. "You *are* selfish," he said eventually, making his opinion of me clear.

I stared up at the sky, trying to find the words.

"But... she came back," Bosh chimed in, trying to help.

"Yes!" I waved a hand in Bosh's direction. "I swear, I'm trying. Don't you understand what I'm offering? What I came here to do?"

When Kadin didn't say anything, I began to pace. "You know, I'm new to this whole thing. But if you insist on going alone and sacrificing yourself instead of letting us help, my gut is telling me the 'unselfish' thing to do would be to tie you down so you can't go anywhere."

"Don't be a fool," Kadin said, but his tone was less harsh, and a smile played on his lips.

"Oh, so I'm selfish *and* a fool now?" I asked, raising one brow but smiling as well to take the edge off.

Kadin gave a soft laugh. "Definitely." He shook his head and sighed. "Alright. I can't believe I'm saying this, but if you swear you won't disappear again, then I accept your help."

"Good." I grinned at them. "Because I wasn't going to take no for an answer."

Chapter 39

Kadin

I HELD BACK A chuckle when Gideon grumbled to me mentally, *How much longer do I need to stay out of sight?*

Rena still thought he'd left.

I only shook my head at him, where he peered out from behind a nearby building. *I never told you to hide. If you don't want to talk to her, then just wait for the signal.* Poor Gideon. The Jinn weren't as supernatural as everyone assumed and they pretended. They were just like us humans. At least when it came to unwanted infatuations.

I could go tell them to start early.

I bit my lip to avoid laughing out loud. Gideon was bargaining with me? *Save your strength to face Enoch.*

No answer.

Fortunately for Gideon, we didn't have to wait long.

The screams floated over to us before the rest of the chaos did. I heard hoof beats on the main road just a few buildings down. A stampede from the stables burst into the streets. The pandemonium grew louder until the herd of escaped animals and people chasing them passed right in front of us. Nearby guards raced down the streets after the animals, and more guards poured out of the barracks to join them.

"That's our signal," I said as soon as they rounded the corner and the frenzied charge was out of sight. Slipping around the buildings, we moved to enter the stables from the side door.

Once inside, I scanned the stalls quickly to make sure they were truly empty. The nearest horse snuffled my pockets, searching for a treat. I waved the others in and we scurried to the back, to an unoccupied stall used to store boxes.

I searched along the back wall until I found the brick that was slightly discolored compared to the rest. Just a bit of pressure there and it scraped against the others as it moved. A chunk of the wall shifted and a dark tunnel mouth yawned open before us, revealing a hidden entrance. Only the first few feet were visible. "In," I waved everybody past me. "Now."

Gideon stopped outside the entrance. "Breaking and entering goes against the laws of Jinn."

I groaned. This was the worst possible time to have this conversation. "You're not using your Gifts," I argued, as Bosh and Rena entered the tunnel. Gideon stood stubbornly outside. "And besides, Enoch is breaking the laws of Jinn with Arie. How come nothing has happened to him?"

Gideon's lips pursed. "I assume the queen is turning a blind eye." He sighed. "I used to be part of the force that watched for Gifts being misused. They've been pulled out of the human world almost completely."

My brows rose. That was unsettling. "Well, then." I waved him forward and this time he allowed me to usher him toward the dark space. "I don't see why we can't break the rules, just this once…"

But Gideon frowned, stopping directly in front of the entrance. "That doesn't make it right."

"Gideon," I hissed, exasperated. "My men can't distract the guards forever. We have this one, very small window to rescue Arie. If you waste it worrying about breaking into a room while Enoch is busy breaking into Arie's mind, so help me, I'll—"

"Yes," Gideon interrupted, holding up a hand. "I see your point." He stepped inside the tunnel. I jumped in after him, yanking the door shut behind us.

It swung back into place on silent hinges, shutting out all light in one swift instant. "Go."

Bosh's voice echoed from somewhere further down the tunnel in a loud whisper. "Does anyone have a match?"

"I can see in the dark," Rena spoke up. "Here, hold hands and I'll lead us."

Behind me, I heard Gideon sigh. "I suppose at this point, there's no reason to hold back," he muttered. A white flame flickered into existence above his palm, lighting up the tunnel for a dozen paces in both directions.

The light blinded me for a moment, but my eyes adjusted quickly, taking in their shadowy faces. The tunnel wasn't wide, only about two paces across, with a ceiling low enough I could reach up and brush my fingers against it. Rena's scowling face was lit up. For once though, it made me smile. We were all here, and we were inside. There was still hope.

"Follow me," I led the way through the tunnel at a quick pace, listening for sounds of life in the castle as we hurried down the dark stone corridor. The walls were thick and silent. I supposed that was intentional.

Outside Arie's bedroom, staring at the back of the mirror that opened into the room, I raised a finger to my lips. Remembering the last time I'd been here, I moved with care.

Once inside, we spread out and searched the rooms quickly.

But Arie wasn't there.

* * *

THE CARPETED HALLWAY OUTSIDE Arie's rooms muffled our footsteps. I pulled back, turning to the rest of them. "Remember the plan?" We needed to stay out of sight until we found either Arie, Enoch, or both of them.

"I'll distract Enoch," Rena volunteered. "I have a few tricks he won't see coming."

"If Rena keeps Enoch from seeing me—" Gideon began.

"When," Rena interrupted.

Clearing his throat, Gideon began again. "*When* Rena keeps Enoch from seeing me, it will give me enough time to entrap him. He won't be able to do anything to anyone."

"And then," I finished, "we'll make sure the enchantment he put on Arie has worn off."

"And if it hasn't?" Gideon asked

"Then it wouldn't be the first time we've kidnapped royalty," Bosh piped up, grinning.

I pursed my lips, looking to Gideon. This would go against his precious code.

But he only nodded back at me. "If Arie's under enchantment, then it's an abuse of power. We can take her to a secure location where we can safely remove the confusion."

I smiled. This could actually work. "Let's do it."

Rena nodded, lifting her chin and stepping out into the hallway first. Gideon hurried to follow, already annoyed with her.

My fingers itched to pull out the dagger hidden in my boot and go find Amir and Enoch.

Instead, I hailed the next servant we passed. Her eyes flared wide when she took us in, and I knew she must have seen me before. "We need to see Queen Arie," I said, "Can you point us in the right direction?"

She lifted a shaking finger to point down the hall. "She was with the Jinni," she whispered. "I'm not sure where they went."

"Thank you," I said, even though it was of no help. Brushing past her, I waited until we were alone in the hall before I spoke. "She'll likely call the guards. We need to split up."

"How will the plan work if we're not together?" Bosh asked.

"We just need to track Arie down. We can meet back here in a quarter hour with what we find, but this way we can search the castle faster."

"I wouldn't advise that," Gideon said, speaking for the first time since the tunnels. "You have no recourse against Enoch's abilities."

"That's why I'll be going with you," I told him, clapping a hand on his shoulder as I began walking. "And Bosh will go with Rena." Bosh nodded, following me. "You two take the lower level," I added, pointing to the nearby staircase. "Gideon and I will take this floor."

Chapter 40

Rena

WE SPLIT UP TO search the castle. My instincts told me this was a bad plan. I mulled it over as Bosh and I descended the stairs. *We can't take Arie's castle back while occupied by a Jinni and a foreign king,* I supposed as we ran down the hall to the next room. Still, as much as I reasoned that our plan made sense, a nagging worry tugged at my gut.

I smelled fresh bread and knew the kitchen was directly ahead, with the common room beside it. Those would be full of people. It was doubtful Arie would be there.

Bosh and I slunk down the back hallway instead, aiming for the small room built behind the throne room where I'd spent so much time with Arie in the last few weeks.

We stole inside, shutting the door just before a servant rounded the corner in the hall. "She's not here," Bosh said, as we peered into the throne room which was equally empty.

I nodded, and we waited for the servant to pass before we slipped back into the hallway, racing to the next room.

It was a grand library full of tall bookshelves that stretched to the left and right. I trailed my fingers across the closest shelf full of books. The dust tickled my nose. It was so dry in here.

"We need to get back soon," Bosh whispered as we entered the room. "You take that side, and I'll take this side." I bit my lip. He was right. We could cover more ground that way.

I clutched my necklace, twisting one of the shells. "Put this in your pocket. It will keep anyone from grabbing you." It was meant for sharks looking for a bite of Mere, to blast the animal away, but it should work for humans too. I pressed the tiny shell into his palm. He accepted it, nodding to me, but didn't move. "Tides be with you," I whispered, turning to go, but he took my hand and pulled me back.

The momentum made me nearly crash into him and staring up into his brown eyes, I instinctively licked my lips. "What's wrong?"

"Nothing," Bosh said, but he didn't let go of my hand. "I'm sure everything will work out fine. We always find our way out of tough places." It felt like he was lying and he knew it, and he knew that I knew it, but I didn't say anything to disagree. "I just wanted to say…" he swallowed, reaching up to touch my cheek, "I'm really glad you came back."

I blinked as he pulled away, hand slipping out of mine as he turned to search his side of the room. "That's it?" I said out loud before I could stop myself.

He paused, turning on one heel, to squint at me. "What were you expecting?"

"Um." Heat flooded my face. "I don't know, exactly. Something... more."

He took one step back toward me, then another. "Did you *want* more?"

My feet were rooted to the floor as he came closer. I opened my mouth to answer, but it was dry and I couldn't think. "I'm not sure, honestly," was all I could get out as he stopped in front of me again, not touching me, but standing significantly closer than humans usually stood when speaking.

"It's okay not to know," Bosh said as a slow smile crept across his face. This made my toes curl. "But there's one way to find out..." He leaned in and gently brushed his lips across mine. It was over even as my eyes fluttered closed. I found it hard to swallow.

"Now you can think about it," Bosh said as he stepped back, winking at me, before taking off down the hall once more. This time I didn't say anything. I just stood there, smiling at his back, reaching a hand up to touch my lips where they tingled.

I would definitely be thinking about it.

Chapter 41

Arie

ENOCH RETURNED TO THE East tower only a few hours after he'd left me there. "What's going on?" I asked him as I stood next to the bed and he tied my hands to the tall post.

He'd let me stay alert and aware of my surroundings since I'd asked him, but the cowardly side of me whispered that I should let him make me forget. It'd be easier that way. Shaking my head to clear the thought, I lifted my chin and stared him down. He moved back and forth around the small bedroom, working with ancient objects I'd never seen before. They had Jinni symbols all over them.

"Why do you help him? Surely you've seen what a fool Amir is?"

A dark cloud passed over Enoch's face. Anger. "A bigger fool than most," he was quick to agree.

"Then, why?" I repeated. "Why help him?"

"I don't have a choice," he said once again.

"Can you say *nothing* else?" I tugged at the ropes, trying to slip out of them, but they were too tight. A flash of inspiration hit me. "*Can* you say nothing else?" I asked again, meaning something quite different. "Is this the work of your queen? A spell of some sort maybe?"

Enoch didn't answer.

"But why would the Queen of Jinn care about the human world?" I murmured, mostly to myself, since Enoch was ignoring me.

He stiffened. I almost missed it.

"Has Queen Jezebel grown so power-hungry she wants to rule the human world too? Or do we have something she needs?"

His thoughts, of course, were silent. Protected in that Jinni fashion that I didn't understand. I had no idea if I was even close to guessing correctly.

The door burst open unexpectedly. King Amir strode in, smirking at me as he passed. "This is a good location," he said to Enoch as he peered over the Jinni's shoulder at his work table and supplies. "No one will hear her scream."

My skin flushed hot and then cold. This was it. They were going to do a Severance right here and now. No trial. No witnesses.

Amir waved at the door as he told Enoch, "Use your Jinni magic. Make sure anyone who comes through that door regrets it."

Enoch lifted his hands. A shimmer appeared over a heavy dresser. It lifted into the air on its own, to dangle in the air directly above the door, presumably to drop on any unsuspecting visitor.

"This isn't right."

"I agree, my dear," Amir mocked me. "You should never have been allowed to possess this kind of Gift for so long. Don't worry. We'll remedy that shortly."

"No," I whispered. "You can't." I threw all my weight into trying to break free, feeling the rope cut into my wrists. Breathing hard, I stopped only to try a different angle.

Enoch still hadn't said a word, stirring something in a small clay jar, then adding another ingredient and mixing them together.

Amir tsked. "It's a shame, really. You could have been my queen. Ruled beside me. Or at least been very comfortable. Now, it's too late." He spread his hands wide as if truly apologetic. "You had to go and tell the kingdom about your Gift, and now the only option I have is to put you on trial myself."

"This trial is a sham," I snapped.

"Sham or not," Amir replied, barely seeming to notice me fighting against my restraints. "It will be over soon enough."

Chapter 42

Kadin

TWISTING THE DOORKNOB SILENTLY, I glided through the door unseen with Gideon on my heels, and closed it softly behind us. We'd searched dozens of empty bedrooms. I scanned the small front room and held a finger to my lips when I heard voices in the bedroom beyond. I pointed to it and Gideon nodded.

He stepped forward into the next room first, and accidentally sprung an invisible trap.

Enoch had somehow known we were there, before Gideon and I even entered the room. A heavy dresser flew through the air and Gideon threw his hands up, flinging it backward, just before it would've crushed him. The momentum knocked Gideon back into the tiles by the fireplace, where he hit his head and slumped to the ground, unconscious.

I dodged the piece of large furniture as it flung itself my way, seemingly with a life of its own, leaping to my feet by the bed.

"Kadin!"

I lifted my gaze to find Arie standing on the other side, tied to the bedpost. *She was okay.* I leapt across the bed toward her, forgetting to look around the room in my haste as I tried to untie the first knot. "It's okay—"

"You need to leave!" she yelled, shaking her head violently. "Get out of here now—"

"Hush, girl. Don't speak another word," a man said from behind me, and Arie's voice cut off mid-sentence.

I whirled to face the speaker and ducked down to grab the knife from my boot in one smooth motion.

"Stop him," said the same voice. It came from King Amir who stood before me in his imperial robes, hands clasped before him. The purple-eyed Jinni next to him waved his hands and the knife I held disappeared, reappearing in his hand.

"You've come to visit me," the king continued. "How nice of you." Something about his voice calmed me. I *felt* nice.

I smiled and straightened.

"Please," he said, returning my smile. "Have a seat."

I found myself moving toward the chair he'd pointed out willingly, even though a part of me whispered that I was here for another reason. I couldn't remember what it was. I smiled at Arie, glad that we were together again, but she frowned at me. Her hands were tied up, which made me uncomfortable.

King Amir moved to block my view. "Remind me of your name, young man."

"Kadin of Baradaan."

"Tell me, Kadin," the king said, pausing as he studied me. He circled behind my chair, placing his hands on my shoulders. The pressure was uncomfortable, pinching me. "Are you and this Jinni here alone?"

"No," my mouth said, before my mind could stop it.

"Who's with you?" he asked, pressing his fingers deeper into my shoulders until the pain made me flinch.

I bit my lip, tasting blood. Why was I keeping it from him? My mind felt like a soft cloud, like a mist, like a slippery bit of soap. I couldn't quite grasp what I should do next. I looked over to Arie, hoping she'd help me. No, wait. I'd come here to help *her*… but with what?

The king released me, and I drew a breath as the pain stopped, though I felt certain there would be deep bruises. He came around to face me, leaning over the table to peer into my eyes. "*Who is with you?*"

His deep voice flowed over me like a powerful wave, and I couldn't fight it. "There are two others." The information felt dragged out of me. Something in me was fighting the pressure to tell him, but losing.

"Who? I want names."

My lips formed the words even as I fought to stop them. "Rena, the Mere, and Bosh, from my crew."

King Amir smiled down at me. "Thank you." He waved a hand toward Gideon, where he still lay unconscious on the floor. "Enoch, take care of the Jinni. And reset the trap."

Enoch's violet eyes flickered with an emotion too quick to name, but he obeyed. The heavy dresser lifted off the floor, flying through the air toward the door, where it stopped to hang above it, ready and waiting.

Crossing the room, Enoch lifted Gideon into a sitting position, leaning him against the wall. Gideon's head fell to the side, still oblivious, as Enoch placed a hand on his shoulder.

A soft film came over Gideon, wrapping him fully like a sheer cocoon.

"Is it safe?" King Amir asked when Enoch returned to the table. "What is that thing?"

"It is a Jinni containment spell. It will prevent him from moving and immobilize his Gifts as well."

As he spoke, Gideon's eyes opened. He glanced at the film over his feet and didn't bother to struggle. With a sigh, he met the other Jinni's gaze. "Hello, Enoch."

Enoch only nodded. Though both Jinni appeared young, there was a slight gray in Enoch's black hair and his face was more gaunt, skin stretched and tightened with age.

"I didn't expect to see you again," Gideon said calmly, as if he weren't restrained and this was just a casual conversation.

"I'm sure not," Enoch replied, leaning back. "In truth, I never thought I'd see you again either."

"Is this necessary?" King Amir interrupted, hands on his hips, chest out. "We have a Severance to complete."

Gideon's expression darkened. "Why are you associating with this human?"

"I can't say."

"Humor an old friend," Gideon murmured. They'd been friends? My curiosity was piqued.

Enoch considered Gideon for a moment. "I truly can't say." Those violet eyes blinked once, then softened. "I've missed you this last year. You were one of my best soldiers."

I stared at Gideon in a new light. That stiff bearing. His strict adherence to rules. All signs of his past life. How had I never seen it? And why in the name of all the Gifts would they have banished a soldier as seemingly dutiful as Gideon?

"Alright, enough." King Amir stepped between them, scowling. He reached into the deep pockets of his robes and pulled out a small object. "I'll tell you why he can't say, and why you won't be able to say in a minute either."

Gideon's eyes widened.

King Amir shoved the object in Gideon's direction and yelled, "Telesmaat!" A shimmer burst out of the little totem and settled over Gideon, thicker than Enoch's previous spell, which evaporated, almost like a heavy blanket. This one slowly disappeared as I watched, but it left a distinct metallic taste in the air.

"I learned how to capture a Jinni and force them into service from the Queen of Jinn herself." Amir waved the strange little totem in the air before tucking it back inside his pocket with a twisted smile. "A little gift in return for my loyalty. Now, stand up."

Gideon got to his feet and stood motionless by the door.

A tiny part of me whispered that I should take this chance to attack while the king's back was turned. But he'd told me to stay seated. So, I stayed. It felt as if a heavy pillow had been stuffed inside my skull.

"You will be very useful," Amir told Gideon, tapping his chin in thought. "In fact, Enoch, why don't we have Gideon perform the Severance instead?"

The only response from Gideon was a muscle twitching in his jaw.

I blinked at them. Why wasn't I following this? They seemed so tense. Gideon's hands were clenched, but he otherwise didn't react.

King Amir turned to smile at me once more. "Tie that one up and make sure he can't escape," he told Gideon, though I hadn't moved. "We don't need any surprises when he sees what comes next."

Chapter 43

Arie

MY MOUTH WOULDN'T FORM words, but I didn't stop trying. King Amir's Gift should wear off much faster than Enoch's. Although I didn't honestly know what I would say, even if I could speak.

Kadin sat tied to the chair across the room and his eyes were vacant, staring at nothing. It broke my heart. He shouldn't have come here. But it meant the world to me that he had.

Enoch and Amir stood at the table conferring. I tugged at the ropes for the thousandth time, trying to slip free without success.

According to Kadin, Rena and Bosh were on their way, but it didn't matter. They wouldn't see the trap Enoch had set until it was too late. And with both Kadin and Gideon under Amir's control, it was up to me to do *something*.

Amir approached. "I could stand here all day and list your crimes." He shook his head at me dramatically.

I ignored him, staring at the wooden floorboards and woven carpet under my feet, hoping he'd come close enough that my foot could reach him.

"For the sake of time, we will focus on the most significant misconduct: a woman who possesses a Gift."

Words rose in my throat, but I couldn't quite manage to say them. I wanted to yell that I hadn't asked for this. How was it a crime if I'd never actually done anything wrong? It had happened *to* me! If anything, the crime was my mother and father's, mixing human and Jinni blood, passing down an unwanted birthright.

But I stayed silent. Tears pricked my eyes. With my hands tied, I was forced to blink them back, struggling to keep my face clear of emotion.

"What do you have to say for yourself, hmm?" He cupped a mocking hand behind his ear. "What was that now?"

Slowly, I lifted my chin and met his gaze, holding it as I took a deep breath in and out. Pushing against his command not to speak, I found my voice. "I… am *proud*… of my Gift."

Amir just raised one brow, smirking at me. He wasn't worried.

But I wasn't done. "You want to know what I have to say for myself?" I asked.

Amir frowned, and his lips pinched together at his words being thrown back in his face.

I didn't wait for an answer. "My Gift is part of me," I declared boldly. "I didn't choose it, but it's who I am." Gideon's words. I was finally beginning to believe them. "And I do not, nor will I ever, use my Gift for evil."

"Yes, yes," Amir glared at me, waving an impatient hand. "That's a pretty speech, but it won't change anything. You need to stop talking now." His Gift floated over me, making my mouth snap shut once more. "Gideon, it's time. I don't want to wait another minute. Begin the Severance *now*."

Chapter 44

Rena

KADIN AND GIDEON WEREN'T at the meeting place. "Something's wrong," I told Bosh, crossing my arms.

He nodded, but didn't stop walking. "Happens all the time on a job," he whispered. "They had a lot more rooms to search than we did. Kadin always says if part of the plan goes wrong, that doesn't mean you throw out the rest of it."

I sighed and followed him from room to room. We reached a quieter part of the castle that seemed mostly uninhabited.

"There's no one here," I complained. "They're probably waiting for us back at the stairs now."

"Just a couple more rooms and we'll circle back," Bosh replied.

Absently, my fingers played with my shells around my neck. Pulling up the necklace, I had a flash of insight. Perhaps this shell would be more powerful on land. "I think I know how to do this faster," I told him.

He'd just closed the door to yet another empty room, when I whispered the words of the spell that would amplify every noise in the surrounding area. I froze at the sound of Arie's voice. "They're here!"

"Where?" Bosh ran back to me, grabbing my arms.

"Um, this way… I think." Listening intently, I followed the voices up to a door. "Here," I whispered. "She's inside with someone else. He sounds mad."

"We can take one guy," Bosh whispered back, grinning. "This will be a piece of cake." He grabbed the doorknob.

"Wait! What if it's Enoch?" I hissed.

Bosh made a face. "Yeah, I guess it could be, but you could take him, couldn't you?"

I took a deep breath. "I think so. I just need to add an extra layer of protection first." I dropped the shell I'd used to listen and picked up another. My protection spells against Jinni were always active, but after my last encounter with the Jinni who'd smashed me over the back of the head with a bottle, I wanted to add an extra layer of defense. Whispering quickly, I allowed the buffer of air to surround me. Nothing could touch me now. "Okay, go."

Stepping inside, Bosh crept through the empty front room silently. My shoes clunked on the hard floor behind him. "Sorry," I mouthed when he gave me a look.

The next moment happened in a blur. Bosh and I shoved through the door of the room, ready to attack, only for a heavy piece of furniture to drop on top of us from above. My spells made it bounce off the air around me, leaving me unharmed. But Bosh wasn't so lucky.

It crushed him, smashing his head and body into the ground hard. The sound of a bone snapping made me cry out. "No!" I shrieked as Bosh screamed in pain. "Bosh!" I tried to shove the heavy furniture off him, but I wasn't strong enough. Gathering the shells at my neck, I searched with shaking fingers for something that would help me lift it, when someone said, "stop her," and the shells around my neck disappeared.

Whirling to face the room, I took in everyone else for the first time. My mouth gaped open. Gideon stood before me, dark and broken, holding my shell necklace in one hand and a flame in the other. His face was stoic. Almost resigned.

King Amir stood across the room, flanked by Enoch. Arie struggled against ropes that bound her to the bedpost, but didn't speak. And on the other side, seated calmly as if nothing were happening despite being tied to his chair, was Kadin. What was going on?

"Somebody help me," I yelled, straining to lift the dresser from Bosh's still body.

"Kill her," King Amir said to Gideon.

I nearly laughed at the ridiculous command. Gideon might not love me, but he also wouldn't kill me.

My confidence faded as Gideon lifted a ball of flame without a word. King Amir smirked as Gideon threw it in my direction.

I screamed and threw up my hands, but without my shells I was powerless to counter the fire. Only my buffer of air saved me. The flames surrounded me in a thick circle. The fierce heat caused a sheen of sweat on my skin within seconds. Fire licked at me, despite the bubble of air. How long would it hold? This was my worst nightmare.

Fear slid down my throat, slamming into my heart, making it hammer like I'd just swum across half the ocean.

"Enough waiting," King Amir said on the other side of the flame. "I said begin!"

Gideon slowly turned to Arie. His skin was almost gray and the room had grown dark as he lifted his hands slowly. He whispered to Arie, "I'm sorry."

His hands stretched toward her, and white-hot light shot out of them.

Arie's scream sounded almost feral. Her head tipped back and her body arched as if something was breaking her from the inside-out before she dropped to her knees. The look on her face physically hurt me. I'd never heard someone make a sound like that in my entire life. Chills ran up my arms despite the flames.

Bosh groaned in pain as he roused, shifting on the floor underneath the dresser. "Rena... What's going on? Why is Gideon helping them? Do something!"

I couldn't answer. My buffer spell still protected me, but the rest of my spells relied on the necklace in Gideon's hand. Everything was going wrong. Bosh was bleeding out, Kadin was still tied to a chair in a trance, and Arie suffered at Gideon's own hand. Gideon—he would *never* do this of his own volition. Someone was forcing him.

The heat around me increased; it was becoming more than I could bear. My eyes teared up from the smoke and I made a decision. Against my better judgment, I cast aside my Mere spells that made me immune to the Jinni Gifts and yelled at Gideon, "What do I do?"

I couldn't tell if he heard me over Arie's screams; his face held an awful, grim concentration, lit up by the white light, as if what he was doing was destroying him in the process as much as Arie.

Coughing, I yelled again. "Gideon!"

"There's nothing you can do," Amir answered, as he calmly watched the process.

Just then, Gideon spoke into my mind. *The amulet. In Amir's pocket.* His face was grim and he didn't turn to me once, but it was unmistakably his voice. *Break it. Break it into as many pieces as possible.*

In his pocket. I shook my head at Gideon, catching myself before I protested out loud. The king was halfway across the room. Even if I managed to somehow steal from him while his back was turned, there was no way I could escape the circle of fire without getting burned.

Arie thrashed on the floor, only held upright by the ropes now. Her cries were growing weaker. When I glanced down at Bosh, his eyes were closed. Kadin still sat in the corner with a glazed look on his face. And Gideon—once he finished with Arie, I had no doubt Amir would turn him on me next.

It's just a little burn, I told myself and nearly choked. I knew better. I'd never seen a burn before, but legend said Mere burned ten times worse than humans or Jinni, and the recovery took twice as long. My feet didn't move.

I took a shallow breath in the smoke, then another. *You can do this. Do it for Bosh. For Arie. For all of them.*

This was the moment of truth.

I leapt through the flames, feeling the fire bite my skin, and gasped in pain. Hair smoking and skirts on fire, I ran to King Amir and shoved my hand into the deep pocket of his kingly robes. It was empty.

"Wh—?" Amir swung around. "You!"

He grabbed my wrist. A big mistake. My barrier spells flung him across the room and he smashed into the wall.

The fire had made its way through the layers of my dress and its sharp heat scorched my legs.

Roll, Gideon snapped at me, eyes never leaving Arie.

Dropping to the ground, I rolled, back and forth. It snuffed out the fire. I took a deep breath of relief before crawling in my shredded skirts over to where King Amir lay sprawled on the floor, and dipped my hand into his other pocket. My fingers closed around something small and round. I yanked it out, immediately falling back, ducking underneath a table, before I dared to open my hand, uncurling my fingers slowly to peer at the little item in my palm.

It was the totem.

Arie's screams of agony pierced the air.

The king groaned as he opened his eyes, blinking at me. His eyes narrowed at the totem. "Give that to me."

I backed up.

He stood, wary of following after what had happened to him last time. "There's nothing you can do to stop this," he said and turned to Gideon, opening his mouth.

"There is one thing I could try," I told the king, making him pause, as I set the totem down carefully on the ground.

"No!" He dove toward it as I lifted my foot and brought the sharp heel of my shoe down on the small clay totem.

It smashed into little pieces.

Gideon immediately ceased the Severance's white light and rushed forward to help Arie.

"No!" Amir screamed in fury. "Stop them now!" He turned to Enoch, but the other Jinni only stared at him with those violet eyes now, no longer bound to obey. Like a cat stalking a mouse, his gaze was locked on the king as he stepped closer.

"Guards! Guards!" Amir yelled, but it was too late.

Enoch pounced. He landed on top of the king, reaching toward the table. The small knife there flashed out of sight, reappearing in his hand, and he stabbed Amir through the chest, skewering him in one swift move. Enoch carefully pulled the blade out and wiped it on the king's sleeve, as Amir's eyes glazed over.

The moment Amir's Gift faded, Kadin broke out of his trance, struggling against his ropes.

I picked up my shell necklace where Gideon had discarded it and stepped up to Kadin, using the sharpest shell to slice through the ropes. He raced to Arie's side. Gideon carefully transferred Arie into his arms, before lifting his cold blue gaze to meet Enoch's.

Without a word, Enoch folded into himself and disappeared, leaving behind no trace. Gideon ran up to the spot where Enoch had last stood, and vanished after him.

I limped over to Bosh's side. My first glimpse of him made me trip in shock. He lay in a pool of blood. The puddle was a dark shade of red, still growing.

With effort, I inverted my buffer spell faster than I'd ever done a spell before in my life, shaping it so that it would happen at my will. I used it to fling the heavy dresser off of him.

I fell to my knees beside him. They grew wet as the blood soaked through my skirts and touched my burns, but I ignored the pain. "Bosh." I shook his shoulder gently. "Wake up." His face was a blur through my tears.

His head wound wasn't the worst of it. My eyes caught on his lower half. The dresser had cut into his stomach and ribs. I knew little about human anatomy, but even I knew that was a bad sign.

He took ragged breaths, staring at the ceiling, not seeing me until I leaned directly over him, taking his hand. I wiped at my eyes furiously. "You can't die," I yelled at him. "You can't!"

"I'm sure it's not that bad," Bosh said, even as he gulped for air like a fish on land.

I squeezed his hand, hoping he'd squeeze back, but it lay limp in mine. His eyes began to glaze over. "No," I cried, sobbing openly now. I knew that look. I'd seen it growing up more times than I wanted to count.

I bowed my head over his. Why weren't any of the Mere spells designed for healing? Kadin was right. We were selfish. Me more than any of them.

"I have an idea," I whispered to Bosh, pulling back just enough to take the Key from around my neck. I pressed it into his hand. "Take this." Yuliya would kill me. I didn't care. There was no guarantee that he would ever give it back to me, but I didn't care about that either. We had to do this together, shoulder the price of the Key together, otherwise the spell to save him would also cost a life.

"Bosh, listen to me," I said, shaking him a little until his eyes fluttered open again. "I need you to do something for me."

"I'm tired," he slurred. "Just let me take a little nap first."

I smiled through the tears. "You can nap as soon as you do this, okay? I promise." I curled his fingers around the spine of the Key, holding them together. "Say my name."

His brows drew together but he took a shallow breath and whispered, "Rena…?"

Just like that my greatest desire appeared before us in an inky black vision. It was simple. We were still in this room, but Bosh stood before me on his own two feet, alive and well, his body fully intact and uninjured.

"Wow," he mumbled, eyes falling shut. "That's us. How did you do that?"

"We did it together," I told him, taking his hand with the Key in mine. "Stay with me now. There's just one more step. It's going to hurt a little… but, well, you're already in pain so I guess it can't be that bad." I could only hope this would work.

We turned the Key together.

Chapter 45

Rena

EACH TIME BOSH'S CHEST rose, I thought it was his last breath. I'd screamed through the agony of the Key taking its toll, but my plan had failed. Bosh wasn't getting better.

Bosh choked. I squeezed him even harder. I didn't know how else to comfort him.

"Rena," he whispered and I pulled back slightly. "You're squishing me."

Not the last words I'd expected. Shifting to see his face, I pressed my hand to his cheek, which had grown cold before, but now felt warm again. The color was returning to his skin. Swiveling to his wound, I found the flesh slowly knitting itself back together.

"Stay still," I told him when he tried to sit up. "You're still recovering."

He propped himself up on his elbows and when he saw his body piecing itself back together in front of him, his eyes grew huge. "Did you do this?"

"Kind of..." I smiled at his reaction as tears dripped down my cheeks. "We did it together." I'd let go of the Key and it was now officially his. I would happily return to the ocean for the rest of my life to make up for it. It was worth the price.

"Where is everyone else?" he asked, trying to see the rest of the room over his shoulder.

I'd completely forgotten about Arie in my panic. She was still in Kadin's arms, unmoving. Had Gideon completed the Severance?

Before I could say a word, a Jinni flashed back into the room.

Enoch.

My hand instinctively rose to my necklace, and I clutched the shells.

"If I wanted to harm you, little Mere, you'd already be dead," he spoke in a soft tone. His calm, so deadly and quiet at the same time, reminded me of Gideon. "The Telesmaat that bound your friend to King Amir bound me as well. Now that I am free, I would like to talk."

Gideon flashed back to the room before I could answer and attacked, snarling at him.

"I was under the Queen's orders!" Enoch protested, but Gideon ignored him, flashing around to kick him viciously in the back. I'd never seen a Jinni so openly dangerous.

Enoch fell and didn't fight back when Gideon tackled him, straining to speak with Gideon's hands around his neck, choking him. "The amulet that bound you to the king... has compelled me... to obey Amir... for months now."

Gideon eased up, but only barely. "And how did a man such as Amir obtain a Jinni-spelled object like that?" he demanded.

"You heard him," Enoch said softly, spreading his hands wide in a gesture of peace. "Same way the Prince of Jinn disappeared and no one has heard from him in over a year."

Gideon took a deep breath, and let Enoch go abruptly. He held out a hand to help the other Jinni stand. "The queen," he replied finally.

"It's worse than you think." Enoch stood tall, rubbing his neck. "If I'd known then what I know now, I would've stood with you a year ago."

Gideon shook his head. "You would only have been banished with me." He gestured in my direction. "Rena has promised to help me get back into Jinn. She has the Key."

I swallowed, standing up. A deep cut throbbed in my leg from the Key but it was nothing compared to the heat of the burns all along my arms, neck, and face.

Preparing myself for Gideon's fury, I opened my mouth to explain that the Key now belonged to Bosh.

But Enoch spoke first. "I've searched high and low. The prince isn't in Jinn. Everything I've found leads me to believe he's somewhere in the human world."

Gideon's expression fell. "That changes everything."

✻ ✻ ✻

MY DEADLINE FOR BEING in the human world was today. I'd avoided the water and even the windows in the days leading up to this, but I feared it was only a matter of time.

Since I didn't have the Key anymore, I couldn't give it to Yuliya. But I would still lose my legs at sundown.

Would Yuliya use a tracking spell to come find me or would she be home, waiting for the Key to come to her? Knowing my sister, she'd leave nothing to chance. Perhaps she was here already, waiting to collect. There was no telling what she would do when she discovered Bosh now held the Key. She could make me her slave or set me on fire. My burns from the last fire were only just finally starting to heal.

I strode down the hallway through the castle in a hurry. I needed to say goodbye to everyone and return to the ocean before sunset, before my last day in the human world ended.

I desperately wished I could stay.

Even now, in the last hour, I couldn't tell them of the bargain, or the spell would break that much sooner.

I didn't know what would happen to these humans I'd come to love, or the kindhearted Jinni I'd realized I didn't actually love at all. I only knew one thing for sure: there was no chance Gideon would be declaring his love for me or asking me to stay.

The day following the Severance, I'd stopped Gideon outside Arie's room. "I did something you're not going to like…"

Gideon took a deep breath and let it out slowly. "Tell me."

"I gave the Key to Bosh. I had to, to save him, but now I can't give the Key to you. On the other hand, he'd probably be happy to give you the Key if you ask him—"

Gideon waved a hand through the air, cutting me off. "No need. If the prince is not in Jinn, as Enoch says, I have no reason to return either."

I scrunched my nose at that. "Do you trust he's telling the truth?"

"I do." Gideon lifted his cane absently, running a hand along the delicate designs. "Enoch is in many ways like a father to me. The only time we ever disagreed was when he thought I betrayed the queen. Now he knows better and has agreed to help me in my search for the prince."

Chewing on my lip, I debated helping him. He was a Jinni after all. But if there was an internal war within Jinn, I knew which side I'd be on. "The Key could still help you find him."

Gideon straightened, blue eyes sharp and focused. "How?"

I led him to Bosh's recovery room, where he still held the Key.

Bosh smiled weakly when we entered and when I mentioned the Key he was quick to offer it back to me.

"No, no," I held up my hands, refusing. "I don't want it." Having it would only mean Yuliya would have it shortly. "But I want you to try something..."

I walked him through using the Key. He spoke Gideon's name over it and the inky black vision appeared. Since Gideon's desire had changed to finding the prince in the human world, it should show him the way. Or at least give him a place to start.

The dark black cloud hung in the air, but nothing appeared inside it.

"That's strange." I scowled, leaning closer. "This has never happened before... Try again."

Bosh did. The same vision appeared. Or rather, lack of vision.

"There's no desire to unlock," I murmured, glancing over at Gideon. "Do you truly want to find him?"

"More than anything," he said fervently, gripping that cane until his fingers turned white. I believed him.

Pondering the empty vision, we stared at it for long minutes until it faded away on its own. "It almost seems like the prince's location is hidden," I said finally.

Instead of seeming surprised, Gideon nodded. "That just confirms my suspicions more. The queen has cloaked him somehow."

"I'm sorry I couldn't help after all," I said awkwardly.

"Not at all," he replied. "This has been most helpful. At least it didn't show us a grave. There's still hope. If anything, it spurs me on."

Each day after that, Bosh had tried to give the Key back to me, but I'd refused. "I don't want it. Just make sure to use it carefully. Only smaller desires, if you want to live."

One day after he'd mulled that over he'd asked, "Could I use it to help Arie?"

I'd sighed and shook my head. "The cost would be far too high." Gideon had said she could pull through. "She has to find the strength on her own."

The entire kingdom was focused on her healing. It felt like the whole world held its breath, waiting to see if she would recover.

Today, I wanted to check on her before I had to leave. When I pushed through the door to Arie's room, she blinked at me almost like she'd forgotten who I was.

"You're awake," I said hopefully, crawling into the bed with her. "How're you feeling?"

She lifted the corners of her mouth in a weak smile, but didn't answer. Her eyelids were low and heavy. Kadin watched from a chair on the side of the room. Between him and Gideon, they kept a constant vigil.

We watched her fall back asleep within minutes. Slipping out of the bed, I pulled the curtains closed around it, moving out onto the balcony with Gideon and Kadin where we could speak without her overhearing. "How's she doing?"

"Not good," Kadin's lips flattened into a grim line. "It's not just exhaustion that's gripping her."

"But that could still be due to circumstances—her father's death, Enoch's mind control, and everything else that's happened," Gideon insisted, as he had for the last week. "No matter how gently Enoch says he treated her mind, there are always repercussions. But there's still a chance that the Severance wasn't completed. And she's strong. Even if her Gift was cut off completely, there's still a chance she'll survive the trauma period."

The first time he'd said this, Kadin had perked up. "Do you know anyone who's survived that stage before?"

"Not off-hand," Gideon had said slowly, clutching his cane until the tips of his fingers turned white. "But we can't give up hope just yet." He kept saying that, but the truth was none of us could really tell what the damage might be.

Now as we stood on the balcony, I could only nod, not saying anything. I hoped she would survive this. I wanted to believe it.

Kadin and Gideon would be here for her. And maybe, someday, I'd find a way to come back and see them all again.

"Have you seen Bosh?"

Kadin nodded from where he stood by the balcony railing. "I sent him on an errand to town, he should be back soon."

"Thank you." I left them behind, slipping past Arie. I considered waking her up to say goodbye, but worried it'd only upset her. They'd figure it out soon enough. And if I were honest, there was really only one person that I needed to say goodbye to.

Bosh entered the courtyard as I opened the main castle doors. We met in the middle under a fruit tree.

"Were you looking for me?" he asked with a grin.

"No," I said, even though I was. Why was I embarrassed? I should say goodbye here and leave. But I couldn't. "I'm going down to the beach. Walk with me?"

Even though it was at least an hour walk, he agreed. Most of it, we didn't speak, or joked about pointless things.

We reached the shore, where I'd thought the waves might calm me down and help me find the words, but even when I stepped into the cool water and the waves crashed into my legs, soaking the hem of my dress, it only agitated me further. I said the first thing that came to mind, "Can I see your wound?"

He laughed. I'd asked a dozen times since he'd been healed. Lifting his shirt, he let me look once more.

The skin was marvelously smooth with only a thin scar that slashed across his stomach. When I touched the red line, fading each day into a dull color, a completely unrelated heat warmed my skin.

Bosh didn't pull away, but his face grew serious for once, unreadable. "I need to give this back to you," he said, pulling the Key from his pocket for the thousandth time.

"No," I said, holding out a hand. "I need you to keep it." I hoped it might make him remember me fondly, instead of recalling all my flaws. And he would be a far better master of the Key than my sister. For once, Yuliya would not get her way.

As if my thoughts had summoned her, I heard her voice, "You *gave* him *my* Key?"

We whirled to face the speaker. Yuliya stood on her own two stumps, wearing a gown she'd made out of ocean flowers and kelp, though it was still far too revealing for a human. Bosh blushed.

"What're you doing here?" I said icily. "I still have time."

"I came to see if you would honor our deal," she spat, glaring at Bosh. "And what do I find? My sister giving a priceless object to a *human*? Does he even know what it does?"

I found myself stepping in front of him. Who knew what Yuliya might do when she was this angry?

But Bosh didn't let me protect him. "I do know," he snapped. "Rena used it to heal me. It saved my life."

"She did *what*?" Yuliya's eyes narrowed at him, swiveling to my face. "How?"

Swallowing hard, I put a hand on Bosh's arm to steady him. He was sweet, but he didn't know who he was dealing with. "The Key shows someone's greatest desire," I reminded him softly. "It doesn't normally heal, but that's what I most wanted it to do, so it did."

"So it truly does whatever you want?" Bosh was finally paying attention. Why hadn't he listened before?

Yuliya's lips tilted upward as she smiled at him, her voice growing soft like a cat's purr, "If you give it back to Rena, she can give you whatever you want. Can't you, Rena?"

Bosh's eyes lit up. He didn't give me a chance to argue, shoving the Key into my hand. "No—" I said, but it was too late.

"Very good," Yuliya said, grinning. "Now, it's time you honor our deal and come home. The day is over; your month is up." She pointed to the sky, where the sun was setting. *How had it gotten so late?* I'd thought I had more time. "Give me the Key, Rena."

"Wait!" Bosh grabbed my arm as I moved to obey. "You said she could give me whatever I wanted."

Yuliya paused. "Whatever you want *most*, yes." She sighed and shook her head. "Fine. Do it, Rena. Then we'll go."

I glanced between them. What was Bosh doing? *Is he like everyone else, just wanting to use me?* I stared down at the Key in my palm, wishing he hadn't given it back to me. There was nothing I could do now. Lifting the Key, I wrapped my fingers around it and whispered his name. *Bosh.*

The vision of his greatest desire appeared before us. Yuliya's breath hitched. It was of the three of us in this moment right now, but as we watched, Bosh held out his hands to me and said one word: "Stay."

And in this vision of his greatest desire, I took his hands with a grin and said, "I will."

Whatever might've happened next vanished as the sun touched the horizon. I hissed in pain as the spell broke. My legs burned as they knit together and my tail returned. Bosh caught me before I fell, holding me up. I wrapped my arms around his neck. I'd never felt so helpless.

Yuliya's face was red with fury. "Give me the Key *now*, Rena!"

My lips parted as her reaction hit me. "I don't think I have to," I whispered. "I think Bosh just gave you the proof you asked for." His arms tightened around me.

"No," she argued, but her eyes were desperate, shifting between us. "You needed to prove the Jinni wanted you here more than anything else. This human doesn't count."

"No," I said slowly, "your exact words were, 'if *he* loves you enough to ask you to stay.' Which means I win."

Yuliya took a step toward me. "You little—"

"She said she's staying!" Bosh yelled, angling our bodies to shield me from her. He still had no clue who he was dealing with. He glanced down at me, suddenly unsure. "Right?"

I nodded.

Yuliya grabbed the shells around her neck. My eyes widened at the one she chose. I thrust the Key out toward her. "Wait! Listen to me!"

Yuliya didn't let go of the shell, glaring at Bosh and I, but she didn't use it either.

"How about one last deal?" I offered, holding the Key in my open palm. Bosh turned slightly so I could face her.

Her eyes narrowed to slits. "What kind of deal?"

"Give me back my legs," I began, "*Permanently* this time… And I will give you the Key."

Yuliya eyed my hand. She let go of the shells around her neck. "What's the catch?"

"No catch," I said, and for once, I meant it. Gideon didn't need it anymore, and neither did I.

She reached out to take the Key.

"Ah," I stopped her, pointing down at my tail. "Legs first, then I swear on the same binding contract that the Key will be yours as long as you honor this deal."

Bosh's head swung back and forth between us as she silently took the shell that gave me legs and murmured a new spell over it. His eyes widened as the magic flowed into it and made it glow.

Yuliya held out both hands, palms up; one with the newly spelled shell, and the other, empty and waiting. When I shifted in his arms, Bosh scooped me up so that my hands were free to make the exchange.

I placed the Key in her palm, taking the shell. In one quick motion, we made the trade.

When I let go of the Key, I expected to feel loss. Instead I grinned in excitement and didn't waste a second. Whispering the spell over myself, I happily suffered through the painful separation of my tail, not turning away from the sight, even when tears filled my eyes.

Bosh stared at the scrawny legs that formed where my tail had been as if he'd never seen legs before in his life. "I guess I should put you down," he said, but didn't.

I shrugged, grinning. "Only if you want to."

A snort of disgust came from my sister. "I can't watch this." I didn't bother to watch her leave.

"Are you sure you made the right decision?" he asked, forehead wrinkling as he slowly lowered me to the ground but didn't let go completely.

He stared down at me and the look in his eyes hit me. It was the look that I'd seen in the eyes of my parents, my sisters, mere-boys, and even Gideon—but *only* in the visions. Never in reality.

"I'm sure," I told him, not letting go either, soaking up the feeling of his arms around me. "I don't need to use the Key to grant your desire, because I want to stay."

Epilogue

Arie

WHEN I OPENED MY eyes, they landed on Kadin in the chair beside my bed. His long legs sprawled out and his head tilted back as he snored softly. He'd been there all night.

The early morning rays lightly touched the stubble on his jaw, but he didn't stir. Exhaustion kept him asleep, while I had slept too much. Even so, sleep tugged at me, begging me to return to it.

I didn't know how many days had passed like this one. At least a week. Maybe two. Maybe more.

That first day, he'd fought the guards outside my room, yelling at them to let him in. I'd lain in bed, numb, hearing his shouts as if from a mile away. Gideon had rescued him, and the guards allowed him in, though they hovered suspiciously.

Their numbers had doubled after the *incident*. I doubted they knew the details; they certainly didn't know how useless they were against Jinni magic. Still, they stood faithfully outside, protecting me.

"I don't blame them," Kadin had said, lips lifting in what he meant to be a smile as he sat next to me and held up a one-sided conversation. "They're just concerned for you. Especially now." He had winced at even this smallest mention of everything that had happened.

I tried to find the energy to nod. Lifting my hand, I touched his, and he scooped it up and held on tight.

After that though, he didn't bother to get permission to enter. He used the secret entrance to come and go, sleeping in the chair by my bed each night and slipping behind a curtain or door whenever a servant or guard knocked and entered.

Sometimes I woke to find him gone, but always Gideon or Bosh was in his place.

"How are you doing?" he would ask each day.

Sometimes it made me furious and I'd ignore him. *How do you think I'm doing? My only family is* gone. *I am* alone. *I am broken.*

Other times, I'd try to smile back at him and croak, "I'm okay." I'd let him hold my hand.

Now, after sleeping through most of the morning, I rolled over to find him awake this time.

"I can't feel it anymore," I whispered, because any louder and I'd be forced to face it.

Right now, I needed to believe I was wrong, that it wasn't true. I needed him to argue with me.

"What if my Gift is really gone? Does that mean…" I trailed off, not willing to even whisper the last part. Kadin already knew. When a Gift was severed, it led to death. Its absence was like the loss of a limb or a lung, and without it…

Kadin leaned forward, taking my hands in his and squeezing. This new, heavier fog in my mind, almost like a rain cloud, lifted just slightly and my chest felt a bit lighter.

Kadin stared into my eyes and instead of arguing like I hoped he would, or even addressing my fears, he simply said, "You're going to be okay."

I swallowed. The clouds settled back in and the dark weight of them pulled me deeper under the covers. Even my bones were tired. "How can you tell?" I managed to say as I sank back on my pillow.

"Because you're here, aren't you?"

"What does that even mean?" I snapped. But the anger exhausted me and snuffed out faster than a candle. I closed my eyes. It wasn't his fault. No one knew what to say.

"It means there's still hope."

My eyelids fluttered, holding in unexpected tears underneath. I swallowed and tried to blink them away, but one slipped down my cheek toward the pillow.

Kadin caught it. "I'm not letting you go again," he said. His voice was low, sharp. Almost angry. "You can't make me. Even if you call for the guards again, I'm not leaving."

My lips twitched at his attempt at a joke and it helped my eyes clear. "I never did apologize for that."

He took my hand and kissed my palm. "No need."

My fingers curled in response. A distant part of me felt warm, but the rest of me was so cold. The shade of this dark cloud dampened the moment. Made it dull when it should have lit me up.

Everyone said I was mourning my father's passing. Even Gideon encouraged me that this grief was normal. Despite everything he'd said about the Severance in the past and how the results were undeniable, he now swore I could get through this.

But I didn't feel okay and this didn't feel normal. Only time would tell the truth.

Summoning all my energy, I pulled myself up until I could swing my legs over the side of the bed.

Kadin's posture shifted in a heartbeat, upright and alert, watching me with those golden eyes. He didn't say anything. He let me lead the way.

I pulled my robe tighter, gathering the little shreds of strength I still had left, and stood. "Can you have someone draw a bath?" My voice sounded weak.

"Absolutely." He jumped to his feet and went to fetch someone.

It was time to face this head on. First, clean up, then face my people.

All I could do was hold onto the gift that Kadin had given me.

Hope.

Likely it was the only gift I had left. Still, it was something. It was a start.

THE END.

...

If you loved this book, support the author by leaving a review—it helps more than you know!

SIGN UP FOR MY AUTHOR NEWSLETTER

Be the first to learn about Bethany Atazadeh's new releases, get exclusive content, updates, and more!

WWW.BETHANYATAZADEH.COM

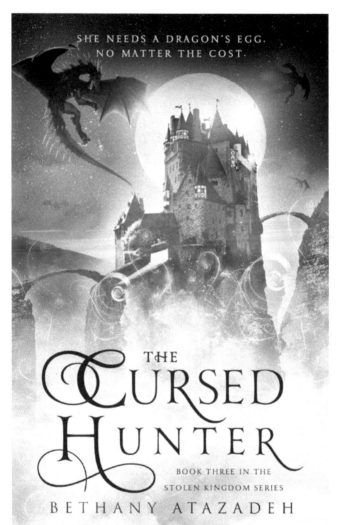

SHE NEEDS A DRAGON'S EGG.
NO MATTER THE COST.

THE CURSED HUNTER

BOOK THREE IN THE
STOLEN KINGDOM SERIES

BETHANY ATAZADEH

PREORDER BOOK THREE IN THE SERIES!
BOOKS2READ.COM/THECURSEDHUNTER

THE CURSED HUNTER

Nesrin Ahmadi needs a dragon's egg, no matter the cost.

The money from its sale could cancel her family's enormous debt and keep them in the lavish lifestyle they're accustomed to. Only one problem. A dragon's egg is incredibly rare; and no one has ever found one fully intact before.

After years of searching, she's about to give up, when debtors come to threaten her family. Climbing to heights she's never dared to go before, Nes risks everything to find an egg…

…and finds a dragon instead.

The Cursed Hunter is a loose "Beauty and the Beast" retelling. Set in a world that humans share with mermaids, dragons, and the elusive Jinn, this is not the fairytale you remember…

BOOKS2READ.COM/THECURSEDHUNTER

GLOSSARY

Amir (Ah-MEER)– King Amir of Sagh, a wealthy neighboring kingdom of Hodafez

Arie (ARE-ee) – princess of Hodafez (means Lion in Hebrew)

Baradaan (Bar-rah-DON) – kingdom where Kadin and Naveed grew up

Bosh (BAH-sh) – orphan adopted into Kadin's crew (persian word for yes)

Daichi (DIE-chee) – member of Kadin's crew

Dina (Dee-nah) – Rena's fourth older sister

Dmitri (Di-MEE-tree) – mereman

Egor (Ee-gore) - mereman

Enoch (Eee-knock) – the violet-eyed Jinni who helps King Amir

Farideh (Fair-REE-duh) – Arie's lady-in-waiting

Gideon (GID-e-un) – a Jinni

Havah (HAH-vuh) – Arie's lady-in-waiting (means sky)

Hodafez (Ho-DAH-fes) – Arie's kingdom (loosely translated in persian it means goodbye)

Illium (ILL-ee-um) – member of Kadin's crew

Jezebel (JEZ-zuh-bell) – queen of the Jinn

Jinn/Jinni (Gin/GIN-nee) – Jinn is the name of the country and the race of Jinn as a whole (i.e. *the Jinn, the land of Jinn*); Jinni is the singular, used to refer to an individual Jinni and also as a possessive (i.e. *a Jinni, a Jinni's Gift*)

Kadin (KAY-din) – leader of the crew of thieves

Lemuel (LEM-you-el) – another Jinni

Mere (Meer) – mermaids and mermen, also known as mere-folk

Misha (MEE-sha) – Rena's second older sister

Nadia (NAH-dee-ah) – Rena's third older sister

Naveed (Nah-VEED) – member of Kadin's crew

Piruz (Peer-ROOZ) – town that Kadin takes them to

Rena (REE-nah) also known as the *Grand Tsaretska Marena Yuryevna Mniszech* (Zar-ret-ska Mar-reen-na Yer-yev-na Nez-zich) – youngest daughter of the Sea King and Queen

Rusalka (Roo-SULK-ah) – the underwater kingdom of the Mere

Ruslan (Roos-lan) – mereman

Ryo (RYE-oh) – member of Kadin's crew

Sagh (SAW-gh) – King Amir's kingdom (persian word for dog)

Sasha (SAH-sha) – Rena's fifth older sister

Severance – when a Jinni's Gift is severed from its owner

Yuliya (YOU-lee-yuh) – Rena's first older sister

Three Unbreakable Laws of Jinn:
1) Never use a Gift to deceive
2) Never use a Gift to steal
3) Never use a Gift to harm another

ACKNOWLEDGMENTS

I wanted to set this book on fire multiple times, but thanks to prayer and amazing people, it survived and might even be an exciting story. (My husband says I shouldn't tell you that, but it's the truth.) I want to thank everyone who played a role in keeping this book out of the trash:

First, my critique partners, Brittany Wang and Jessi Elliott. If I am the Story Architect, then they are *the Story Engineers and Electricians* who specialize in problem solving and connecting all the moving parts. Both of you are so talented and bring a completely different perspective to the story that I either didn't consider or didn't *want* to consider haha! Brittany, you've read this story multiple times now, just like all my previous books, and yet each time you always come up with new ideas and encourage me to keep going! Jessi, the timing of your reading this book was nothing short of miraculous, thank you for being so detailed and thorough! I'm so thankful for both of you. Your friendship means more than you know.

To my beta readers, *aka My Construction Crew.* You helped me to both build this story up and tear it down, depending on what it needed—a good chunk of the beginning and the entire second half were completely rewritten thanks to all of you! I had such a wild deadline and each of you agreed to read in a very short time frame, which meant the world to me. Make sure to watch for lots of changes inspired by your notes and questions! Huge shout out to: Amelia Nichele, Athena Marie, E.C. Woodham, Elizabeth Hamm, Kyra Hunter, Lia Anderson, Peggy Spencer, Valerie Wheeler.

To my proofreaders, *aka The Last Line of Defense.* I was extremely nervous to share this book with the world. I'm incredibly thankful to have people willing to triple check that this story is truly ready. Enormous thank you to Brittany Wang, Kris Cox, and Rachael Martin for catching all the last-minute boo-boo's.

I also want to shout out my Patrons, *aka My Support Network.* During the last year that I've been on Patreon, 191 amazing people have supported me. Their support has encouraged me and helped me focus on writing this story, so I feel that it's extremely important to give them credit. To all my Patrons, thank you SO much. You rock! Make sure to check out our "Patron Key" (designed by the fabulous Mandi Lynn from Stone Ridge Books) on the next page to find your name!

Last, but certainly not least, I'm extremely thankful my husband can handle the insanity of being married to a writer who talks about characters like they're real people and has way too many deadlines. Not only that, but he continues to encourage my writing and my dreams—thanks babe! And Penny, our corgi, continues to encourage frequent breaks to play ball, which is obviously very important as well. Finally, thank you God for this amazing support network and another story out in the world!

THANK YOU TO ALL MY PATRONS!

Aaron Dumas • Adam Beswick • Adara Rosewood • Aisazia • Alex Longmore • Alexandra Michaud • Alicia Arial • Allison Aldridge • Alx LeFrey • Amanda Creek • Amber Pineau • AmeliaNichele • Andrea Alvarez • Angel Guice • Anna Zappia • Anne MacTavish • Ashley S. • Ashley Price • Ashley Shiflett • Athena Marie • Author Brittany Wang • Benjamin W. Stratton • bookworm l • Breny • Bri Leclerc • Bri Spicer • Brianna Remus • Bridie Blake • Britt • Caffeine and Composition • Cam Meze • Carla Calvert • Cassandra • Cassidy Joy Kottke • Cassie S. • Cassie Kelley • Catherine Girard-Veilleux • Ceara Nobles • Cheryl Gilmore • Chloe Vasby • Claerie Kavanaugh • Courtney Corboy • Cynthia Carbonneau • danielle hippman • Dannielle Oag • Dede Nesbitt • Devin Berglund Joubert • DjanB • Elijah Parks • Elfia Barnes • Elizabeth • Elizabeth Amos • Elizabeth Robinson • Ella Winters • Emily Wade • Emma Woodham • Erika • Erika Gill • Erin Merriam • Esther Diaz • Eve Terry • Falan Rowe • Fatimah Rashid • Fiona Bennion • Hailie T. • Hannah Jane • Heather Venkat • Holly Davis • Ingrid • J S Roberts • J.M. Ivie • Jack Silver • Jade Yap • Jade Young • Jamie Rennie • Janet Y. Perkins • Jasmine • Jenai Logan • Jenna Hale • Jennifer Acres • Jessica Jurcan • Jessica Renfro • Jessica Sayers • Jessie Jones Wilbanks • JJ Otis • Jodie Duxbury • John Jeng • Jonathan Hargus • Julia McKernan • Kasie Cox • Kassie D. • Katelyn Spedden • Katherine K. • Katherine Barrett Ryan • Kathryn Marie • Katie Cavinder • Katie Rodante • Katie Wilson Author • Kayla J. • Kayla Eshbaugh • Kaylee White • Kelly Martin • Keylin Rivers • Kimberly Tornberg • Kirie-lea • Kirsten Hicks • Kris Cox • Kristen Shafer • Kristina Allardice • Kristina Meta Kristensen Kihdan • Kristy Walker • Kyra Hunter • Lacy Hess • LadyDiva00 • Laura Pu • Laura Richter • Leilani Lopez • Leslie Arambula • Lisa Farver • Lisa Hoffman • Liz Henderson • Logan LeDuc • Malin Victoria Så,vik • Mandi Lynn • Margarita Lapina • Martin Marquez • Mary Long • Melanie Clark • Melissa Frederick • Melissa Frey • Michelle Cantwell • Michelle Patrick • Mickey Miles • Morgan Espinoza • Natalie D. • Natalie Roberts • Nathalie Strappazon • Nichole P. • Nichole D. • Nicole Wallace • Orla Byrne • Pascal Quintero • Peggy Spencer • PG Yons • Poppy Williams • Rachel Pena • Randy Bishop • Ravenclaw Pride • Rebecca Armstrong • Rebecca Kelsey Sampson • Renee Dugan • Rosa Snapp • Rox Alvarado • Ru Owen • Ruby Honan • Ryan Medina • Ryn Willis • Samantha Traunfeld • Sara Blomqvist • Sarah Giles • Sarah Lee • Scribbling Kat • Shawneen Leigh • Sondae Stevens • Stephanie Durocher • Stephanie Housley • Stephanie Van den Bos • Stuart Jackson • Susan Watson • T.E.Graves • Tatiana H. • Tenisia Davis • Tim V • Timothy Miller • Tina Canon • Tracey Glass • Tyler Q • Valerie Johnson • Valerie Skinner • Vanessa A Mcmillon • Veronica Agostini • Victoria Ellis • Vivien Reis • Wendy Rogers • Whitney Vandiver • Zoe

Bethany Atazadeh is a Minnesota-based author of YA novels, children's books, and non-fiction. She graduated from Northwestern College in 2008 with a Bachelor of Arts degree in English with a writing emphasis. After graduation, she pursued songwriting, recording, and performing with her band, and writing was no longer a priority. But in 2016, she was inspired by the NaNoWriMo challenge to write a novel in 30 days, and since then she hasn't stopped. With her degree, she coaches other writers on both YouTube and Patreon, helping them write and publish their books. She is obsessed with stories, chocolate, and her corgi puppy, Penny.

CONNECT WITH BETHANY ON:
Website: www.bethanyatazadeh.com
Patreon: www.patreon.com/bethanyatazadeh
YouTube: www.youtube.com/bethanyatazadeh
Instagram: @authorbethanyatazadeh
Facebook: @authorbethanyatazadeh
Twitter: @bethanyatazadeh

CPSIA information can be obtained
at www.ICGtesting.com
Printed in the USA
LVHW050233260420
654424LV00001B/220